There are places we were never meant to go...

The DEEP

#1 Bestseller

michaelbrent
COLLINGS

For more information on Michaelbrent's books, including specials and sales; and for info about signings, appearances, and media, check out his webpage, Like his Facebook fanpage or Follow him on Twitter. You can also sign up for his email list for deals and new releases.

PRAISE FOR THE WORK OF
MICHAELBRENT COLLINGS

"… prepare to be creeped out." – *San Francisco Book Review*

"Move over Stephen King... Clive Barker.... Michaelbrent Collings is taking over as the new king of the horror book genre." – *Media Mikes*

"[*Crime Seen*] will keep you guessing until the end…. 5/5. " – *Horror Novel Reviews*

"It's rare to find an ending to a novel that is clever, thought-provoking and surprising, yet here Collings nails all three…." – *Ravenous Reads*

"*Crime Seen* by Michaelbrent Collings is one of those rare books that deserves more than five stars." – *Top of the Heap Reviews*

"I barely had time to buckle my mental seatbelt before the pedal hit the metal...." – *The Horror Fiction Review*

"Collings is so proficient at what he does, he crooks his finger to get you inside his world and before you know it, you are along for the ride. You don't even see it coming; he is that good." – *Only Five Star Book Reviews*

"A proficient and pedagogical author, Collings' works should be studied to see what makes his writing resonate with such vividness of detail...." – *Hellnotes*

"[H]auntingly reminiscent of M. Night Shyamalan or Alfred Hitchcock." – horrornews.net

"*The Haunted* is a terrific read with some great scares and a shock of an ending!" – Rick Hautala, international bestselling author; Bram Stoker Award® for Lifetime Achievement winner

"[G]ritty, compelling and will leave you on the edge of your seat...." – horrornews.net

"[W]ill scare even the most jaded horror hounds. " – Joe McKinney, Bram Stoker Award®-winning author of *Flesh Eaters* and *The Savage Dead*

"*Apparition* is a hard core supernatural horror novel that is going to scare the hell out of you.... This book has everything that you would want in a horror novel.... it is a roller coaster ride right up to a shocking ending." – horroraddicts.net

"What a ride.... This is one you will not be able to put down and one you will remember for a long time to come. Very highly recommended." – *Midwest Book Review*

"Collings has a way with words that pulls you into every moment of the story, absorbing every scene with all of your senses." – *Clean Romance Reviews*

DEDICATION

To...

The people who didn't believe in me,
because sometimes idiots are necessary paths to
finding people who really *do* believe in you,

to Devin, who was nice to me before it was cool,

to Mindy, who taught me how to hug,

and to Laura, FTAAE.

Contents

"Ocean is more ancient than the mountains, and freighted with the memories and the dreams of Time."

- H. P. Lovecraft

"What would an ocean be without a monster lurking in the dark? It would be like sleep without dreams."

- Werner Herzog

"Below the ocean lies the last great undiscovered wilderness on Earth. And the greatest dangers yet unknown to mankind."

- Unknown

BENT

~^~^~^~^~

The world is called Earth. Which is strange when you consider that over seventy percent of it is covered by water. But it is named for the place humanity lives, the places we walk and eat and sleep and defecate and fornicate.

Still, we can *die* anywhere. And the ocean provides an easier death than almost anywhere else. After all, though we descend from water, we long ago lost our gills, our fins, our ability to do more than stumble about in the dark rivers of the deep.

That being said, there are worse things than dying. Worse things than going into an ocean or a sea and feeling your lungs fill with water and knowing a wet and lonely death has come for you.

No, the worst thing that can happen to any diver isn't drowning. It's not simply dying.

It's getting bent.

Every serious diver knows this. Every careful diver takes measures to avoid this.

Normal air is nearly eighty percent nitrogen. And when breathed on the surface, that nitrogen is inert. In and out, and nothing in our bodies is the wiser. When breathed in the deep, in the blues and then grays and blacks of the world below, the nitrogen gathers in a diver's blood stream. It isn't let out through breaths, but through the skin. If a diver rises too quickly, molecules of nitrogen gather together and form large bubbles in the body.

Depending on where the bubbles choose to form – around nerves, near joints… in the brain – those bubbles can cause pain, seizures. Not just death, but *agonizing* death.

This is decompression sickness. The bends, as it's more commonly called.

All this pounded through Debi Richardson's mind as she swam to the surface. Not much of a swim, actually. She was clawing at the water, yanking panicked handfuls of liquid toward herself, kicking the lopsided kick of a diver who has lost one fin.

Don't get bent. Gotta stop. Gotta wait.

The way to keep from getting bent is to wait. To simply and quietly hang at predetermined spots in the deep, letting the nitrogen leave your body in bubbles so small they will cause no pain, no damage. Debi's dive computer had readouts that told her how long she should wait, and at what depths. It was a tool that was nearly as important as the tanks on her back and slung from her sides.

Stop. Stop. Gotta stop.

Debi Richardson didn't. She couldn't.

She knew she was past the first deco waypoint. Knew she should stop. Knew she was risking it all.

She kept kicking. Kept clawing at the water, kicking up, up.

The water was lightening around her. Going from the black –

(why couldn't it have stayed dark why did I have to see?)

– to the gray to the dark blue.

I'm too high. I'm too fast.

She kept climbing. Kept grabbing those handfuls of water and yanking them down, yanking herself up in the process.

Her pulse thundered in her ears, blasting through her mind. Another symptom of deep diving: nitrogen narcosis, the rapture of the deep. That damn nitrogen again, getting into cells, causing them to expand and short-circuiting the signals between brain and body. It was like being drunk – loss of mental acuity, vision problems, inability to problem solve, motor skills impaired, euphoria, inability to concentrate on more than one thing at a time.

It's coming it's coming it's coming.

Darkness gathered in the corners of Debi's vision, even as the water around her lightened. She was narced out of her gourd, but that went away when you ascended. She just had to get high enough, get –

(*AWAY!*)

– to the boat.

But there's no one left on the boat. They're all dead.

She kept climbing. Clawing. Didn't matter. Didn't matter that they were all dead above. All that mattered was what lay below. What was coming.

She pulled up.

Something touched her foot.

She didn't look down. Didn't have to. She knew what it was, what it had to be. The touch was light, almost friendly. It tickled a bit. A feather-touch on the foot that had no fin, like a friend had found her and was playing a trick.

But this was no friend.

Debi screamed. The regulator popped out of her mouth, bubbles escaping along with a shriek that momentarily overcame the jackhammer sound of her own heartbeat.

She didn't bother trying to get the regulator back in her mouth. She clamped her mouth shut. Managed to remember that much, at least, managed to avoid sucking in great gasps of water and ending it all right there.

The tickle became a caress. The caress became a touch.

She screamed again. This time she *did* suck water.

She inhaled. Gagged. Vomited. The water around her clouded with bile.

She climbed. Pulled her way up.

One of her hands found the inflation button on her buoyancy compensator.

Why didn't I think of that before?

'Cause you're narced, Debi, baby. You're whacked outta your nut.

SHUT UP, IT'S COMING!

The vest-like apparatus on her back and sides began inflating. Suddenly she was no longer clawing at the water. It felt like she was actually gaining purchase, climbing with purpose as the buoyancy compensator did its job and pulled her higher. She yanked open a pair of pockets on the vest, and two sets of weights dropped out. Now she wasn't just floating up, she was *flying*.

You'll bend.

Maybe not.

Yes.

She didn't care.

The touch hadn't repeated. She hadn't felt... *it*. Maybe she had gotten away.

She managed to get the regulator back in her mouth. Gagged out a last hard *chunk* of water, then sucked deeply at her air.

She looked at her dive computer. It seemed hazy. Wavy in the brightening water. It danced before her, seemed to change color.

Narced.

It said she was thirty-two feet down.

Debi started to think she might make it.

Then the first pain hit.

She let go of the readout on her dive computer as her fingers suddenly felt like someone had bent them in half. The regulator fell from her mouth again as she screamed – this time not in surprise and terror, but sheerest agony.

The pain traveled up her hands, to her arms. Writhing paths of electricity that told the dim part of her brain that was still functioning that the bubbles had found their way to her spinal cord, maybe even her brain.

Her feet started kicking a different kind of kick. No longer pushing the water, but thrashing back and forth in uncoordinated motions, seizure-spasms wracking and wrenching them so hard that she felt her right knee pop out of its socket.

She was still screaming. Still a single exhale.

She broke the surface. Shrieking. Sucked air. It hurt. It was agony.

Her body curled in on itself, the protective posture in which we first know life in our mothers' wombs and in which so many of us take our last breaths.

I'm dying. Going to die. Going to die PLEASE GOD PLEASE DEAR JESUS PLEASE MOMMY AND DADDY LET ME DIE!

The buoyancy compensator kept her face-up on the surface. She wasn't going to drown. She wished she would.

She felt something pop, and half her world went dark. Whether that was because her eye had a bubble or because one had found its way to another part of her brain, she couldn't say.

Does it matter?

She was still screaming.

A thought inserted itself. Managed to slip through the cracks of her agony, to find its way to the bits of her brain that could still cobble together rational thoughts.

She thought of Sue. Her sister, so much the same, and at the same time so very different. Light of hair where Debi was dark, laughing and bubbly where Debi was introverted and could be downright moody at times.

But both curious. Both driven by needs to know.

Sue would have gone down with her. Would have looked. Would have *seen.*

And so Debi was suddenly glad. Even in her agony, her searing pain, she found a spot of brightness. A white slightly lighter than the white pain that had enveloped her. She was glad her sister wasn't here. Glad she would die alone.

Another pop. Her world went completely dark. Nothing to see, only pain to feel. The drumbeat of her pulse still slamming through her skull.

And something touched her again. Her foot. Then her leg.

She couldn't see. But she could feel.

And in the next moment, Debi found out how wrong divers really were. The worst thing wasn't drowning. It wasn't dying.

And it wasn't even getting bent.

The touch wrapped itself up, around, and *through* her.

Debi wouldn't die alone after all.

She had time for one more scream. Then it pulled her down. Down to the deep, down to the dark.

And then she was gone. The surface was an unbroken mirror in the day. A calm blue sheet that showed nothing of what hid beneath.

FISHED

~^~^~^~^~

Sue Richardson looked over the blue and wondered – for the thousandth time – what she was doing here.

She knew she was hoping to find Debi; at the same time knew there was no possible way she could do that. Hoping to find Debi by going out on a dive boat in the general area she had been headed when she disappeared… it would be like finding a molecule in a haystack.

No, she wasn't here to find her sister.

So what *was* she doing here?

"What's up?"

The voice sent a pleasant tingle through her, and on the heels of that came a vague guilt. The tingle was because she recognized the voice of Tim Palmer. He was five-ten, slightly balding, and he had a body that was far from the kind that you would see on the average underwear commercial. But there was something about him that made Sue's blood race a bit faster when he was around.

Maybe it's because *he's not an underwear model.*

Sue herself was beautiful. Not as stunning as Debi – her sister had an exotic look that had men tripping over themselves to get to her – but she had never had trouble filling up her dance card. Usually with men who were attracted to her face and her athletic figure – then got quickly turned off when they discovered there was an actual mind behind them.

8

And that was it. Tim was aware she was beautiful – she had seen him check her out covertly once or twice – but he wasn't creepy or lecherous about it. And once he got those few looks out of his system, he had just treated her as... what?

A friend.

Tim was one of those people who bring others into his orbit, who make them part of his family. Sue got the feeling he would gladly invite her over to Christmas dinner if he found out she was alone for the holidays... but what made that matter was the sense she got that he would invite *anyone* over for the feast, rich or poor, smart or stupid, beautiful or ugly.

"Are you trying to hypnotize me?" he said.

Sue realized she had fogged out a bit. She had been staring at him, and now she blushed. Which was totally unlike her: another pleasant effect of being around Tim.

"What if I am?" she said. She meant it to sound funny, the teasing of a friend. It came out biting.

Tim didn't withdraw or seem offended. He grinned. "Don't make me a chicken. I hate that."

"You've done this before, then?"

"Lots of times. *BA-GAWK!*"

Tim's sudden cluck, delivered at high volume and accompanied by a frenzied flapping of his arms, was so surprising that Sue was completely silent. She just stared.

Tim grew solemn. "See, that's why I don't want you to make me be a chicken with your mad hypnosis skills. The last guy never made me *not* be a chicken." He sighed. "It's awkward at funerals."

That last was too much. Sue laughed. The laugh broke something inside her. Not in a bad way – it was like it shattered chains that had hung around her soul since she first heard about Debi. She didn't think she had laughed much since hearing her sister had gone missing. Maybe not at all.

It felt good.

Tim grinned at her. Then his face grew serious. No mockery, none of the urbane cynicism she saw in so many of the people she worked with back in what she thought of as "the real world." Just simple concern.

"You okay, Sue?"

She nodded. Opened her mouth. She was going to tell him about Debi. Not just about her missing, but... *everything*.

"As good as can be, I guess."

"You want to finally tell me what's eating at you?"

Of course he didn't know. No one did, really. She and her father had booked the first boat that was going in the general direction they required, and had paid the captain extra to make a quiet side trip. But he was the only one who knew about the side trip – and not even he knew *why*.

"I –" she began. But before she could say more than that....

"Sonofabitchbastardbitch!"

The voice that interrupted her was as intrusive and irritating as Tim's had been welcome and inviting.

Sue didn't know much about Geoffrey "Don't Call me Geoff" Taylor III, other than that he was very rich, he

10

worked in commodities, and he was very rich. Those were the three bullet points he kept coming back to, and he stayed on message with the tenacity of a well-trained presidential candidate.

Currently Geoffrey was at the stern of the boat, a fishing rod in his chubby hands, looking at the thing like it had betrayed him – worse, had *disrespected* him – when it failed to bring in something roughly the size of Jaws.

Tim rolled his eyes covertly. "His Lordshipness heaveth a mighty rod," he whispered to Sue.

She giggled. Well, almost. Again, she thought that Tim was more than he seemed to be. He looked like just a middle-aged dive leader, no one of import, no one of interest. But he was, in fact, very interesting; and just in the twenty-four hours the boat had been underway she had begun looking forward to the times they could bump into one another.

"Sonofabitchbitchbitchbastard!"

"He's got a way with words," said Tim.

"Shakespeare is green with jealousy," she agreed.

"Well, he's dead, so maybe green with decay?"

"As long as he's green."

"Sonofabitch!"

"Dude's very limited in his cursing."

The new voice that joined them was low, even, slow. Not slow in any way that communicated stupidity. It was the slow of the waves, the gentle roll of a voice that has spent so many hours and days and weeks atop the surf that the ocean has become a part of it. Jimmy J – and that was what everyone called him, though Sue had no idea why, or what the "J" stood for – was in his late twenties. He looked like the prototypical surfer, with long blonde hair that shagged a bit at the shoulders. He was broad-chested, with narrow hips and tan skin that set off his blue eyes. The kind of look that just about any girl would go ga-ga over in about three seconds. And it didn't hurt any that he was affable, genuinely warm in his attitudes and funny in a laid-back way. He was also clearly devoted to Tim.

Join the club.

Jimmy J poked Tim's shoulder. "One of us better go help Duke Luckyfingers before we sink under the awesome weight of his vocabulary."

"I think it's your turn," said Tim.

"And *I* think these many years at sea have addled your gray cells, *kimosabe*."

Tim held out a fist. Jimmy J grinned. Held out a matching fist. "Your beautiful butt is mine this time."

"Flattery will get you nowhere."

Sue listened to the banter with a smile pulling at one corner of her lips. The two sounded like more than coworkers. They were more like best friends – even brothers.

Their fists bounced. Once, twice. On the third drop, Tim opened his hand flat while Jimmy J kept his tight.

Tim's grin widened as Jimmy J sighed. "In what world does a piece of paper beat a rock? Like, is it titanium paper? Is it on fire? Does it have *superpowers*?"

"You're stalling," said Tim.

"Damn right."

"Sonofa –" began Geoffrey.

"Fine." Jimmy J held up his hands. "I'm going." He stepped out of the salon, joining Geoffrey on the deck. "You okay, Geoff?"

Geoffrey didn't look away from his ineffective casting. "It's Geoffrey, you twit! I told you that!"

Jimmy J looked over his shoulder, grinning at Tim and sending a wink Sue's way. "Right. Geoffrey. Like the Toys 'R' Us giraffe."

Geoffrey began a new round of "sonofabitch"ing, this time directed at Jimmy J as he moved toward the irritable (rich) commodities trader. The two men huddled together, and in a moment their voices disappeared in surf and wind.

Then Jimmy J must have had the audacity to suggest moving on to a more fruitful venture – like searching for the Loch Ness Monster. Because Geoffrey shouted, "No, I will *not* stop. I –"

Suddenly, his whine was cut off by the only-slightly-higher whine of the reel unspooling. The sound set Sue's teeth on edge for some reason. On some deep level she wanted to scream at Geoffrey, to shout, "Just let it go!" The feeling surprised her. She prided herself on being rational – with everyone but her father, at least, and he was a very special case – so the sudden, deep urge to shriek a warning was out of character; nearly alien.

But it was there. It was real.

Let it go, Geoffrey!

Let it go!

"I caught something!" Geoffrey was screaming. "I told you! I told you I'd –" Then his voice slammed to a halt as the line spun so fast the rod nearly yanked out of his hand. And nearly yanked Geoffrey overboard along with it as the commodities trader refused to surrender the rod.

Jimmy J grabbed hold of Geoffrey, and that helped. But only for a moment. Then both of them started skidding toward the dive platform – the flat back end of the aft deck.

"Uhhh... Tim?" Jimmy J's voice was almost comically high, the first time Sue had ever heard him leave what she thought of as his "Dude Voice" behind.

"Duty calls," said Tim. He hustled over and added his strength to the already-straining muscles of Jimmy J and Geoffrey.

Sue wondered – suddenly and less fleetingly than she would have supposed – how strong he was. And how his arms might feel around her.

"Mr. Raven!" Tim shouted.

A voice floated down from above. The boat was divided into three parts: the middle level was the common level, holding a salon, galley, and one of the two bathrooms. Belowdecks held the berths, galley storage, and a bathroom/shower combo. Above was the wheelhouse, from which the boat's owner piloted.

Mr. Raven was a squat man who looked like he was in his late fifties. Though a lifetime in the sun had turned his skin to something like old leather, and he could have been considerably younger. Still, young or old he had the soul of a cantankerous eighty-year-old. He seemed to view the passengers as something to be tolerated rather than appreciated, their money their only redeeming factor. He stayed up in the wheelhouse most of the time – even slept there – and no one seemed overly mournful about that fact.

"Yeah?" shouted Mr. Raven. Sue didn't know his first name, had never heard it spoken. She occasionally wondered if he even *had* one, or if he had once lost it – along with his sense of humor – to long years eking out a living on the sea.

"Cut the engine!"

"Why?" came the shouted reply. It sounded muffled, and she suspected Mr. Raven hadn't bothered to even look at what was going on, let alone leave the wheelhouse. But a moment later the engine cut and the boat began its lumbering drift to a halt.

"Told you!" Geoffrey was still crowing. "Told you I could…."

Sue smiled as Tim and Jimmy J moved to help the commodities trader and got roughly pushed aside for their troubles. "Mine!" he screamed. Sue wanted to laugh. No doubt he thought he sounded tough and strong in his righteous claim of ownership to a massive catch. In actuality he sounded like an infant.

She shook her head and turned to the salon.

And had to consciously struggle to keep every muscle from contracting as she came face to face with one of the passengers. And probably the only one she liked less than Geoffrey.

Mark Haeberle was in his thirties. One of those people who carried a sense of danger about him, like a dark cloud centered over one small location. His eyes were dark, his black hair perpetually mussed. Whenever she saw him, her skin felt like insects were writhing across it.

She had caught him looking at her a few times on the first day of the trip. A wasted day, with the ocean too choppy for Mr. Raven to permit diving. They spent the day in the salon, reading or playing cards or just shooting the breeze.

But Haeberle stayed apart. He had arrived at the last second, tossing his gear on board the boat just as it was pulling out, shouting for them to wait. But other than that he had hardly said two words to anyone. He had simply sat. Watched.

The watching gave her the creeps.

He grinned at her. The smile was wide – too wide. Not the reassuring smile of a stranger who means no harm, not the warm smile that Tim wore. It was… predatory. The smile of a wolf looking at the herd, scoping out the weak, the weary, the old.

"Sorry," he said. His voice was a whisper. "Didn't mean to scare you."

But she got the feeling he had meant to do just that. As though checking what her reaction would be, what kind of person she was.

"You didn't," she said. She forced her shoulders to loosen, consciously made herself stand in a relaxed pose that she hoped would give lie to the near-panic he seemed to cause somewhere deep within her. "Just startled is all."

His smile widened. "Liar liar," said the smile.

He moved out of the room, onto the aft deck. He didn't join the still-arguing trio of Tim, Jimmy J, and Geoffrey. He stood apart, staring at nothing. He wasn't there to help.

So what is he doing?

Scouting the competition. Alpha.

What if he decides there is no competition?

He'll take what he can. What he wants.

She shivered. Turned away.

The stairs that led belowdecks were thudding that solid *clump, clump, clump* that signaled someone coming up.

A moment later Cal's head appeared. Then the rest of him.

Sue felt her shoulders tense again. Didn't bother trying to conceal it this time. Her father knew how she felt, knew that it wasn't likely to change. There was too much history there.

Cal Richardson was fifty-eight. Salt-and-pepper hair that hid his age, eyes that were awake and aware. He was fit and trim – starting to fade a bit with age, but only in tiny increments. Women were still attracted to him, men found him easy to be with.

But not you, Sue. No, you have to be the one person in the universe who can't stand being with him.

Life's a bitch, eh?

Her father stopped at the top of the stairs. Just stood there, and she couldn't figure out why until she realized it was because of her. Because she was here.

"Hey, Sue," he said.

"Hey."

The exchange was awkward. Nearly as painful as complete silence would have been, if not more so.

After a few seconds, her father cleared his throat. She got the feeling that if he'd been wearing a button-up he would have pulled at the collar nervously.

"You wanna get a beer or –"

"No," she said. "I don't want to get dehydrated."

"Oh. Sure. Right." He looked downcast. "Right, that was stupid."

There was an even longer pause, and Sue wished her hips and knees were on reversible joints so she could kick herself in the butt.

He's trying.

So what?

So give him a chance.

Right.

"What if we just hold the cans?"

Sue didn't answer. She didn't even understand the question, and after she replayed it in her mind to make sure she hadn't missed something – she hadn't – it still didn't make sense.

"What?"

He smiled. This time it was a bit less strained. "I'm just looking for an excuse to stand in the sun with my daughter. Beer was what came to mind. But no one says we actually have to *drink* it."

Sue felt her own face shift. A position so strange she almost couldn't place it.

Are you smiling? At him?

I think you might be, Sue-girl.

Smiles had been in short supply since the news of Debi.

"Well? What do you think?"

"Sure."

The foredeck wasn't nearly as big as the aft, but it was large enough for them to stand and watch the ocean as it drifted toward them, passing below the still-moving keel of *The Celeste*. The boat was a queer mix of luxury and utility: a dive boat that tried to cater to serious divers, many of whom took an almost perverse pleasure in their ability to weather Spartan conditions; and the overnight dilettante, who expected hot showers and well-cooked meals.

Tim was an excellent cook. Another point in his favor.

"Sonofabitchbastardbastard!" Geoffrey could still be heard, shouting his rage at the universe. It was at least somewhat muted over here.

Sue scanned the horizon. Back and forth, back and forth. Looking....

For what? You hoping to see a boat? A raft? A single diver, alive in one of those made-for-Lifetime miracles?

"You think there's any chance?" she said. She was speaking to herself, mostly. A conversation she had had every day for the last three weeks, though it was a bit quieter, a bit more desperate and at the same time a bit weaker with every passing day.

It almost surprised her when her father answered. "I... I'd *like* to think so."

"That doesn't answer my question." She turned to face him when she said it, putting him on the spot as much as she could with only the force of her gaze.

"I don't know what happened, Suzy-Q," he finally said.

"Don't call me that," she snapped.

It grated. She hadn't been called Suzy-Q by anyone for years. The last one had been Debi. They fought.

They always fought.

Family trait.

Her father looked pained. She wondered if he would move from distress to anger to the usual end of their conversations: a fight that would have them no longer speaking for some unknown time. Probably.

He surprised her. "Sorry," he said. He looked at the deck. They were almost motionless on the water now, only the gentle swell of deep ocean rising then falling, rocking them, soothing them. "I don't know what happened to Debi," he continued. "Could've been anything. She could have had a gear malfunction. Maybe she went too deep and got narced. Maybe –"

"No. None of those happened. Not to Debi. She was too careful for any of those things to happen. You know that. Besides, it wouldn't explain why her boat and the rest of her crew were never found, either." She stopped. Looking. Looking at the waves and the water and the nothing that they represented.

"It's that damn place she went to work for. All their experiments. All their stupidity," she said.

Her father was shaking his head before she finished. Of course he was. "We don't know if that had anything to do with it, Sue. We'll probably never know."

He punched the rail that surrounded the deck, a waist-high piece of wood polished by years of sea and wind and the sweat-slicked palms of countless passengers. The motion startled her with its sudden violence. She felt herself drawing away from him. Tried to stop it. Couldn't.

"Dammit." He spat the word. "I wonder why we bothered coming. It's been three weeks, no one's heard from her or her boat, no one –"

"So what, we just give up?"

"Sue, if the Coast Guard and six naval vessels couldn't find her, what chance do we have on a single dive boat where most of the passengers don't even know we're looking for someone? It's, it's…." He threw his hands wide, his body giving eloquent voice to his frustration, his impotent rage.

Then he sagged. Suddenly Sue saw her father as he rarely permitted anyone to see him: a man beyond his prime. A man who held himself straight and strong, but at a cost.

He's getting older.

He'll die someday.

She was a bit surprised how much that realization bothered her. She didn't want him to die.

Debi was dead. He was the only family she had left.

"I don't even know why we're here," he said again.

She reached out to him. He didn't see it. And because her hand stopped a few inches away from his shoulder, he didn't feel it either.

Just do it. Give him some comfort.

He doesn't deserve it.

He's lost someone, too.

That last thought was what drove her. What decided her. She would reach out. She would begin the process of mending... whatever they had. Not a relationship, not exactly. But perhaps it could become one. Someday.

Her hand moved closer.

"I told you! I told you I'd catch something! I –"

Then her hand froze. Because Geoffrey stopped his triumphant screams, and began an entirely new kind of shrieks. The shouts of a man in pain, in terror.

The banshee wail of something horrific.

Sue's hand dropped. Her father turned. His eyes locked with hers.

Geoffrey was still screaming.

Sue and her father ran toward the screams.

CAUGHT

~^~^~^~^~

Tim Palmer was not born to the sea. The water came to him as a rebirth. A baptism that was as close to a spiritual awakening as any he had felt in his life.

He started his life – his adult life, at least – as a lawyer. Just one of a thousand tiny cogs in the grist mill-wheels of a big-city firm, toiling away in a small office with a view of a smoggy skyline and bragging rights because he could look down on the tops of the buildings around him. Small thing to brag about: the tops of the buildings were ugly. All piping and air conditioning units. The ugly unseen portions of grand monuments of steel and glass that stood like pillars in a modern Stonehenge that, ultimately, was as mysterious and unknowable as the one of ancient days.

One of his friends – his real friends, not the other associates who smiled shark-smiles and secretly plotted to sabotage his cases and thus get ahead of him on the hamster-wheel race to partnership – got him a day trip on a dive boat. "Go," he said. "Get your nose out of the Milton case. Breathe real air. Exercise. I can't remember the last time I saw you outside and I'm entertaining serious concerns that you might in fact be a vampire."

Tim had no intention of going. He was in the middle of discovery on the case – a complex intellectual property case over the infringement (alleged!) of a patent detailing the creation and manufacture of a new kind of synthetic cork. Things were too busy. He had just received over fifty thousand pages of correspondence, engineers' notes, and a series of very polite "screw you" letters from opposing counsel. He intended to prepare at least *seventy* thousand documents to return in response to their document demands, along with an even more politely worded "bite me" letter.

But the unthinkable happened, two days before the trip: the case settled. It had been going on for almost four years, neither side giving an inch. Then, suddenly, all those marvelous billable hours just went up in smoke.

Tim found himself with the curse of free time. Nothing to do on the week*days*, let alone the week*end*.

He went on the day trip.

The first few hours were spent going over the scuba gear, practicing in a pool. He hated it. He wished he could get back to his small but comfortable office, the soothing clutter of a case that had spun charmingly (expensively) out of control. He missed his secretary, and the way she talked to people so he didn't have to.

Then the group went out.

The ocean was different. The first five minutes of open water utterly entranced Tim. He saw nothing of import, but the *feeling*... it transported him.

Minute six he wondered how he had ever felt comfortable in the confined space of his office.

Minute eight he wondered how two businesses could spend four years and over six million dollars fighting over *cork*.

Minute ten he wondered how he could have been a part of that fight.

Minute eleven he decided to quit.

Minute one-hundred-twenty-one – exactly one minute after leaving the water – he called his office and gave notice.

He had no plan. No idea that he would become a diver, let alone a dive leader for a respectable dive outfit on a boat like *The Celeste*. But that was what he did. He had plenty of savings – hard to spend money when you never ventured forth into the real world – so he lived off his bank account until he was certified as a diver, then got odd dive-related jobs around the pier until he was certified as a dive master.

And then this job.

He was happy. Beyond happy. He was fulfilled. He had something he realized he had never felt as an attorney, billing five hundred an hour to clients so wealthy they could not only afford it, but expected to pay no less.

He had purpose.

And that purpose was to spend as much time as possible in the waves, and to help others do the same.

He loved every minute of it. From the great-grandmother who had gifted herself to her first dive at the ripe young age of ninety-two, to the family of two lovely parents and six even lovelier children they homeschooled, who rented the dive boat for three delightful days of learning and hands-on science, to that one time – a beautiful memory – when a group of six women on some kind of bonding trip rented the boat and spent the whole day *not* diving but for some reason fawning over him instead.

He loved it all.

But there *were* moments he loved *less* than others. Cleaning out the berths after any group of men between the ages of fifteen and thirty-five was involved always turned into a chore that had him smelling like beer from the elbows down, and he sometimes wondered how *any* woman could stand to marry *any* man, based solely on the still-lingering evidence of gaseous emissions he ran into in the closed cabin where the berths were.

And, of course, there were moments like this: moments where he had to submit to the driving will of some moron who knew how to dive – barely – and somehow thought he (it was *always* a he) had the keys to understanding the universe. Generally this person was the least competent person on the boat.

It certainly held true in this case. Geoffrey "Don't Call Me Geoff" Taylor III might not have been born with a silver spoon in his mouth, but he had certainly nurtured the growth of a solid gold stick up his ass.

"You sure those should be stowed there?" he asked first thing, pointing at some air tanks that Tim was putting into a space that was – wait for it – specifically designed for stowing air tanks.

Tim plastered what he thought of as his "asshole" face across his expression. The "asshole face," or just "face" if he was in a hurry, was so named because it meant he was prepared to deal with an asshole, and to kiss that asshole's... well... ass.

Just part of the job, he thought. Then grinned even wider, and said, "Gosh, sir, I really think so. But if you believe there's been a problem can I recommend you talk to the captain about it?"

"Where *is* the captain?"

Tim shrugged. He knew exactly where Mr. Raven was, of course, but he suspected this time-waster's "knowledge" base would proceed along the path of least resistance. "Gee, sir, I'm really not sure. He could be in the galley, or in the wheelhouse, or maybe –"

"Yeah, yeah, I get it. You don't know." Geoffrey sneered, as though this lack of knowledge was the final nail on a coffin built of sheer stupidity.

But as obsequious as he was, or as jolly, or as over-the-top "ol'-buddy-ol'-seamate-me-lad" as he got with Geoffrey, the other guy's dick factor just rose slightly every time he opened his mouth.

Now was no exception.

"I told you," Geoffrey crowed. "I *told* you."

Mr. Raven had already cut the engine, which might make pulling in whatever Geoffrey had caught a bit easier, but also resulted in the man's voice carrying that much farther across the ocean.

Life is nothing but double-edged swords.

"I told you! I told you I'd catch something!"

"Ease up, bud," said Jimmy J. "Give it some slack, then –"

"Shut up!" Geoffrey barked. "You didn't even think I'd find anything, so you obviously –"

Tim was interrupted in his momentary self-reminder that it wasn't okay to pitch paying customers overboard by Geoffrey suddenly pitching backward into his arms. Whatever he was yanking had apparently darted toward the boat, creating abrupt slack against the combined pulling of Geoffrey and Jimmy J.

Jimmy J went down on his butt on the deck. "Ow," he said, sounding more startled than in pain.

"Okay, reel it in," said Tim. He wanted to punch himself when he did, knowing it would bring an inevitable response. As it did.

"Don't tell me what to do!" shouted Geoffrey. "I'm the one –"

His voice pinched off and his mouth opened to a circle so perfect it was almost funny. But any laughter Tim felt was chased away by the look in Geoffrey's eyes. The gloating, the triumph, the sense of superiority – all were gone.

In their place: fear. And maybe more.

Geoffrey raised a hand. Pointed.

Started to scream.

Tim saw why. He didn't scream, didn't even feel the urge. But his stomach dropped so hard and fast it was a wonder he wasn't driven right through the deck of the boat.

He picked up the rod. Began reeling in. Wondering how the thing had darted and zigged so hard and so fast.

Musta been The Celeste. *The thing must have hit our wake, been caught in some weird turbulence.*

That made sense. But something in Tim's still-fallen stomach cried out.

Just drop it. Cut the line and leave it!

Can't do that.

28

You can. You should. You must!

He ignored the voice that counselled to leave the thing in the water.

Geoffrey's screams had dropped off a bit. Not completely, but enough that they were no longer piercing shards of broken glass pressing into Tim's ear canals. They had downgraded to thumbtacks pressing into his ear canals.

Jimmy J had seen Geoffrey's catch. He moved to the man, whispering in his ear. Trying to calm him. Jimmy J was good with people, and Tim knew if anyone could calm Geoffrey down Jimmy J could.

But Geoffrey kept screaming.

Tim kept pulling.

He felt something behind him. A presence. Nothing unusual, just the normal "someone else is here" feeling we all get from time to time. A sense left over from primal times when awareness of other people was not only important, but critical to survival.

Tim flicked a quick look over his shoulder. Saw who had come out of the salon.

Haeberle.

The guy gave Tim the creeps. He had brought excellent gear with him, and had signed on as an experienced diver. But he had fumbled his way along when stowing his gear. He seemed a bit ill-at-ease when the thin strip of land dropped below the horizon.

He was also huge, and seemed to like that fact. There are large men who exude cuddly happiness. They are teddy bears, normally so affable it's almost ridiculous.

On the other end of the spectrum are men who are big and muscular and seem intent on making everyone around them know that it is by grace, patience, and largesse alone that they are allowed to survive. These large men stand a bit too close, a bit too straight. Intruding into personal space and standing with arms crossed over broad chests.

I own your ass. That was what they said – or tried to – with every movement, in every moment.

Haeberle was one of the latter type. He hadn't said more than fifty words the entire trip, but every one of them had been delivered in a low, slow, menacing voice. "Where do I bunk?" sounded more like, "I better get first pick of berths." "What can I eat?" felt more like, "If I don't get some food *now*, there will be trouble."

And he creeped the women out, Tim could tell. Not just Sue, but the other female fare, Mercedes. She was in her forties, attractive enough but unassuming and quiet. Every time Haeberle moved across a room either of them was in, he seemed to somehow change course just enough to bring himself within a foot or two of where they were. Looming above them. Seeming to challenge them with every movement.

Tim did not like the guy. Not because he caused trouble – he hadn't – but because he seemed like the kind who, when trouble came, would sit back and laugh. If not join in the mayhem himself.

The line was still hard to reel, but getting easier as *The Celeste* slowly drifted to a halt. Geoffrey's screams started to ramp up as his "catch" drew closer.

"Easy, man," said Jimmy J. "Let's just take a big ol' glass of Calm Down Juice, okay?"

Geoffrey's cries continued unabated. Got louder.

Haeberle stepped suddenly over to him. Stood close, stood tall.

"Quiet," he said.

He spoke in a voice so low that Tim could barely hear him. But Geoffrey must have seen something in the man's face that scared him more than the bundle that Tim was pulling in. His screams ended mid-shriek, gulped down before they could emerge.

"Thanks, man," said Jimmy J. He flashed a smile at Haeberle. Tim marveled again at how well his friend worked with the passengers.

"I didn't do it for you." Haeberle suddenly looked like violence was on his mind. Like he would like to let loose and tear someone – maybe *everyone* – apart. "He was getting on my nerves."

The big man threw a last hard look at Geoffrey, then moved to join Tim on the dive platform. Looking at what he had.

A moment later Sue, her dad, and Mercedes came out of the salon. All joining him on the platform, water sloshing over their feet. Watching what he was doing.

None of *them* screamed, at least. That was good.

Tim pulled it closer.

A body. Clad in the neoprene suit of a scuba diver. A tank trailing from it, attached by a hose that had tangled in the body's compensator and other gear.

The body bobbed in the waves. Facedown, the fishing line traveling under it, obviously caught on the front of the dead diver's body.

Other than the disarray of the tank and tangles, the body could have been just some snorkeler, face down in the waves. The suit looked unmolested. The arms trailed, clad in thick rubber sleeves that fed into heavy gloves that bound over the wrists.

Just a diver.

But he knew that was a lie. Knew it even before the body bumped against the dive platform hard enough to draw splashes and shouts from anyone who was –

(*alive*)

– awake, even barely conscious.

Then a swell moved over the mirror of the ocean. An unexpected wave that rolled the ship up and down, that pounded the diver against the dive platform... and flipped it over.

Geoffrey started screaming. Clamped it down when Haeberle grimaced at him, but couldn't quite contain his whimpering.

The body had no face. The soft tissue had been eaten away, corroded by water and by the tearing of small creatures that would have gone for the softest bits of this unexpected feast. Yellowed skull poked through in some spots. The rest was a uniform mask of waxy brown, the half-pickled flesh of someone too long adrift in the sea.

Geoffrey's hook was set deep in the body's eye socket.

Tim heard a gag, someone retching behind him. Not Jimmy J, not Geoffrey – who was still wheez/crying behind them. Which left Haeberle – not likely – Sue, Cal, or

Mercedes. He didn't look, but his bet was on Mercedes, simply because neither Sue nor Cal seemed the type.

Especially not Sue. She was... special. Together. Interesting in a way that both baffled and delighted him.

The body bumped against the platform again. The platform was nothing more than a part of the aft deck that had been built out a bit to allow for easier ingress to the water. It hung about a foot over the water, a ladder at each end. But each time the waves rolled up and down, it smacked into the water with a wet *splut*, and the body seemed to time its forward motions so as to collide with the platform.

Tim suddenly had the weird feeling that the body was trying to get onto the boat. Still dead, still beyond any help, but trying nonetheless.

And when it got aboard....

He quashed that thought. It was ridiculous, it was beyond reason. He didn't believe in ghosts, didn't believe in spooks. Certainly didn't believe in dead divers climbing like wet zombies aboard his boat.

But he did believe in physics. In the power of waves and water, and realized that if the body swung forward at the wrong moment it would come *under* the platform. Pummeled down, under the boat. Who knew what damage that might do – to the boat or to the body?

He had to go in.

Without thinking about it – thinking wasn't a good idea considering what he was about to do – Tim shucked off the flip-flops he'd been wearing. That left him in a t-shirt and board shorts. That was good enough.

He dove in.

He splashed into the water close to the body, on the opposite side of the still-trailing fishing line. He didn't want to get wrapped up in the thick line, designed for nabbing sport fish.

How stupid would that *be, to drown a foot from the boat.*

Heeding his own advice, he gave the trailing line a wide berth, trying to pay attention to it and to the body, but at the same time close his vision to the grisly sight of the corpse's non-face.

He got two out of three. It seemed like he couldn't look *away* from that face. He paddled toward the body, and with every inch the visage got that much worse. Not just the brown, semi-congealed gel that had replaced the skin covering the skull. Not just the hook biting deep into one dark, abandoned eye socket. The lips were gone, so was the nose – either chewed away or melted into the viscous brown of the rest of the head. The teeth were still whole, biting together and grimacing in a death rictus that went up beyond the gum line, exposed by the lips that had dissolved or been chewed away some time ago.

He was at the body. Grabbed it. He felt suddenly as though it might grab *him*. Just as it had tried to get on board the ship, now it would grip him, hold him close, sink into the deep. The ocean floor was about eight hundred feet below them here, and Tim shivered as he grabbed a handful of the wetsuit, his mind darkened by a vision of death at those crushing depths, dragged below by a dead man with no face.

The body didn't move. The flesh below the arm of the suit was both stiff and oddly flexible. Like the rubber of a tire – tough, but bendable. Not the feel of an arm bending at the joints, but of an arm bereft of bone, toughened to something not-quite-flesh.

The body rolled face down again. He was glad – the motion hid that awful face from his view. But then he shivered. Nothing to do with the cold water all around him. Rather, it was the idea that now the thing was calling others. Other dead divers, clutching from below, reaching up... up....

Get a grip!

He heard Mercedes retching again. Focused on the sound. That was reality. That was a normal reaction to an ugly death.

Focus. Pay attention to what's real.

He saw, now that the body had rolled face down and he was up close, that the wetsuit had tears up and down its length. Rips on the back and arms that hadn't been visible before, but as the body bobbed in the ocean they shifted, glinted. Dark water – or dark *something* – oozed out of them when they ground against one another.

"Jimmy J, help me here!"

"You want me to *touch* that thing?"

Tim almost laughed. It was such a perfect, completely Jimmy J thing to say. Delivered with utter seriousness, even as the kid grinned and moved to the edge of the dive platform.

Tim held to it. It was real. Not the images of grasping hands, the idea of a corpse come to life.

This was reality. A boat, a friend, passengers that would need reassuring.

His duty to whatever unfortunate diver this would prove to be.

He pushed the body forward, timing his motion so that the swells didn't push him too far – he didn't want to end up under the dive platform, either.

Jimmy J reached out. Snagged the corpse by its left arm.

"Got it," he said. "Easy... here...."

Jimmy J pulled, but didn't make much headway getting the corpse out of the water. Tim figured that between the weight of the body itself, the extra drag of the ocean, and its gear, it was probably an impossible task.

Jimmy J must have come to the same conclusion. He looked at the closest passenger. Haeberle. The big man just watched, arms crossed over a barrel chest and making no move to help. "No, don't worry," Jimmy J said. "Stay there. I got this."

Movement behind Haeberle. Sue darted forward, followed by Cal. "Sue, don't –" began the woman's father.

"Do you see the logo?" she nearly shouted. "Nelson Chemical."

And with that he felt the weight stop dragging at him. Felt the corpse begin to lift.

It was only thirty seconds until his world would explode.

IMPACT

~^~^~^~^~

Perceval Raven – now known only as Mr. Raven to friend and foe alike – had once been great, and would be great again.

That was the thought he clung to, the belief that was so deep it approached personal ideology.

I have been great.

I will be again.

Perceval Raven had been bullied in school. Beaten by his father. Abused by his mother.

He had risen above it. Risen above by falling below.

When he was eighteen he escaped. Left home after finally taking one hit too many, realizing at last that he was actually bigger than the old man. What had been a beating became a fight. What was a fight became a one-sided pummeling. Giving his father back one punch for every single one he had ever received. With interest.

After breaking both the man's arms, pulling one from its socket, fracturing ribs, blowing apart one of his eye sockets with the force of his blows... after all that, Perceval kept going.

"Stop, Perceval! Stop, Percie!" His mother screamed from a corner in the room as the beating – this time with Perceval on the right side of the fists –

(*My idiot Sunday School teacher was right! It is better to give than receive!*)

– continued. The sound shifted from hard smacks to sick, meaty thuds. Bones became powder. Mother screamed.

"Stop, Percie!" She didn't seem to realize how many times she had borne the brunt of the old man's attacks. She was trying to get her son to stop get him to stop stop stop *stop*!

She ran at him. Grabbed his upraised fist. "Stop, Percie!"

He threw her off. "Don't call me that! Don't ever call me that again!"

Perceval. The lamest, queerest, most pansy-ass name possible. No wonder he got beat up as a kid – not just by the old man, but by *everyone*.

Not again. Never again.

She glailed at him, hands reaching for him. "Percie!"

He punched her. Right in the face, right in the center of the nose. Punched her so hard she just fell over. He saw the lights – the fevered, strange lights that had visited him in the darkness so many times as he grew – go out. Dead, dark eyes. She fell forward, body limp, smashing down nose-first with a *CRACK!* on the cheap linoleum floor.

"Don't call me Perceval."

Crying. His father was crying.

For some reason that took the air out of him. Tired him. He didn't want to hit anyone anymore. Hadn't wanted to in the first place. They had made it happen. *Them*, not him. With their touches – some hard, some soft and all the worse for that – their taunts, their goddam naming him *Perceval*.

He would never go by that again. Would never let anyone know his name again. He would go by Raven – it was a comic book character he liked, and he thought it fit him. Dark, dangerous.

He washed the blood off his hands.

Left his home.

Did not look back. Did not check to see if his father could make it to a phone. Did not feel for a pulse on his mother's neck. He just didn't care.

Raven was born.

He ended up on the docks. Ended up doing heavy work. Ended up laboring with the strength of his back, earning a subsistence by the sweat of his face. Whatever jobs he could get, whatever rough work was offered.

He met a low-level pimp and drug dealer who needed someone strong. Raven began to break bones on the side. It paid better.

Then he learned to dive.

A year later, he was a legend. More than that, he was *great*. Twenty-one, barely a year after his first dive, and he was already making a name as one of the great deep sea divers. He dove the *Andrea Doria*, and did it before Trimix became widespread, before divers could go down three hundred feet and more without nearly the risk of getting bent. Dove the *Doria* and brought up the captain's log book, a sign from a galley long thought unreachable, and a China tea set that was nearly untouched by age.

He dove the Blue Hole, the Devil's Cave. He went from caves to wrecks with ease and skill. Brought back ships' bells from two hundred feet, porcelain from beneath Asian waves.

He was great. Only in his twenties, and beyond mortal understanding. He was a God of the deep.

Then, somehow, it changed. A series of romances that went awry, a string of dives that went wrong – several of them accompanied by diver fatalities that earned him a reputation as bad luck.

He began to drink.

Suddenly he was forty. He owned a dive boat, he brought others to dive sites, but he resented them. He resented the dilettantes for their disgusting lack of knowhow. For their inability to understand the mysteries and the appeal of the deep.

And he hated the few who truly understood – the ones who were as he was, as he had been once upon a time – even more. Because they were climbing heights untouched, and he wasn't on the mountain with them. He was just watching. Sitting at the bottom and wishing he could do what they could do, knowing he couldn't and never would again.

But still – he would be great again. He knew it. It was inevitable. Because he had been born to greatness, and the universe would turn itself to him, would bend to accommodate that fact.

And when he heard the cries, heard the shouts of crew and passengers alike... he knew.

This is my chance. This is where I become Great again.

He left the wheelhouse and climbed down the ladder on the side. Took in the scene quickly, efficiently – the way great men always do.

Tim in the water. Jimmy J wrestling with something, along with the father-daughter fares. Geoffrey – an insolent prick who thought greatness was something you bought, something you *earned* instead of something you were simply born to – was sprawled on the deck. A fishing rod near him, pointed at whatever the others were wrestling with.

Mercedes kept hitching in breaths then letting out raspy gasps. She was one of those people Raven's father would have called "lambs in insects' clothing." Someone meant to be used and abused, then tossed aside when whatever entertainment or purpose she could give was used up.

The last man, Haeberle. He stood near the dive platform, watching. He was a man whom Raven couldn't quite pin down. He was dark, massive. Someone that Raven wouldn't have wanted to get in a bar fight with, even in the days when he regularly did such things.

He might – *might* – be Great. Time would tell.

Raven took it all in, even as that thrill continued up and down his back. This was something big. Something that would return him to his rightful place in the sun.

Mercedes took in another of those ragged gasps. She looked green. "Vomit over the side if you have to, sweetie," said Raven. "Less to clean."

She looked a shade greener, but nodded. Visibly got control of herself. Looked away from the dive platform.

Raven nudged Geoffrey with his toe. "What have you found for us, Geoffrey?"

The twit opened his mouth to answer, but instead of words out spewed a torrent of vomit. That morning's half-digested breakfast, the odd sausage bit poking up here and there.

Raven's face twisted. "Good God," he said. He was about to tell Jimmy J to clean it up, but before he could Jimmy J spoke to him. Irritating. One more thing that impeded his progress in life. A small thing, true, but every tiny moment, every minute obstacle in Raven's path – unacceptable.

"We found a body, Mr. Raven," said Jimmy J. "Floating free."

That almost made Jimmy J's impertinence worth it. "How interesting," said Raven. He scanned the horizon. Looking for where the body had come from and seeing nothing. That meant... "I wonder if there's any salvage to be had."

The body was probably new enough that any sunken boat it belonged to – if there *was* a sunken boat – probably wasn't up for grabs. It would have to be returned, and even if it *were* available for the taking, it was under eight hundred feet of water.

But Raven knew people who purchased such information. Locations of wrecks. And they weren't particularly picky about the wreck's age. There was profit to be had for men who knew how to sweep in and strip the carcasses of dead boats. To take all that was of worth and leave only a skeleton of once-value, once-greatness.

All things great would someday be once-great. All but Raven himself.

The body made its way to the dive platform, hauled up in a dripping mess by Jimmy J, Sue, and Cal.

Raven moved toward the body, intent on inspecting it. He saw a logo and a name on one of the arms: Nelson Chem. That was interesting. Could mean a research vessel, could mean something considerably bigger.

He had to restrain himself from licking his lips. This was it. He could feel it.

Tim was still in the water; now moved toward the port ladder to pull himself up.

WHUD.

Something like muffled thunder sounded. Only no, thunder came from above. And this was a sound – muffled, yes, but powerful, nearly *frightening* – that came from below.

He saw Tim, still reaching for the ladder.

And then a huge wave slammed into Raven's employee, and *The Celeste* herself.

The wave didn't roll across the horizon, didn't hump up from somewhere far away and push into them. Nor was it a normal swell, but a twenty-foot monster that could well destroy the boat.

And it had simply *appeared*. Not during a massive storm or *any* kind of inclement weather. The skies were clear, the sea had been calm.

Raven had a moment to think, Impossible!

Another moment to see Tim fly into the ladder, to see it catch him on the jaw with a force Raven could nearly feel from the deck.

Jimmy J, Sue, and Cal all rocketed back, skidding across the deck toward the front of the boat. Sue and Cal caught each other in a knot of tangled limbs, hands and feet and legs and arms wrapping around one another like a two-headed octopus curling in on itself in the face of danger.

Jimmy J kept his hold on the corpse. It plowed into him, driving him back. Dead weight slamming on him almost as hard as the wave itself.

Haeberle took a huge step and seemed for a moment like he might – impossibly – retain his balance. Then he, too, flew toward the wheelhouse. He slammed into Geoffrey, who was screaming again. Geoffrey bit out a panicked, "Bastardbitch!" before both of them went down. Geoffrey slammed face-first into the deck. A crunch that reminded Raven of the sound his mother made when she hit the floor. That cheap linoleum floor.

Mercedes. Useless woman, always cringing ever-so-slightly when you spoke to her. A beaten dog, a bitch with no bite. But she was a paying customer so when she tipped half over the starboard side of the ship, tipping with the roll of *The Celeste*, Raven reached out a hand and managed to snag a handful of her shorts.

She probably won't even thank me for it.

He braced himself against a pipe on the side of the wheelhouse structure, holding fast while the wave tipped everyone off their feet. Remaining upright and heroic while even *The Celeste* herself nearly spilled over, went nearly perpendicular to the sea. Of course. He was destined to stand when others fell.

Then, abruptly, the wave was gone. It didn't curl its way across the surface and disappear from sight. One minute it simply *was*, another it simply *wasn't*.

All was calm again.

"What the hell was that?" growled Haeberle. He stood, disentangling himself from Geoffrey's panic-hold. He left the other man curled on the deck. Stepped away from him as one might step away from a pile of dogshit.

Raven approved.

"Forget what it was, get this stiff off me!" Jimmy J was struggling with the corpse, which had inexplicably managed to land crotch-first against the diver's face. It was funny. Raven didn't giggle – giggling was for fools and homosexuals – but only through force of will. Another ability of the great: to control themselves and their emotions in the face of anything.

Then he saw something that nearly made him lose his composure. Not the body's face, not its mangled wetsuit – he had seen both, and worse, in his long years at sea.

No, for an instant it appeared as though the diver *moved*. Not like it was regaining some impossible form of life; not like it was going to stand up and begin ambling around the deck and shooting the breeze.

The body... *writhed*. Something under the suit moved, like there was a snake beneath the neoprene. Like a serpent had taken up residence in the corpse and eventually eaten it away to nothing.

"Ow!" Jimmy J wailed.

Cal and Sue managed to pull themselves apart, the two-headed octopus becoming father and daughter once more. Cal hurried to Jimmy J and tried to help him out from under the corpse.

"You okay?" said Cal. "What happened?"

"Dead guy bit my arm!"

For a moment Raven felt a thrill of fear. Just a moment, a *frisson* that ran up and down his spine.

Did I see something?

No. Not possible. Just water escaping the suit.

Just water.

Sue spoke as Cal and Jimmy J kept wrestling the corpse. "Where's Tim?'

Then she ran. Raven's gaze tracked her – not merely out of curiosity, but because she was a fine bit of tail. Someone that would have thrown herself at him a few years ago.

Time'll come again, Rave.

She dove off the back of the dive platform with a splash. Raven wasn't sure why at first, then he saw Tim, face down in the water and a spreading blot of his own blood surrounding him.

Cal watched his daughter go, shouting, "Sue!" He left Jimmy J to deal with the –

(moving? writhing?)

– corpse of the unknown diver on his own. Ran after his daughter as she grabbed Tim under his chin and yanked him toward the boat.

A moment later another splash signaled someone else joining her. Jimmy J helped her manhandle Tim's limp body toward the dive platform.

Raven thought he heard Sue say, "Thanks," but the word was consumed in the sea and the splashing as the two of them pushed Tim forward.

"Like I'm gonna let Timmy get felt up by a pretty girl without getting a piece of the action," Jimmy J said, the words coming out in jagged exhalations as he pushed Tim the rest of the way onto the platform. Cal helped pull, and a moment later Raven joined them – wouldn't do to have the paying customers think he wasn't willing to help should one of them go over.

Sue pulled herself up. "He going to be all right?"

Tim's eyes fluttered at the same moment. "What happened?" he mumbled. A cut on his chin – the only one, as far as Raven could see – welled up. Head wounds could be nasty, even when superficial. Raven didn't think the wound would need more than a bit of gauze, maybe some liquid bandage from the first-aid kit.

That was good. He didn't need some workman's comp claim. Or the hassle of finding another dive leader.

"Ladder hit you, man," said Jimmy J as he pulled himself onto the dive platform as well. He squeezed Tim's shoulder. "Glad you're still with us."

Tim groaned. "Feels like I got kissed by your big fat girlfriend."

Jimmy J's shoulder squeeze turned into a punch. "Impossible. My girlfriend has no lips. 'Ol' Snakeface' is what I call her."

Tim rolled his eyes. Winced. "Gross," he said.

Raven rolled his eyes as well. "He's fine," he said.

He went to the more interesting of the two objects laying on the deck: the body. Cal was already there, looking at the corpse with Haeberle. Cal looked at it with the interest of a detective who has found an important clue. Haeberle stared at it with a look that Raven didn't understand, couldn't quite place. It was almost... *hungry*. But more than that, too. Something dark. Disconcerting.

Raven shifted his attention to the body itself. Strangely relieved to look away from Haeberle.

The body was on its back. Waxy brown un-face. Teeth grimacing through chewed-away lips.

"What the hell happened to him? Or her?" said Haeberle. His voice trembled, but Raven didn't think it was fear he heard. It was –

(*hunger*)

– something else.

"It's not a her," said Cal. He spoke quickly, sharply. Raven remembered the extra money he had been paid to come to this particular area. Remembered reports of the boat that had gone missing here a few weeks ago. Realized they must be looking for someone. So when he said, "It's not a her," he really meant to say, "It's not the 'her' we're looking for."

Raven glanced at Sue. She was looking at her father, but with the pronouncement she looked back to Tim, holding a cloth to his chin.

Raven's lip curled as he looked at the body. He wasn't interested in such grotesquerie, other than as a means to an end.

"I'm more interested in just what happened on the sea than what happened to a corpse some time ago."

And that was the truth. Even though the corpse signaled an opportunity for money – something Raven was always on the lookout for, especially when it was easy – he felt more than a little discomfited by an event he had never seen or felt or even *heard* of before.

Where did that wave come from?

Where did it *go*?

He climbed up the ladder that led from the deck to the small balcony behind the wheelhouse, then went in.

The wheelhouse was small, nothing fancy needed to pilot a boat of this size. Pilot's and navigator's chairs. Radio. A few consoles, a computer terminal hooked up to the bottom finder, GPS chartplotter, a printer that he used to print out invoices. When he had started there had barely seemed to be enough room for all the electronics. Now it took up little space – everything was getting smaller. The world included.

Easy for a man of greatness – or greatness to come – to conquer.

He checked the bottom finder: a sonar sensor built to help find – and even identify – fish below the boat. It also measured bottom contours, structure details, thermoclines, and more. Its usefulness was limited over water this deep, but it still might –

He stopped moving. His entire body tight as he saw what was on the display of the bottom finder. He flicked the screen. Same. Same thing that made no sense.

"That's not possible," he said.

And it wasn't. Even less so than finding a dead body in the middle of open ocean. Less even than a wave coming out of nowhere and disappearing as fast as it came.

He turned off the bottomfinder. Booted it up again.

Same thing.

He checked the result on his other instruments.

"Impossible," he muttered again. Because what he was seeing was just that.

But the instruments all agreed.

The impossible was reality.

He licked his lips. Not sure whether he was frightened or excited. Perhaps it was both. Life was full of moments fraught with both danger and promise.

This was his moment.

He felt it.

FIND

~^~^~^~^~

Jimmy J didn't like dead things. That was one of the reasons he wasn't a butcher. His dad had been a butcher, his uncle. His grandfather.

And they weren't *just* butchers, either. Grampa Jim started out with a butcher shop in the sixties, but by the early seventies he had eight shops and a meat packing plant. By the eighties – when Dad started, they were the fifth largest meat wholesaler in the nation.

Jimmy J was supposed to follow in their footsteps. To work at one of the corner shops they still owned, then work his way up on a predetermined course that would lead inevitably to a big office overlooking the floor of one of the plants. Security, even riches.

But the idea of cutting up all that meat, spending day after day looking at dead flesh that was supposed to turn into steaks and hot dogs and McBurgers. The thing was that Jimmy J *liked* eating those things. And he didn't know if he still would after watching the "before" part of his favorite "afters."

So he ended up on the sea. There are two kinds of people who end up working in the ocean – three if you count the scientific types, like Sue and maybe her dad seemed to be. But he didn't count them. They were just professors who used the ocean as lab projects. Maybe they loved it, but only in tandem with their love of science. Not a *pure* love.

So the other two people who you found at sea were people born to it, or people whom the sea had adopted. Jimmy J was the latter. He wasn't the son of seafaring folk – no fishermen or even Navy in his background. But he felt the water in his veins, felt the lust and love for the rolling ocean the first time he set foot on a boat. Grammy J almost shot him when he told her he wanted to be a diver, then almost slit her own wrists out of guilt for giving him that first day trip as a birthday present.

The sea was magical. The sea was his, and he belonged to her as well.

He never looked back.

Still, at this moment he kind of wondered if he would have been better off at the butcher shop. Certainly butcher shops never exploded beneath you, never sent you flying into dead bodies that seemed to bite you – his arm still hurt from where the unknown something had pinched him.

Mr. R suddenly exploded out of the wheelhouse. Dropped down the ladder to the deck and ran past Jimmy J. He was mumbling, and Jimmy J focused on him – something to distract himself from what had just happened, and the dead body that still lay disconcertingly close.

"What's wrong, Mr. R?" he said.

"Not possible," Mr. R was mumbling, over and over. "Not possible. Not...."

Mr. R looked at the body, still oozing water and black muck onto the deck. Jimmy J realized that Haeberle had moved close to the corpse and was poking it with grim fascination.

Geez, that guy gives me the creeps.

And he did. He was big, he was way too intense to be out on something as tranquil as the open ocean was

(*Or at least as tranquil as the open ocean should be.*)

– in weather like this.

Then the big guy stopped poking. He reached for the corpse's hand. For a second Jimmy J had the weird feeling that the big guy was going to hold hands with the dead dude. Some kind of love affair that only the psycho could understand.

Then Jimmy J realized there was something *in* the dead guy's hand.

Haeberle reached for it, but another hand darted in. Mr. R. He had a look on his face that Jimmy J didn't like. Hot and bothered and excited all at once. Like he had spotted a particularly good-looking girl at a party. But not one he was interested in striking up a conversation with, just someone he wanted to screw and then drop.

"What are you doing?" said a voice. Sue. Cool chick. She had spotted Mr. R and Haeberle and apparently also the fact that the Señor Deado was holding something. But she didn't look like she was interested in handholding.

Neither was Jimmy J. His right arm tingled, with a core of pain on his forearm. He glanced at it; saw nothing. No bite, no irritation. But it still hurt, and he wondered what had got him.

"Mr. R," he said, "I don't know if you should touch – "

"Shut up, Jimmy," said Mr. R. It was nearly a snarl. Rabid enough that Jimmy J actually fell back a step.

Mr. R had his hand on the dead dude's hand. Pulling at the fingers. They wouldn't open.

Mr. R grunted. Jimmy J's jaw dropped as he heard a shearing crackle. Fingers breaking. "Uh, I really don't –"

"Shut *up*, Jimmy."

More crackles. They made Jimmy J's teeth feel like they were turning inside out, made his tongue go dry in his mouth.

Bad juju.

Then Mr. R yanked something free. Held it up.

It was a disc. Crusted in algae. Some of it fully black.

And some of it glinted in his hand.

Gold.

Jimmy J wasn't a treasure hunter, wasn't a technical diver like Mr. R had been six hundred years ago. He was just a dude who loved the ocean. But even he knew what Mr. R was holding. This wasn't just gold, it was *treasure*.

Mr. R looked at the body. So did everyone else.

What happened to you, Dead Dude?

Mr. R's eyes were half-closed, like he was thinking something he didn't want shining through. The look made Jimmy J's teeth continue their slow inward turn. So did the look on Haeberle's face.

Jimmy J suddenly knew the big guy wanted that gold piece. And wondered how bad. If he'd be willing to kill to get it.

Nah. Don't be dumbtastic, dude. Not for a piece of gold.

How 'bout for a lot of pieces?

And that made Jimmy J cold, because he thought the answer to that question was probably a big fat "yes."

MOTIONS

~^~^~^~^~

Sue wanted to turn over the body. To take a good look at it, to find out what had happened to it.

And if it could tell her anything about what had happened to Debi.

But they ended up putting that off. Because of what had happened in the ocean. Because of the gold.

Because of whatever Mr. Raven wasn't telling them.

That he wasn't telling something was obvious in his carriage, in the rigid way he moved. Something had him upset – or excited – and it wasn't just the gold piece he hadn't let go since they found it.

Everyone was acting strange. That was to be expected, she supposed. Not every day a rogue wave slams into your boat, almost capsizing you. Not every day you find a dead body in the waves. Not every day you find what looks like pirate's booty in the hand of that dead body.

But there was more to the strangeness. A feeling in the air, making everyone jittery. Something was wrong. Not just what they knew about, but something they *didn't*.

Her examination of the body had to wait. Mr. Raven insisted on getting the body off the deck. Jimmy J replied that he'd be happy to do so, as soon as he made sure Tim wasn't going to die.

Tim had waved him off, expressing "I'm fine" with the motion. But even that small movement caused blood to well out of his cut chin. Jimmy J told him to "shove it, *mi compadre*." And Sue thought that was great of him.

Jimmy J disappeared into the salon, then reappeared with a first aid kit. He slathered Tim's chin with liquid bandage, which hardened into a translucent second skin. Then he slapped a butterfly bandage perpendicular to the cut. "Just to make double sure you don't bleed to death."

"I'm not going to bleed to death."

"Sucks for me. If you do, I call your stuff."

Then Mr. Raven insisted that something be done about the body. Jimmy J picked up the feet with a sigh. Looked at Haeberle.

"What do you want?" growled the big man. His eyes flashed dangerously.

Jimmy J didn't seem to notice. Or maybe his easygoing nature was just impervious to threatening looks from homicidal-seeming giants. "You're a big strapping boy. Mind helping?"

Haeberle looked like he was going to tell Jimmy J to shove it up his ass, then looked around at the alternatives. Tim: still a bit woozy-seeming. Cal: old. Mr. Raven: the guy in charge. Geoffrey: still whining about all that had happened, kind of curled up on the side of the deck and mumbling to himself with an occasional "no fair" and "bastard" being the only real words Sue could make out.

Mercedes and Sue: women. Somehow she knew that meant they couldn't be counted on – in his mind, at least – if they were even worthy of consideration at all.

So he growled and grabbed the body by the shoulders. Face curling as more black ooze spilled from the cuts, ran off the waxy substance that was all that remained of its face.

"Where?" he grunted.

Jimmy J looked at Mr. Raven. "Storage," said the boat's owner and captain.

The two men went into the salon, then Jimmy J directed Haeberle toward the stairs that led down. Mr. Raven followed, and a moment later so did Tim. He tottered for a moment, and Cal grabbed him. "Lean on me," said Sue's father.

Tim nodded thanks. "Little woozy."

"Yeah, you fought a boat with your face. Brave," said Jimmy J.

"Dumb," he said.

"Yeah, pretty dumb," Jimmy J said with a grin and a wag of his eyebrows to indicate Tim had won the argument – but was that such a good thing?

Sue followed them all. They left Geoffrey and Mercedes on the deck. Mercedes moved to check on Geoffrey as they passed by, and Sue heard him voice a last "bastardsonofacrap" before she went down the stairs.

By the time she was at the bottom, Jimmy J and Haeberle were already disappearing into the storage room opposite the cabin where everyone slept. A crinkling sound came to her, and when she looked in the storage door, she saw the body being laid out on a blue tarp.

It was a tight fit. The storage room held everything from extra scuba tanks to netting to the dry goods food. It was all on the walls, in sturdy cage-shelves that had managed to contain most of it when the wave hit the boat. But there was some stuff dripping, a few boxes and cans that had exploded in their sections and caused a mess.

The body took up most of the narrow space between the two rows of shelving and storage. Just enough room to stand at the head, where Jimmy J was, room at the foot where Haeberle stood, and to maybe squeeze one more person in.

Haeberle looked at the body again. Then, suddenly, he lurched forward. Before anyone really understood what he was doing he had begun slapping his big palms all over the corpse.

Sue felt her eyes widen in tandem with everyone else's.

What's he –?

He's frisking the corpse.

He's looking for more gold.

She had barely managed to process these facts when Haeberle finished. He sighed, a quick, hard exhale like that of a moderately irritated rhino. Then he left. Apparently not interested in the corpse if it had no more treasure to yield.

Sue slipped inside the storage room. She leaned in to the body. This time someone had enough wits to question the move.

"I don't think we should –" began Tim.

"We need to find out what happened," Sue replied.

"I kinda agree, man," said Jimmy J. He pointed at the wounds that covered the body: the weird gashes across most of the body's trunk, arms, legs. Still oozing dark goo. "I never seen anything like that before. Gives me the creepy crawlies."

Sue realized everything he had just said was ambiguous: he could be advocating for her to look at the body, or he could be siding with Tim.

Even though the latter was more likely, she chose the interpretation she preferred.

Two against one, Tim. You lose.

She wondered absently if he'd get upset. And if he *did* get upset would he want to talk about it? Maybe more?

Down, girl. Down. One thing at a time.

Plus there's a dead body right here. Not the best time to ask a guy out. Yeah, there's that.

One of the shelves was magnetized and doubled as a small emergency tool box. A number of objects stuck tightly to it, including a folding utility knife which she grabbed and flipped open. Then a fast move and a faster swipe with the knife, and she had cut a long slit in the wetsuit, from the nape of the neck to just above the groin.

She had never seen anything that would cut a wetsuit the way this one had been slashed: long, thin cuts all over the body. She thought there might be a chance the body had gotten stuck in a cave or wreck, and the slits were the result of the diver wrestling his (or her – there was no real way to tell at this point) way out of a tight squeeze.

Maybe a propeller? Maybe he wandered into range of his boat's prop as it was starting?

No. Neither would account for these gashes in the suit.

So she cut it open.

Looked.

And almost screamed.

There was nothing in the suit. Just some bone sticking up from the pelvis, others from where the arms apparently still extended into the sut.

But where the trunk was: nothing. No flesh at all, save a few smeared clumps that she suspected would turn out to be entrails upon close inspection.

How? I touched the thing. Touched the chest. It was rigid. There was something there, I know it.

But if so, where had it gone?

The opening of the suit released a strong odor: the suit smelled like the sea inside. But not the good, clean smell of deep water. This was the rotten smell you encountered when wandering near piers or groynes on the beach: decomposing animals and seaweed, water left stagnant, perhaps the offal of animals (human included). It was tangy, unpleasant.

Tim broke out of his paralysis first, leaning in to look closer at what everyone could plainly see.

Jimmy J was a close second. "What the hell? What the *hell*?"

Her father spoke, startling Sue. She had almost forgotten that he was behind her. Which was appropriate given how much time he'd spent with her as a child.

"What could do that?" he asked. "Shark?"

Tim shook his head. "Not without eating through the suit as well. This… I don't know. I've never heard of anything like this."

For some reason –

(*Imagination. It's my imagination.*)

– the corpse, eyeless face staring at the ceiling of the storage area, seemed suddenly to be smiling. The exposed teeth hadn't moved –

(Had *they?*)

– but her imagination changed the death-grimace to a smile of hidden import. The dead diver knew what had happened, but it's face seemed to chant, "I'll never tell, I'll never tell, what you don't know might kill you, but I'll never tell."

The face suddenly disappeared from view as Tim flipped the slashed pieces of the suit back over the nothing at the center of the body, then covered all of it with blue tarp. The dark eye sockets, the grimacing teeth, the waxy brown once-flesh – all disappeared under a crinkling blue sheet of thick plastic.

She was glad. The face, the empty hole where a torso should have been… it was all so disgusting, so *wrong* that she wished she could excise the memory of it from her mind.

At the same time, though, she hated that she couldn't see the thing. Because what if it did something? What if it was doing something even now, beneath the tarp that shielded it from view?

Did the tarp just move? Did something move under it?

Did the body move?

No. Of course not. She resisted the urge to throw the tarp aside. There would be no change in the corpse's position, no chance it could be moving under its own strength.

It was dead.

One of the people on Debi's boat was dead.

How, when, why? Still mysteries.

Sue had found something that should have been a major clue. Should have drawn her closer to answering the question of what had happened to her sister.

Instead, it seemed like she had more questions than ever.

The tarp settled a bit more. Crinkled. There was that illusion of movement under the tarp again.

No. Just imagination.

Just imagination.

Imagination.

She shivered.

"Okay, everyone," said Mr. Raven. Sue started. For a moment she had almost forgotten there were other people around. It had been just her and a corpse. Just her and the

—

(*moving*)

– silent dead.

"I need to see everyone in the salon," said Mr. Raven.

"Why?" said Jimmy J. His voice sounded dreamy, like he was falling asleep, or perhaps just waking up. Sue couldn't tell if that was because he was reacting to the shock of the body, the wave, everything that had happened; or if she was just hearing things wrong. Her senses seemed to be playing tricks on her.

"If I tell you now, Jimmy, I'll just have to repeat it to Mercedes and Geoffrey." His expression turned in on itself. His eyes grew flinty and even colder than they usually were. "But we need to talk about something important."

Tim nodded at the tarp-covered corpse. "I think we've got plenty to talk about right here."

Mr. Raven laughed. Just a single bark, nearly a cough. No brightness or humor in it. "This?" He gestured at the body on the floor. "This is shit. I have something *important* to talk about."

Tim's gaze joined Sue's. She could see him asking himself what the boat owner wanted. And she could see that he was terribly worried about it.

So, she realized, was she.

What could make a dead, weirdly eaten body into a non-issue? Into "shit"?

Mr. Raven turned away. Went to the stairs that led to the salon. Climbed up and disappeared.

The others followed. Only Tim and she remained.

He gestured. *After you.*

She left. Not because she wanted to hear what Mr. Raven was going to say.

She thought she had seen the body move again.

Impossible. Just the tarp settling down.

Just the tarp.

64

DEPTH

~^~^~^~^~

The dying sun pushed pink fingers into the room. It cast a dull glow about the salon, a new night's darkness fighting the last light of a sunny day. Darkness winning, as must be, as was inevitable.

It was the kind of thing that might be beautiful, but just as easily eerie and strange. Everyone's skin was yellowed, jaundiced by the lowering sun. Eye sockets became hollowed by the long shadows cast.

It was, Tim thought, like a group of skeletons had gathered for a strange party in the salon.

They were all there, even Geoffrey and Mercedes. Haeberle stood beside the narrow staircase that led up to the wheelhouse. He held the gold piece, turning it over and over in his hands and occasionally rubbing it against his now-streaked shirt, cleaning it as much as he could. He wore a distant, calculating expression that Tim didn't like.

Geoffrey had been sitting at the small table where people could eat meals or play cards or just b.s. during the parts of the trip when they weren't actually diving. Now he stood and reached toward Haeberle.

"Hey," he said, "give someone else a chance to look at –"

He fell silent as Haeberle looked up at him. Tim could see why. The other man's expression had gone from cold and distant to completely present, with barely-contained mayhem dancing like flame across his visage.

"I suppose you're wondering why I called you all here," said Mr. Raven. He was standing directly in front of the steps to the wheelhouse, as though to remind everyone that he was the owner, the captain. Tim thought it likely that was purposeful. Mr. Raven liked people to know he was in charge.

Coming from anyone else, this line – so overused in movies and TV shows that it had become cliché – would seem like a joke. But not from Mr. Raven, and not now.

Tim felt his lips pucker. "*I'm* wondering why we haven't called in what happened."

He had tried to get Mr. Raven to go up and call in the discovery of the dead body, and maybe to radio any Navy vessels in the area to find out what was with the wave that had so battered them. Mr. Raven ignored him.

"The law is quite clear," said Mr. Raven. "We're required to report certain injuries, or if someone goes missing. But someone long dead?" He shook his head. "That's... a gray area." He waved, dismissing the subject. "In any event, we have something strange to deal with."

Jimmy J rubbed his arm. He had gotten a long strip of gauze from the first aid kit while Mr. Raven was herding everyone into the salon, and now his forearm arm was wrapped in white. Tim didn't understand why he had done this until Jimmy J had told him about the sharp pain he felt when the body fell on top of him. The other dive leader showed Tim his arm and sure enough, there was a long thin slash on it.

"I didn't see it at first, but I guess I must have cut myself on the guy's equipment," said Jimmy J. "Not much blood but it hurts like your momma on top of me."

Now Jimmy J didn't make any jokes. He just rubbed his arm when Mr. Raven said there was "something strange" to deal with and answered with a very direct and serious, "No shit."

Mr. Raven shook his head. "Not the body. I'm talking about the ocean floor."

Tim felt himself perk up. What did Mr. Raven mean?

At the same time, though, he felt something akin to panic roll through him. Whatever it was, it wasn't going to be good. He could feel it.

"What about it?" said Geoffrey. "It's sand and sand and sand, right? We haven't even found many fish to look at. Which, by the way, has made this dive a huge bust and a huger waste of money." He crossed his arms and looked like nothing more than a man-sized child about to throw a tantrum.

"My apologies for the lack of fish, Geoffrey," said Mr. Raven in a tone that indicated he couldn't possibly care less about the other man's displeasure. "But of more concern is the fact that the ocean floor is currently one-hundred-fifty feet below us."

Tim froze. So did everyone else – except Haeberle, who kept turning the gold over and over in his big hands.

"Mr. R," Jimmy J finally said. "That's... that's wrong."

"We're over an eight-hundred-foot shelf, Mr. Raven.," said Tim.

Mr. Raven shook his head. "No, we *were* over an eight-hundred-foot shelf," he said. "But whatever caused that wave also seems to have caused a massive shift in the ocean floor."

"That's not possible," said Sue. She was seated at the table with her father, and Cal slammed his fist down on the cheap wood as if to punctuate her sentence, to accentuate the truth of it.

"That's ridiculous," he said.

Mr. Raven nodded. "I agree. But the sonar, the bottom finder, the fish finder – every piece of equipment I have confirms it. So the question isn't if it really happened, the question is...." He looked around the salon, meeting each person's eyes in turn. "What are we going to do about it?"

Geoffrey snorted. "We get the hell out of here. We go home."

"I second that," said Mercedes. As usual, she was sitting by herself on a chair bolted to the wall. She sounded worried, as though voicing her opinion was not merely uncomfortable for her, but actively dangerous. Still, Tim was glad to hear her voice. She had listened intently and courteously to instructions and requests on the dive trip, but had barely said three sentences the whole time. Tim had started to worry about her – not that she would cause trouble or be a danger on the boat, but rather that she might be heading *into* trouble and/or danger when she got off it.

"So let's go," said Geoffrey. "I'm tired and bruised and I don't –"

"That's not all, is it?" said Haeberle. His deep voice seemed to creep through the cracks in Geoffrey's permawhine. Strong, quiet – because if you were strong enough you didn't *have* to raise your voice.

Mr. Raven smiled a Cheshire smile.

Tim remembered that the Cheshire cat had been Alice's sometime guide, but one of very little use since the area she traversed was one of dream or perhaps nightmare. A place where nothing made sense.

"No, indeed," said Mr. Raven. "That's not all by a long shot."

And down the rabbit hole we go.

Mr. Raven pulled a crinkled piece of paper from his pocket. It hung there in his hand like a damaged bird, something injured but still possibly dangerous. Tim took it when no one else moved to do so.

"What is this?" he asked.

"A printout of what the 3-D sonar found at the bottom – the new bottom – here."

Tim felt breath on his shoulder. Jimmy J was leaning over him. A bit of a space invasion, but that was Jimmy J for you. And under the circumstances Tim couldn't blame him for wanting to see what Tim held.

Jimmy J pointed at a spot in the center. "What is that?"

Tim shook his head. *Curiouser and curiouser.* "Looks like –"

"Is that a ship?"

Tim started. He had been so intent on the printout that he hadn't even heard Cal stand and join him and Jimmy J.

"I think it might be, yes," said Mr. Raven.

Something clicked. Tim jerked at the sound.

Easy, man. Calm down.

It was just Mr. Raven, turning on a light that hung from the center of the ceiling. Tim realized that his eyes stung from looking at the printout, from the gray on gray and then gray on black that the paper had become.

Night had fallen. The thin fingers of the sun had drawn into a dark fist and disappeared into the black of open ocean.

Mr. Raven held out his hand to Haeberle, obviously waiting for the man to give him the coin. Haeberle pointedly ignored him; kept flipping the coin over and over, pausing to clean it a bit more every so often.

Mr. Raven's hand withdrew. He looked perturbed. Beyond perturbed, actually. Close to enraged. He took a few visibly deep breaths. Then said, "I wonder... I wonder if the ship might be where this coin came from?"

Tim kept looking at the bottom profile. The mass in the center that, sure enough, seemed to be the right shape to be a vessel of some kind. It could also be a pile of rocks, some coral – anything. But maybe....

Jimmy J pointed at another mass beside the one in the center of the sheet. "What's this stuff over here?"

Tim shook his head. "Doesn't matter. This is all academic. Maritime law is so complicated, chances are whatever's down there ends up belonging to some government, or the descendants of the passengers or the insurers."

Mr. Raven nodded. "I agree. Which is why I haven't called it in."

He let the implications of that statement hang in the air.

No one knows.

Just us.

We have it to ourselves.

And this gold piece came from somewhere.

Tim heard the chain of thought as clearly as if Mr. Raven had laid it all out for them verbally, with Power Point presentation and music for dramatic effect.

He thought it was insane.

And there was a powerful urge to follow along with the idea. It is human nature to seek, to explore, to look for what is unknown and conquer it through understanding what it *is*.

It is also human nature to hope for the easy way. To desire a windfall, the kindness of fate falling disproportionately upon us. It is why the lottery plays in almost every state, why we bet money on horses and why the slot machines rest not one minute of one day in Las Vegas.

Tim was more than a little disconcerted to find himself falling into both categories of human normality.

What is down there?

What if it's a treasure?

But he shoved them away. Pushed them from him and re-established what he had to think of as sanity.

He opened his mouth to voice his objections. To say how dangerous this would be, how little chance there was that anything lay there except the bottom of the ocean – a bottom that had risen almost seven hundred feet in a matter of seconds.

And as if to aid his recall of the moment where the world blew up around him, the ocean rising and slamming him face-first into the dive ladder, a sound rolled through the salon – through the entire boat.

Tim had a moment of recollection, an instant where his body remembered where it had heard this sound before and clenched in readiness.

Then the ocean swelled below them. Just like it had before, when he was pushing a dead body onto the boat. Only this time it was more powerful, if that were possible. It felt like a giant fist slamming into the bottom of the boat, ramming the entire craft upward and then even more violently dropping it out from under them.

Tim felt himself curl into a ball – the position we hold when we enter the world, the posture to which we return when we fear we might leave it. Something hit his shoulder, hard –

(*the ceiling holy hell I just hit the* ceiling)

– and then he bounced away from it as gravity seized him and yanked him downward again.

The boat tilted madly to port, then held there a long moment. Tim tumbled sideways, feeling someone barrel into him – Sue, her arms going reflexively around him – and then a long –

(*too long too long we're dead too long*)

– moment of dead air when the boat continued listing to the side, hanging at a forty-five degree angle over the water, deciding whether or not to fall.

Then, slowly…

… it tilted back to center.

The motion seemed slow to Tim's adrenaline-soaked vision, but it must have been fast because he lurched to the side – and now he was holding Sue, instead of the other way around – and almost broke himself in half against the salon table.

Something crashed somewhere in the boat. The unmistakable sound of breakage.

And then nothing. No motion, no more headlong falls up and down and side to side. The gentle sigh of the ocean was all that could be heard for a peaceful second, a soughing that sounded like parchment skin rasping over sun-bleached bones in his mind.

Then: groans.

Jimmy J groaned the loudest, following the sound with, "Anyone dead? I think I'm dead."

Tim managed to stand, helping Sue from her position flat on her stomach to her hands and knees. He tried to help her stand, but she waved him off. Apparently she wasn't ready for that just yet.

"You okay?" he said.

"I think so. Just gonna stay here for a sec."

Tim moved to Sue's father. Cal had been tossed below the salon table, and had somehow wrapped himself around the steel pole that bolted table to floor. Tim helped him out, slowly. The man grimaced with every movement, as though he'd been bruised from head to toe. He probably had.

Mercedes was on her feet. She helped Geoffrey, who was *sonofabitchbastard*-ing in a low voice. Haeberle was flat on his back and Tim moved next to him, but the man knocked away his hand when it was offered. "Back off," he snarled, then rolled to his stomach and pushed himself to hands and knees. Stood.

Jimmy J was helping Mr. Raven to his feet. The boat captain made no noise, but his face was white as a summer cloud.

Tim shouldn't have said anything. He should have waited, at least.

But he was rattled.

He was bruised.

He was *scared*.

He looked at Mr. Raven. "Still think we should stay here?" he said.

Mr. Raven looked at him. And Tim couldn't tell if the white skin of his face was blushing in embarrassment, fear... or rage.

DAMAGED

~^~^~^~^~

Haeberle watched Jimmy J's head and torso rise out of the access port in the middle of the aft deck. Darkness ruled in the space below the deck, but he knew what was down there. The engine. The first thing they had checked after the wave – or whatever it was – struck them for the second time.

"Well?" said Tim. He looked cocky, even when waiting for news that might determine the course – and length – of their lives.

Not that Haeberle was truly worried. He knew that he wasn't going to die. He couldn't. When he died the world ended, and that was not acceptable in the grand scheme of things.

No, he wasn't worried. But Tim irritated him. Because if everything around Haeberle –

(*I hate that name, why did the guy I killed have to be named* Haeberle, *of all things?*

Just go with it, just remember that you're *Haeberle, at least for now.*)

– was a figment of his imagination, if he really existed in a universe that had sprung into being with his birth and would fade away to nothing when (if!) he died, why in God's name would his dream have coughed up something as annoying as Tim Palmer?

Haeberle decided to waste the guy. Not now. But soon.

It would be fun.

"That... thing, whatever the hell it was, banged the everloving crapola out of the engine. Something's bent, I can't really tell what." Jimmy J sighed, rubbed his chin with his hand. "We ain't going anywhere." He shook his head. "What about you? Any luck on the radio?"

"There's a Navy cutter on its way," said Tim.

"How long?"

"Three days."

"Are you *serious*?"

"So we go," said Haeberle. He was standing in the doorway to the salon, and as he said the words he felt someone else behind him. Geoffrey.

Tim turned to them both. His face curled in an expression that was divided equally between incredulity and what Haeberle chose to interpret as fear.

It had to be fear. Everyone feared him, secretly at least. Well, not everyone. Women didn't fear him, they *loved* him. He had yet to meet a woman who didn't want him – his body, his love. The two on the boat were no different. Sue was a piece. Mercedes wasn't bad, either. And they both wanted him, sure as the sun raised on his head every day. Sure as it lowered at night, and sure as all ended each night when he slept, only to be resurrected in his dreams and in his waking life the next day.

"What the hell are you talking about?" demanded Tim.

Yes, he'd definitely have to die. No one talked to Haeberle like this. Even if "Haeberle" was just a name, the man behind it demanded better than this. Demanded respect. Demanded *awe*.

Haeberle shrugged. "Tomorrow. We go to the wreck."

He stepped toward the middle of the deck. Behind him, he felt Geoffrey –

(Gutless asshole.

But at least he's respectful. Afraid.)

– Mercedes, Sue, and Cal –

(Another one who doesn't show the proper fear. Another one who deserves death.

– follow him out of the salon. Mr. Raven came out a moment later.

"You're nuts. We're not going down there like this. We're waiting for the naval vessels to –"

Haeberle cut Tim off. The look of surprise, anger –

(terror!)

– in the dive captain's eyes was delicious. "We wait for them and we have no chance to get whatever's down there."

Everyone froze around him. Total statues, like he had fallen asleep without knowing it and they had taken up their own nightly position of unmovement, unlife.

"So you want to steal whatever's down there?" Mercedes said. As always her voice was soft, defeated, broken – sexy.

Mr. Raven broke in before anyone else could voice an opinion. "No, no. I think he wants to *salvage* it. There's a difference. If it looks new, we wait for the cavalry to claim and restore it to its owners. But if it's old...." He shrugged.

"We still wait for the cavalry. But we get some work done first."

Mr. Raven grinned. A smile that Haeberle might have seen on his own face when he practiced smiling in the mirror. Wide, sincere, and a little dangerous.

He wondered if Mr. Raven might be a part of him. A bit of his own subconscious made flesh. That bore thinking about.

"Yeah," he said as soon as Mr. Raven had finished. "That sounds good."

Geoffrey spoke up, and said probably the only thing he'd ever said that was worth the breath it took: "I'm in."

Jimmy J was still mostly in the engine access port, and now he leaned forward and put his elbows on the deck. Entirely too relaxed. Disrespectful. "I don't know, Mr. R," he said.

Tim nodded his approval. "We're not outfitted for this –"

Another voice broke into the conversation. Sue. He expected resistance from her – and her resistance just made her that much sexier as she played hard to get on every single level – but she surprised him. "I'm in," she said.

"Sue!" her father shouted. Prick. The old guy looked at her in shock. "Did you hear him? Whatever's down there is a hundred-and-fifty feet under us! And setting aside the fact that it should be *eight* hundred, we don't have any Nitrox or Trimix on the boat. We'd be diving with regular air and at that depth that's *insane*. That's guaranteed narcosis, that's maybe death, maybe bends."

Sue rounded on her father. "What if Deb's down there? Or at least, what if that's her boat on the bottom? What if the diver we found came from whatever's below us, and we have to see that place to understand what happened to him?" She got quiet. She chewed her lower lip. Very hot. She looked like she knew her way around a good kiss and probably more. "You saw what he was wearing," she finally said. "Who he worked for. Just like Deb." She stared at her father. "We have to know."

"Then let the Navy figure it out," he pleaded.

Mr. Raven broke in, voice silky-smooth and reasonable. "Ah, but if we do that they'll set up a perimeter, investigate the wreck and the ocean floor indirectly, then peripherally, then go down only after days or perhaps even weeks. And even then they won't go *inside* any wrecks until they have made a concrete determination of ownership. Again: weeks, perhaps months." He smiled that reasonable, slightly predatory grin again. "Do you want to wait that long?"

Cal threw up his hands. A full-body gesture that said, "I can't reason with you people." Haeberle was really starting to hate this guy.

"One-fifty is deep into Narcville," said Jimmy J. He frowned. "No way we should go down there."

"Jimmy J's right," said Tim. "This is a bad – a *terrible* – idea and I don't want any part of it."

"Then none for you."

Everyone – every*thing*, the entire world – seemed to grind to a halt when Haeberle said that. His voice was as low as he let it go. Just on the verge of a lack of control, when he –

(beat raped killed and laughed over it all)

– let his most primal, most powerful self rule for a time.

Jimmy J was the first to speak. "What do you mean?"

"No one gets a share of the treasure unless they go. That's it."

"Sure you don't mean *me*, Mr. Haeberle." Mr. Raven was still smiling. The smile had more teeth now. And Haeberle was about to say, "No, of course it doesn't," because at this point he was fairly certain that Mr. Raven was just one the figments of his mind that were locked off from his direct consciousness. Then Mr. Raven said something *wrong*. "It would be a long swim back to land, wouldn't it?"

Haeberle froze. So this was one of the dream-people who existed to challenge him. Who existed to be put in his place.

But not here. Not now. Sometimes it was easier to go along. Or to pretend to. "I think I can live with the captain getting an appropriate share," he said.

"Fine." Raven's shark-toothed grin widened. "Then I suggest everyone get some rest. Tomorrow will be a big day."

And everyone moved, in ones and twos, to the stairs that led down to the berths. Tim and Jimmy J kept trying to convince everyone not to commit to such a foolish goal.

No one listened.

Of course not. Because I want to go, and in the final analysis all of them are me.

Jimmy J and Tim returned to their examination of the engine. Haeberle watched them for a while. Thought how easy it would be to kill them. Just a sharp blow on their necks, a stab with the right tool.

He finally turned around. Headed downstairs as well.

Not now.

The time isn't right to do it.

No, not now.

But soon.

WOUNDED

~^~^~^~^~

Jimmy J finally headed to his berth. Tired. Exhausted, actually.

And a bit scared.

Not about the fact that they were floating dead in the water. The Navy would find them easily enough, and there were plenty of stores to get them through until then.

No, he was worried about the other thing.

His berth was a bit different than the others. With Mr. R's permission he had removed the top bunk in the back corner of the sleeping area. Then he'd swung a hammock across the gap that was created.

He hadn't always slept like that, but then he saw *Master and Commander: The Far Side of the World*, a movie about ocean-faring men at the turn of the nineteenth century. They all slept in hammocks, slung so close they rubbed each other in the night.

Jimmy J wasn't fond of the idea of banging up against a sweaty shipmate all night long. Nor did he want to include the majestic realism of scurvy, beatings for insolence, or the buggering of other crewmembers when the ship's voyages got a bit on the long side.

But the hammock thing was cool.

His hammock was totally radical, bright red and green and yellow so it looked more than a little like a Rastafarian relic, even though Jimmy J had gotten it for ten dollars during a day trip to Baja California.

At night he pulled the edges close to him. They curled in, almost covering him like a blanket. He felt secure in his hammock. And like a real sailor.

Usually.

Now, though, he felt very insecure. And being a sailor was far from his mind.

The only thing he was really interested in was his arm.

He'd worn a long-sleeve shirt for most of the night, mostly because the spot where something jabbed him when the stiff fell on him was sore and achy. He figured if he wore a lightweight, long-sleeve shirt it would help him forget about the discomfort.

It didn't.

Every small motion he made caused the cotton to rasp across his arm. It felt like sandpaper, and more than once he had thought of screaming. Thought of asking Tim or maybe Sue to take a look at whatever was going on.

But he didn't.

He wasn't sure *why* he didn't. He went to ask them a few times, once even going as far as tapping Tim on the shoulder.

"Yeah?" Tim said.

And Jimmy J didn't answer. Just shook his head and moved away, scratching his arm.

Now, laying in the pea-pod shape of his hammock, he pulled up his right sleeve. Then peeled away the bandage that covered his wound.

People around him were all snoring, and the light he clipped to the ropes near his head was a dim one, not enough to wake anyone.

But it was enough to see the wound.

There was a dark spot at the center, maybe a quarter-inch across. Like he had been bitten by a one-fanged vampire. Around the wound there was a ring of crusted blood, and around *that* was a larger ring of yellowish shores that freely wept a dark fluid.

"Ew."

The word sounded infantile, even to Jimmy J's ears. But it was all that came to mind. Especially when he saw the long black threads that spread out from the sores, reaching toward his hands, questing for the flesh of his chest.

He thought he saw one of them move slightly, but it was just his imagination. Just a trick of his light that swayed slightly with the motion of his hammock.

Still, the wound was *beyond* gross. And clearly needed attention.

He leaned forward, intending to slip out of his hammock and go to Tim. To ask him if he'd ever seen anything like this, and if he had what to do about it.

Then he turned back again. Slumped into his blanket. An exhaustion grabbed him. Hauled him by brute force back into his hammock.

He closed his eyes.

A last series of thoughts:

It's probably nothing.

No, something!

Nah... just....

And he slept and dreamed sweet dreams and did not feel the things burrowing through his flesh.

SCHOOL

~^~^~^~^~

Tim stood at the rail that surrounded most of the aft deck and looked into the dark water as though it might offer some answers.

None came. Of course not. The ocean had been what started all this, and whatever mysteries it held were mysteries it held *close*.

The ocean was a strange thing. A harsh lover from which all life had been born, which life she could reclaim at her whim. Biblical stories talked about the flooding of the whole earth, and while Tim had his doubts about that event, he did *not* doubt that the many waters that covered most of the earth were far more powerful, beautiful, and capricious than the land. She gave, she took away.

And now… now she held such secrets as he had never seen.

The water, exploding below them.

The ocean floor, casting itself up hundreds of feet in an instant.

The allure it carried for so many in the ship.

That last was one he truly didn't understand. Diving was one thing. Diving a hundred-fifty feet was another. And diving that far into a world that had suddenly begun to act so strangely? Madness.

Splashing broke him out of his reverie. A shiver rolled through his frame, and for a moment he was gripped by the dread certainty that one of the passengers had fallen over the side. Was struggling in the dark water that surrounded the boat, unseen and soon to be lost.

Then reality poked a hole in the waking dream. The splashing wasn't that of a panicked man or woman. Wasn't the splashing of *any* kind of man or woman, panicked or not.

He turned on a deck light, illuminating the area on deck and a small halo of light around the back of the boat.

He saw. Saw, but didn't believe.

Fish surrounded the boat.

That in itself wasn't so extraordinary. He had seen huge congregations of fish before, schooling together for protection from the larger fish – tuna, marlins – that constantly attacked and tried to eat them. He had even been in a boat one night off the coast of Mexico, surrounded by thousands of Humboldt Squid as they attacked prey and one another with abandon. Their huge bodies slamming into anything that moved – even the boat Tim had been on – was one of the only times he had been afraid of the ocean.

Until today.

And what he saw right now only added to the unease –

(fear)

– he'd been feeling since they found the body in the water.

It wasn't a school of fish. It was something else.

Millions of fish spun in silvered flashes through the water. As far as he could see, their bodies twirling through the water, surrounding *The Celeste*. But they didn't simply swim. They flapped at the surface in a carpet so thick Tim was fairly sure he could have walked across them like a strange kind of living land. A single organism whose cells were so large they could be seen by the naked eye.

And stranger perhaps was the fact that the fish around the boat were not of a single kind. Not sardines or threadfin or fusiliers or salema or any other single fish. This was a spinning, whirling mass of fish composed of what seemed like millions of different individuals from different species. Reds and yellows battled for space with silvers and greens and blues. Small bodies flickered between large. Sharks and other predators swam alongside smaller fish that would have been their food in other circumstances.

But they weren't eating each other. They just swam. Spun. More than a few flew into the air, swimming up from the deep so quickly that they went briefly airborne before slapping back to the water's surface.

They swirled their mad dance. A maelstrom both terrifying and beautiful, a hurricane of color with *The Celeste* in its eye.

Then, just as fast as they had come, they were gone. One moment they were everywhere, then Tim blinked and the water was calm again. The only sound the gentle slap of the ocean against the hull of *The Celeste*, as though reminding him that he floated not in air but in the neverwhere between air and water, the dividing line between the places humanity was meant to be and realms beyond its ken.

The ocean was dark.

He was alone.

And the light went off.

The nimbus that surrounded the boat disappeared, and Tim felt terror pierce his skin, felt his stomach ball up into a tight knot.

He hadn't touched the light.

So who had?

The darkness was thick, so complete that there was no telling where air ended and sea began. Not by sight.

But as dark as it was, Tim felt... something. A presence.

He turned.

There was someone behind him. A form in the dark salon. He couldn't make out features. But he felt like whoever it was was watching him.

"Jimmy J?"

The shadowed figure remained motionless.

"Jimmy J, if you're trying to scare me...." Tim's throat went suddenly dry. His tongue felt like a brick in his mouth. "You're doing a great job," he managed. He had hoped to deliver the words as a joke. An invitation for whoever was watching him to laugh and clap and scream, "Gotcha!"

Instead the dark figure moved away. Silent, and something in its motion – strange, rolling, graceful but not *normal* – made Tim's stomach tighten another notch. He felt suddenly like he might urinate, might lose control of his body.

The form moved down the stairs. Toward the berths.

Sue.

It was a strange thought. He had only met the woman a few days ago, had only come to know her on this one trip. But she was the one he thought about. The one that motivated him to move.

What if something happens to her?

What do you think is going to happen?

He had no answer.

But the question moved him after the figure. Into the salon, moving fast enough that he barely missed slamming into the extended edge of the table in the dark space. Hustling toward the barely-there glow of a few dim lights belowdecks.

He ran down the stairs. Stood in the slim passage between the galley storage and the sleeping area.

The door that led to the berths was closed.

Click.

Tim frowned.

There weren't many options down here. Not many places to go. Just the berths, or storage, or the head.

Had the door to the galley storage clicked?

But why would anyone go in there?

Suddenly Tim didn't care. No, he cared, but he didn't *want* to know. Didn't want to keep following whoever –

(*whatever*)

– had led him down here.

But he kept moving. He had to. People depended on him to show them a good time, to keep them safe. And while the former seemed to have disappeared as an option over the last few hours, the latter still remained as his responsibility.

He went to the galley storage door.

What are you expecting?

Nothing. I'm sure it's nothing.

He felt the words as a lie.

He opened the door.

Dark. Not just the dark of above-decks, the dark of a sky full of stars, the dark that reminded you that you were at least a part of something, even though that something was grand and terrible and huge beyond conception. The dark in the storage room was complete. No portholes to let in the slightest glimmer of light, no lights on inside.

Just black.

And Tim heard no movement. No scrape of shoe on floor, not even a breath.

He reached in and flicked on the light. It was dim – the batteries were draining. But he had to see. Had to see…

… nothing.

There was nowhere to hide in the small room. Just the stores, dry goods, canned goods, some dive equipment.

And the body on the floor.

He stared at it. Trying to remember.

Was it like that before?

Of course it was. It had to be.

The body still lay under its tarp. Quiet, lifeless, silent.

But Tim could see its head – some of it at least. And could see something that made him go nearly as still as the dead man.

The head.

The hair.

Did we lay him facedown?

No, we didn't – did we?

Yes. Yes, we must have. Because that's how he is now. Or maybe someone looked at him. Maybe someone flipped him over to cover that awful mess that he was, the gutted shape, the body that had no body other than arms and feet and head.

Yeah. Someone moved it.

Someone.

He stared at the body. Realized he was holding his breath, realized blood was pounding through his head with drum beats that had begun to speed up.

He let out the breath. Sucked in another.

Didn't breathe.

Sure. Someone moved it.

But he didn't believe it. Not even when he turned the light out and stepped out of the storage room and closed the door. He expected to feel a cold hand on his arm, a scratching voice in his ear. Expected his doom.

None of it happened, though. The dead stayed dead. The light went off, but no monster appeared in the darkness.

Tim stepped out of the room.

Closed the door.

Latched it.

BUBBLE

~^~^~^~^~

Getting ready for a deep dive – and one-hundred-fifty feet qualified – is vastly different than getting ready for a recreational dive.

Most deep divers favor drysuits instead of the traditional wetsuits. The function of a wetsuit is to allow a thin layer of water into the suit that will be warmed by the body's heat, keeping the diver warm. But at one-hundred-fifty feet the water is pressing down on the diver at over four atmospheres – more than four times the pressure per square inch that it does at the surface. The pressure crushes wetsuits flat, squeezing out the warmth and allowing the diver to feel every degree of cold the deep has to offer. Drysuits are water-tight, and the buoyancy control device (or BC) pushes air into them, just enough for the body to keep an insulated layer of air between the diver and that biting – potentially deadly – cold.

The same pressure that crushes wetsuits flat also crushes air into and out of the body. On the surface, a diver might take in .6 cubic feet of air with every breath. At one-hundred-fifty feet, that same diver will have sucked three cubic feet of air with every breath. Deep divers don't take the one tank that people see scuba divers using on television – they have several slung to their backs, several more to their sides.

Nor is that the only extra equipment needed. Deep diving requires a BC buoyant enough to deal with the extra weight; a dive computer built to deal with the tremendous pressure of a deep dive; dive gauges rated to hold up under that all-encompassing pressure, and special oil-filled mechanical gauges if going too deep for air-filled gauges to withstand implosion.

Perhaps most important of all save the air itself: the dive computer has to be recalculated to allow for stunningly short times at the bottom, with correspondingly long times to decompress on the way up. It will take three to six minutes for a diver to drop in a controlled manner to a depth of one-fifty. The diver will then have perhaps twenty to thirty minutes at the bottom before she has to begin her assent, which can take up to several hours.

Sue had the gauges, she had the extra tanks – *The Celeste* had extra in its hold, enough for everyone to stay down twenty-five minutes at the bottom and then return with full decompression – or deco - stops.

The boat didn't carry any drysuits, and none of the passengers had brought one. They would all be operating on the razor's edge between discomfort and hypothermia.

Mr. Raven had printed out calculations of bottom times, deco times and depths, and passed them out. Sue did her own calculations to verify his were accurate. They were.

She felt worry creeping in. One-hundred-fifty feet was well within the level that people could – and did, and would continue to – dive on air alone, as opposed to specialized gas mixes designed for deep dives. But it was also deep enough that some very bad things could – and did, and would continue to – happen to the unprepared.

She pulled on her wetsuit, helping her father occasionally with his and getting help in return. Most experienced deep or "technical" divers would give you a polite "Back the hell off, buddy," if you tried to help them. Every diver had a specific way of putting on gear and getting ready for a dive. No one was there to help each other, and dive buddies for a deep dive were rare.

There were reasons for that. Reasons Sue preferred not to think about right now.

Regardless, her father and she *could* work together. Even though not what you'd call a doting family, they were family. That allowed for a measure of cooperation.

Geoffrey and Mercedes were nearby as well, both pulling on their suits and accepting the extra gear and tanks that Mr. Raven was handing out. Geoffrey was an ass and Mercedes had spoken few words on the trip. But now that they worked to suit up, both had a measure of confidence and competence that gave Sue hope for them and for the dive.

This was a dangerous level. Anyone who wasn't sure what he was doing was going to be in trouble.

Is it fair of me? Fair to weigh in on the side of doing this? Did my vote to go make Mercedes go? What if something happens to her? To Geoffrey?

Would it be my fault?

Should I drop out? Say "never mind" and try to convince them to stop this before it begins?

Someone could die. This kind of dive kills people who don't know what they're doing.

That led her to Haeberle. The big man was fumbling a bit. Either because of nervousness or something else, he was having trouble. Not a lot, not enough to call great attention to himself.

But some.

And if you were nervous at one-hundred-fifty feet...
if you were careless... if you were incompetent....

He caught her looking at him. Most people having
trouble with their gear would be embarrassed. Would look
away. Focus on their work and pretend nothing else
existed.

He didn't do that. His face broke into a wide grin, so
wide in fact that it was well beyond a leer and into
something even more uncomfortable. Haeberle looked like
he was gazing at his next meal.

She forced herself to stare back. Not long, but long
enough that she hoped he got the idea that she wasn't
scared of him.

Which was a lie. The guy definitely scared her.
There was something wrong with him, something that was
going to burst like a bubble sooner or later, letting the
world see what was inside. And she suspected it wouldn't
be pretty.

A hand reached around Haeberle, turning him and
then helping secure some of his rig.

Tim.

Sue felt some of the fear leach out of her. She hadn't
thought he was going to come, but he was already dressed
and holding a rig at his side, his tanks and gauges and dive
gear ready to be slung on in one large motion. Jimmy J was
behind him, dressed to dive as well.

"You coming after all?" she said.

Tim looped Haeberle's octopus regulator – an extra regulator for "buddy breathing" if someone ran into trouble – out of the way, keeping it from tangling.

But no buddies at this depth. It's everyone for themselves.

She tried to get rid of that thought. Tried to forget everything but the chance – however slim – that what waited below might be answers. Might tell her what had happened to her sister.

"Jimmy J and I talked," Tim said, snapping Sue out of her reverie. "You guys are going to need us down there."

Haeberle knocked Tim's hands away with a snarl. "I got this," he said.

"I know you do. Just thought I'd help. But...." He looked uncomfortable. "Before you get totally geared up, could you help me with something? I need to bring a few extra tanks from storage and I could use your help."

Haeberle kept glaring for a moment. Then nodded. The movement was quick and jerky, like he was forcing it against his better judgment. It was also ferocious.

Yeah. He's going to pop.

Just don't be around when it happens.

It won't be pretty.

SOON

~^~^~^~^~

Haeberle followed Tim into the salon. And seethed.

Of all the people on this ship, Tim and Raven were the two who most irritated Haeberle. He was tempted to go to sleep and dream them away and then wake up without them to hassle him, to constantly prick at his reality, like mosquitoes invading a peaceful picnic.

Even Haeberle – the *real* Haeberle, the one he was pretending to be – had been less irritating. Hell, *that* guy had been downright fun. Strangling him, beating him to death, dropping his body into the sea.

The new Haeberle –

(*the real Haeberle now, face it, nothing is real until it's you, until you do it, until you own it*)

– crossed his arms and waited for Tim to speak. Waited to decide whether the other man would live or die.

Tim didn't speak, though. Just looked at him like he was less than a God, maybe even less than a man.

You're going to die, Tim. You'll die and be gone from life, gone from my dreams, gone from everything.

The thought almost made him smile. Almost.

"What do you want?" he said instead. "What is this?"

Tim finally spoke, a small shake of his head that made Haeberle feel like he was being *pitied*.

(*dead, dead, dead, you'll die you'll die, I'll kill you and maybe dream you back and kill you again, you prick*)

"Have you ever been diving at all?" said Tim.

The question nearly caught Haeberle unawares. Of course he had – in his previous life he'd actually dived quite a bit, which had made his discovery of the other Haeberle –

(*the fake Haeberle*)

– a man who was about to go on a conveniently offshore dive trip, just that much more proof of the universe's love for the one man at its center.

"Of course," he said. "This is a *dive* expedition, isn't it?"

"Yeah." Tim wasn't backing down. "But you're all thumbs. So my question remains: You ever dive before?"

Haeberle felt his muscles clench. Imagined snapping Tim in half and throwing him overboard.

Then he realized what this was. This was the universe again, bending to his will. To his whim. Tim wasn't here to hinder him after all. He was going to help.

"Yeah," he said, and felt the fight leave as fast as it came. Tim was just another element of himself, and it was insane to get mad at yourself, wasn't it? "I've dived. But not this deep."

Tim shook his head. "Then you're not going."

Haeberle actually took a heavy step toward Tim.

How. DARE. He?

"I am," he said. "Nothing's going to stop me. Least of all you."

Another step. Looming over Tim now. Letting the other man feel the presence of the God of this place, this sea, this *world*.

Tim just shook his head again. "You'll die. There's no light down there, it's cold, it's an entirely different thing from recreational diving. You'll get narced and make a bad decision and –"

Haeberle frowned. It *had* been a while since his last dive, and a lot had happened since then. Plus when he got mad it was sometimes hard to think. Things got foggy, his thoughts got fuzzy.

Bad things happened.

Not to Haeberle, of course. Everything happened to him for the best in this, the best of all his possible worlds.

But bad things. And the fog was falling fast. Tim seemed to bring that out in him.

"Narced?" he said, interrupting the lesser man.

"Nitrogen narcosis," said Tim. "It affects everyone, *everyone*, who goes this deep. Nitrogen gets in the way of proper brain functions. Anyone down there is going to be a functioning drunk." He shook his head again. "And then there's whatever's down there. Wreck or underwater reef or whatever this insane ocean has puked up at us…. You get tangled on something, you die. You run out of air, you die. You lose your tie to the anchor line and you'll get swept away by underwater currents and never find your way back to the boat and die. You come up too fast and –"

"Yeah, I know. I get it. I'll die."

Tim laughed. Just a quick machine-gun rattle of a laugh, barking at the ceiling like Haeberle had said the most monumentally stupid thing possible.

I'm going to kill you, Tim. And screw whether you're here to help.

"No, you *wish* you die," said Tim. "You come up too fast and you get bent. The nitrogen in your tank air gathers in bubbles around your joints and nerves and causes the worst pain imaginable. It blocks blood vessels and causes ruptures, blood can explode out of your nose, your ears, your mouth. You get an embolism. And then, after all that, *then* you finally die in agony."

Now it was Haeberle's turn to laugh. None of that could happen to him. It was impossible for a universe to cripple its creator. "I'll risk it," he said. He felt genuinely jovial, as though reminding himself of his immortality was enough to drive back his irritation, even a bit of the fog that had clouded his thoughts and covered his memories.

"I'll risk it," he said. Grinned a toothy grin. "Treasure's too fun an idea to give up on."

"Then you're an idiot."

The declaration came so simply it didn't even penetrate for a moment. Then it did, pricking Haeberle's good mood and deflating it so rapidly he coughed to cover his surprise. Then he straightened and took a last step to Tim. They would have been nose to nose if they were the same height. As it was, Haeberle looked right down at the man.

A king.

A lord.

A God.

"The last guy who called me names ended up in the hospital," he whispered. His left hand clenched into a fist. The right dropped to the hilt of a knife he had strapped to his thigh.

"Fine," said Tim. "You're not an idiot." Tim glanced down at the knife. "But are you going to be so *smart* that you attack the only guy on the boat who's ever tied the anchor onto a deep water wreck?"

The knife actually came an inch out of its sheath. Stayed there a long moment, long enough for five or six bull-like breaths to explode through Haeberle's nostrils.

Tim shouldered past him. Went to the door. Haeberle didn't watch him go. But called out, "Timmy?"

He could sense the other man freezing, sense his irritation at being called such a childish name. He let Tim wait a moment, let him stew, before finally saying, "People – all people – have their day. Their times. But those times pass."

Tim didn't say anything. But a moment later he pulled open the door and left. Haeberle heard the door click behind him.

He smiled.

Soon, Tim.

START

~^~^~^~^~

Everything was wrong, and the dive wasn't even started.

No one had drysuits. No one had the right experience. No one had TriMix or Nitrox: gases specially mixed for deeper dives that all but eliminated the mental and physical dangers of getting narced or bent.

Worst of all, the attitudes were wrong. Everyone was jittery or scared or unsure or a mix of all three. Only Jimmy J seemed calm, and even he had never been quite this deep – his dive experience maxed out at one-hundred-thirty feet.

Other than Mr. Raven, Tim was the only one who'd really done this before. And he hadn't liked it. Going down past one-thirty, you started to feel drunk, started to hear drums in your ears, started noticing things and wondering if they were really there. Divers called it the "rapture of the deep," but it hadn't felt too rapturous to him. Mostly weird and off-putting and scary.

The worst moment came when he tried to grab his trip computer and had to take four swipes before he got it into his hands. Being below one-thirty didn't just mean loss of acuity; it brought physical impairment as well.

And there was no cure, no way to vaccinate oneself against the rapture. Experienced divers knew that the best way to operate at great depth was to have done everything that might be necessary on the dive so many times that the responses were automatic. Thinking was compromised, so muscle memory had to reign. Dilettantes need not apply; only those with intimate knowledge of necessary procedures could be reasonably safe.

Which all meant that this group was in danger the second they touched down, if not before.

"Okay," he said to the dark shapes that had once been lithe and trim people but were now hulking masses of equipment strapped to wetsuits with hoods pulled over heads, masks on faces. "Here's how it's going to go. Mr. Raven is going to drop the anchor and try to catch it on whatever's down there. If he does, I follow the line down and try to secure it. I'll explore to make sure it's –"

"Hey!" The outburst came from Geoffrey. Naturally. "How come you get first shot at the treasure?"

Tim wondered of the others could hear his teeth grinding. "I don't want first shot. I want to make sure you don't die five minutes after splashdown. I could care less about *treasure* – which I doubt is even down there. I just want to make sure you all come back alive." He paused for Geoffrey's comeback. Surprisingly, none came. The man just nodded and then sidestepped a bit as a swell moved the boat.

Tim tensed. What if this was another one of those sonic boom/tsunamis? What would they do?

Nothing happened. The boat settled. He heard Mercedes let out a whoosh of air and knew she had been thinking the same thing as him.

And we're going down there.

He shook his head. "Jimmy J?"

The young man stepped forward. He gulped visibly as the entire group swiveled to face him. That was a first, too. Jimmy J was usually utterly relaxed and at ease in any situation. Perhaps too much so: Tim had lectured him any number of times about appearing more professional. He never got anywhere with it. So the fact that Jimmy J looked white and hyper-alert under his suit… it unsettled Tim.

Jimmy J rubbed his arm. The arm that had been hurt yesterday. As he did, a glazed look came over his eyes. Tim would have guessed the kid was stoned if he hadn't snapped to in the next second – and if Tim didn't know that Jimmy J never took drugs. Didn't even drink – it wasn't good for a diver, and Jimmy J loved diving above all other things.

Tim kept waiting, and Jimmy J looked uncomfortable again, and then started as he realized what was expected of him. "Oh, right." He turned to look at the group. "You've all programmed your dive computers for tank changes and ascend times, right?" Nods. "You follow those or you'll either run out of air or get bent on the way up." He turned to Mercedes and Haeberle. "Some of you guys are using some DCs we had on board since yours weren't rated for this depth. They'll beep – loud – to let you know you have five minutes before you need to start back up. You go any later than that and you either run out of air down there or you have to come up too fast." He grimaced. Faced Tim. "Small postscript to that: if I get bent, please shoot me in the face with a harpoon. Seriously."

Tim ignored that one. What was he going to say? "Don't worry, you'll be fine"? He could only hope that wouldn't happen. No promises this deep.

"Remember to control your breathing," he said to everyone. "At one-fifty everything is under pressure, even your lungs. That means each breath you take pulls almost five times the air from your tank. Breathe fast and you run out of air even faster and your dive computer calculations will be off. And if you run dry on your first tank while you're narced, chances are you'll panic and make a whole load of crappy decisions."

He looked at Haeberle the whole time he delivered his speech, hoping to convince the other man to stay – or at least to take his obvious ignorance a bit more seriously.

Haeberle remained impassive. A small smile touched the corners of his lips, then even that was gone.

"Yeah, yeah," said Geoffrey. "We know all this. We're not newbies, you know."

"Okay," said Tim. "Then try this for some new info: don't touch *anything*. Especially if it's a wreck. And above all, don't go in."

Geoffrey frowned. "How the hell are we supposed to find any treasure if we can't go in?"

"You can find a thousand ways to die faster than you can find a single 'treasure' in a wreck," said Tim. "Even the outside can be dangerous. You don't know what can tangle you, what can collapse. If you go inside, you touch a single thing and it will likely create a cloud of sand or oil or rust or all three that'll make it impossible for you to find your way out. You could lose your line. You could die."

Mercedes piped up. Well, not piped up – her pipes seemed fixed permanently at the "quiet" position. But she spoke. "Sounds like we could die no matter what.

"That's why you shouldn't go," said Tim with a nod.

Mercedes shrugged, and in the shrug and the look on her face Tim saw that there was something driving her to do this. Something quieter but no less compelling than the things which drove Sue, Geoffrey, and Haeberle.

"Fine," he said. And then, because there was nothing else *to* say, he added, "Let's get started."

BEGINNING

~^~^~^~^~

This is how the dive began.

First: dragging anchor.

The average scuba diver can swim anywhere from one-half to 1.5 knots per hour underwater – a knot being a little over a linear mile. Underwater currents of four knots per hour are not unusual. And water being over eight hundred times denser than air, this means a diver swimming as fast as he can into a current will actually be dragged *backward* at a rate of 3.5 knots per hour. If swimming *with* the current, that augments his normal pitiful speed of 1.5 knots per hour to to *five* knots per hour.

Both of those mean a diver can be assured of being yanked away from starting points – and having a good chance of it being impossible to return.

Then you add in the ascent, which can take several hours. Several hours of being dragged at least a few knots per hour away from the spot where you dove... and the diver may surface up to six miles away from his dive boat.

Even one mile away, a dive boat will be utterly invisible to the surfacing diver – and vice-versa. The diver will likely be stranded. Marooned on a microscopic island that consists only of his gear and his own body. And soon to die of hypothermia, lack of water, exposure, or the tender attentions of underwater sea life.

To combat this, deep divers tie on to the ascent line. They then have a way of pulling themselves to and from where they need: let out the line to go in the direction of the current, then pull back to the line when it is time to ascend – and stay clipped to the ascent line the whole way up.

This is why Jimmy J released the drag anchor before anything else happened. The drag anchor was a four-pronged grapple designed to grab onto underwater outcroppings, either natural or man-made. Mr. Raven would pilot the boat in a straight line over the mass on the bottom, dragging the anchor along the bottom until it caught. If it didn't, he would turn and try again. Dragging the anchor was one of the time-consuming and somewhat stressful parts of a deep dive, since one never knew how long it would take or even if the operation would be successful.

A few feet above the anchor, Jimmy J attached an emergency strobe. It blinked a steady flash, two per second. If anyone got separated from the line, the strobe might help them to find it again in the darkness of deep water.

At what he guessed would be about twenty feet below the boat, Jimmy J attached an emergency air tank to the line. The tank would allow a diver in trouble to wait at a final deco level before ascending all the way. Hopefully this would provide a failsafe against running out of air, against a possibly fatal case of the bends.

The anchor fell, trailing its thick line. The passengers and dive crew watched it reel out. Waited.

In the wheelhouse, Raven piloted the boat with a steady hand. He also frowned at the nearby printer. A single paper lay there, stained from the sweat and grease that perpetually coated his fingers.

The printer had recently spat out something... interesting. Perhaps helpful. Raven felt like he stood on the edge of destiny. A return to the greatness – financial, emotional, reputation-wise – that he had once enjoyed.

The paper was, he decided, not merely interesting, but helpful.

He felt it likely that things were finally going his way again. Felt it in his bones.

Back on the deck, the passengers and crew saw the line twitch, felt a minor tremor as the boat was jerked a bit. The engines cut immediately, and Raven leaned out of the wheelhouse.

"We hooked?" he shouted.

"Looks like!" Jimmy J responded.

Raven nodded once, curtly, then leaned back into the wheelhouse. He looked at the paper again, and only one word kept going through his mind:

Interesting.

On the deck, the divers began final checks.

The dive was ready to begin.

FALL

~^~^~^~^~

Tim felt a gentle tug. It was Jimmy, pulling lightly on his back tank to make sure it was secure. Of course it was, and of course Jimmy J knew it would be. Tim recognized the action for what it was: concern. Jimmy J was making a final check because it was all he *could* do.

People always act to control... even if those actions are fruitless gestures. Even if people *know* they are fruitless gestures. Because lack of action is an admission that we are not captains of our ships, that we are simply huddled in the hold in a storm-tossed sea, hoping for the best, a large part of us expecting the worst.

So when Jimmy J tugged on his back tank, Tim knew he would find it perfectly secured, the hoses in place, all as it should be. But he let Jimmy J proceed – it made them both feel a bit better. And "a bit" was the best either could hope for.

"You sure you want to do this?" said Jimmy J. The words a whisper that barely carried above the slap of the waves against the hull of the boat.

"Not much choice if I want to keep everyone safe," said Tim. He realized he was doing the same thing Jimmy J was: pulling on his gauges to make sure they were firmly attached, looking at his hoses, eyeballing his regulator.

It's okay, man. It's okay.

Right.

"What about the fish thing?" said Jimmy J. "Weird."

Tim had told Jimmy J what he had seen last night: the thousands, hundreds of thousands, *millions* of fish swirling on the surface. A school of disparate pupils so massive as to be unheard of.

What caused that?

"Fish always gather at wrecks," he said. "Coral grows on them and an ecosystem moves in."

He knew that was a stupid excuse for what amounted to a natural impossibility. Not only were masses of fish like that unknown, but there couldn't *be* any coral growths. Coral reefs took thousands of years to grow, and the place below them hadn't even existed before yesterday.

Jimmy J shook his head, giving voice to Tim's own thoughts: "This isn't a wreck site, man. This is Mother Earth puking on us."

Tim felt a chill that had nothing to do with the stiff breeze that blew. Because Jimmy J was right: this wasn't a wreck site. Wreck sites didn't just appear, didn't just rise up from an eight-hundred-foot drop and settle at the diveable but dangerous level of one-hundred-fifty feet.

He shook his head. Not sure if he was shaking his head at Jimmy J, or to give a silent voice to his own need to insist that this was a good idea. All evidence to the contrary.

"I know," he said. "I know. But my job is to make sure these people come back." He clapped Jimmy J on the shoulder. "And yours is to make sure *I* come back. Don't forget that."

And then, before Jimmy J could say anything else, anything that might –

(*terrify him*)

– dissuade him, he lumbered to the dive platform, put a hand to his mask to hold it in place, and stepped off.

The water hit him as a mix of pleasure and pain, the internal opposition that was the sea. She was life to everything on the planet, but also a force that could kill with impunity. As large-scale as tsunamis that buried entire islands, and intimate as a rolling tide that pulled a child out to sea and buried her forever under a trillion tons of liquid.

He waited a moment, bobbing on the surface, but didn't look at the boat. He didn't want to see the worry on Jimmy J's face –

(*and maybe – hopefully? – on Sue's?*)

– or look at the boat that represented his last and sanest opportunity to turn away from what he was about to do. He knew this was all wrong – they were going in for the wrong reasons, at the wrong place and time... but wasn't this his job? Not just to show passengers a good time, to b.s. with the dilettantes and toss out interesting facts to weekenders, but to *guide*. To *protect*.

He let air out of his buoyancy compensator and let the sudden decrease in his personal buoyancy drag him under. He swam quickly to the dive line.

And began his descent.

Down here, at this level, it was a different world. At ten feet the sea was light blue. Empty and formless as the void that God had to work with. The only sounds were the bubbles that escaped his regulator as he breathed. He inhaled, he exhaled.

His heartbeat started to sound in his ears. Palpitations that banged a drumbeat through his body.

Bubbles leaked from his BC. Slowly letting him fall.

The light began to leave him.

He began to fall from the light.

Below him lay his destination. Below him lay the unknown.

Below him… lay the dark of the true deep.

MARK

Raven looked at the paper on the printer. Still where he had put it, shoving it back on its tray after he printed it, as though to deny what it had shown him. Because it had scared him. He had to admit that to himself, if to no one else. What he saw on that page was a new element in a situation already fraught with unknowns.

But a moment later, holding the page, about to call the naval vessel, about to let them know what he held… a moment after that he put the paper back. He thought.

And, thinking, he realized that this was no curse, no stumbling block in his path. No, it was one more stepping stone. One more step in his path to fame, fortune. To money and power and women throwing themselves at him the way they had when he was young and strong.

There are many different kinds of strength.

He leaned out the wheelhouse. Everyone was on deck, most of them leaning toward the dive platform as though they could see through the bottom of the boat and spot Tim's dive.

Raven grinned tightly. He hadn't been surprised when Tim volunteered to go first. The man was noble to a fault – meaning he had more than an iota of nobility. Being noble was just code for putting the needs of others above your own. The worst kind of foolishness.

The one person who *wasn't* looking toward the sea, but rather sat on one of the benches bolted to the deck, was the man Raven wanted to see.

Figures. Bastard doesn't care about anyone but himself.

Just like you, Rave?

Birds of a feather.

And with that thought, any last doubts over what he was going to do disappeared completely.

"Haeberle?" he called to the man.

"What?" Haeberle answered. He didn't look up. Just kept staring straight ahead. Raven wondered what the man was staring at. Then decided he didn't want to know. Then decided he didn't give a damn.

"I wonder if I might see you in the salon?" said Raven. He started down the ladder to the deck.

"No," said Haeberle. Surly as always. Intractable.

Not this time.

"Please, *Matthew*," said Raven. "It's important."

Haeberle – or the man who called himself Haeberle – stiffened. "What did you call me?" he said. He glanced at the others, who took no note of the conversation the two were having.

"I'm sorry, didn't I call you Mark?" Raven had seen Haeberle smiling at Sue and Mercedes. Had seen the shark-grin the man lavished on them, the smile that said, "I will own you completely. You're already mine, you just don't know it yet."

Now Raven smiled that way at the big man. A shark-grin – the humorless, deadly smile of a *great white* – of his own. "I thought I called you *Mark*. I'm sure I wouldn't call you anything but your given name, after all."

He turned and went into the salon. Knowing Haeberle would follow.

Yes, this was going to work out after all.

Everything was.

ENGULFED

~^~^~^~^~

Tim dropped…

… dropped…

… dropped…

… into darkness.

The water was first blue, then darkened to the cobalt tones that reach out to capture the sun as twilight falls. Then even that color fell away. Twilight deepened to the uniform gray of a world without direction or differences. Just an entropic mass, the only thing guiding him in the right direction was the anchor line he held tightly in his hands.

Then… black.

Tim switched on a light attached to his shoulder. It sent out a slim dagger of brightness into the black, but the dark around him was stronger by far. The light only extended a short distance. Surrounding him with a sickly halo and shooting out directly in front of him a few additional feet before being beaten to a premature death by the raw power of a dark, empty sea.

And then not so empty.

His light caught something. A flash reflected back to him. It was so out of place in the loneliness in which he found himself that he couldn't place it.

Another flash.

Another.

Another another anotheranotheranother.

Now he understood. But before he could respond, he was engulfed.

It was just like the other night. A huge school of silver fish, about the length and thickness of his arm. They absorbed him into what seemed a single mass, a gigantic organism whose cells were not the microscopic variety but large and hostile. They batted against Tim with tails; he felt fins flutter all over his body.

He felt his body clench, and at the same time his gut felt loose, achy. He had to concentrate on not losing control of his bowels. Voiding himself in a wetsuit wouldn't be fun.

The fish swirled, whirled, slammed into him harder and harder, nearly bruising him with their impact. Visibility was next to nothing. He held to the anchor line so tightly his fingers ached.

Then he saw something else. A larger shape flashing in front of him, slipping in and out of his light so fast he wasn't sure whether or not he imagined it.

Then the shape came again. Bigger than the silver shapes. Much bigger. Blue-green-gray, a huge series of featherlike fins atop its back, an extended snout that lengthened into a thin spike with a deadly tip.

A sailfish. Not unusual for them to be attracted to schools of fish. They would use their sweeping back fins to separate large groups of fish from the edges of a school, then would turn on their tails and gulp down great mouthfuls.

But this sailfish didn't seem to be eating. It flared in and out of Tim's view, in and out of his light. It swam jerkily, almost panicked. Like it was trying to shake free of an invisible hook, the drag of something unseen. And every time it appeared it seemed closer to him.

Where Tim's stomach had felt loose only a moment before, now it drew into a painfully tight knot. Sailfish could swim almost seventy miles per hour, and if this one barreled into him, even with a sideswipe it could be a crippling blow.

If it hit him with that sword point....

Then the sailfish was joined by another. And two more. And then dozens. All flapping, fluttering their way through the water in lieu of the graceful manner for which they were famous.

One came so close its dorsal fin slammed into Tim's chest as it turned away. He felt the breath explode out of him, almost lost his regulator.

Almost lost his grip on the anchor line.

If that happened he would be lost for sure. He was at near-neutral buoyancy right now: his weight was almost exactly that of the water around him. Which meant there was almost no sense of gravity. If he lost his line he wouldn't know up from down. He could swim straight down and end up caught in a current that would drag him away from any hope of returning to *The Celeste*. He could swim straight up and be bent before he knew what was happening.

There was only one thing to do.

He loosened his grip on the line.

He opened the pressure release valve on his BC as far as possible. The air bubbled out of the vest's bladder.

He dropped like a rock.

UNDERSTANDING

~^~^~^~^~

Haeberle entered the salon, and experienced a rare emotion: fear.

Did he really call me Matthew?

Was it a mistake?

Could he know?

Then he was into the small room, closing the door behind him and facing Raven. The smaller man had arms across his chest, a smug look on his face like he owned the universe.

That chased the fear right out of Haeberle's mind.

Bastard.

Sonofabitch.

I'll kill you.

He felt his body tensing, felt his muscles – the envy of all men, the object of lust of all women – ball into dangerous masses. Fear was gone, because. He. Was. *Power.* Raw energy, greater than any wave, more terrifying than any earthquake.

I'll kill you.

Aloud he said, "What is it?"

Raven uncrossed his arms. He dug something out of his pocket. A white paper, creased and with faint dark stains on it where he had clearly been handling it.

"When I contacted the Navy about helping us they had a very interesting question to ask about my passengers. Even sent me a picture that I printed out."

He held out the folded page. Haeberle took it, and when he opened it cold –

(*fear terror oh shit oh damn I'm in trouble*)

– rage engulfed him. White, terrible. The muscles that had been clenched before now started twitching.

He had to concentrate on not flying across the cabin and ripping out Raven's neck with his teeth.

Not now.

Soon.

The page had a picture of him at the top right. Beside was the name "MATTHEW JERROD" in large bold letters. A name he knew well. His old name, his old disguise.

One of the wonderful things about being him was that he could be anyone he wanted. When you are the only real person in a sea of imagination, be anyone you choose to be. So he had chosen to be Mark Haeberle, and just like that Matthew Jerrod had ceased to exist.

But here was that other person, that previous self, Matthew Jerrod staring up at him from this paper.

Below the name, the old him, was a long list. Words like WANTED and KIDNAPPING and SEXUAL ASSAULT and MURDER written, accusations that were ridiculous on their face. How could you steal a person who existed only to serve your whims? How could you rape women who clearly desired you?

How could you kill someone who wasn't *real*?

But for all its ridiculousness, the paper made him uneasy. He crumpled it. Wished it away, and was surprised that it didn't puff right out of existence.

How can that be? What's happening?

And the answer came right away: He must *want* this to be happening. He must desire this moment on some fundamental level.

Why?

Time will tell. Give it a minute.

His muscles unclenched. A little.

Raven watched him crumple the paper. Didn't ask for it back. "Did you kill the real Mark Haeberle? Take his place to get away from the manhunt, wait 'until the heat died down,' as I believe your kind say?"

Haeberle's muscles seized again. "'Your kind'?"

Raven ignored both the explicit question and the threat implicit in Haeberle's tone. "That would explain why you aren't the experienced diver we were expecting."

Break his neck. Slam into him and thumbs around his throat so he can't scream and twist and he's dead and I pull him to the front of the boat and dump him and no one's the wiser.

I could do that.

He almost did. But something held him back.

This moment had been brought to him. All the moments of the past few days came to him: killing the old Mark Haeberle, stashing his body, running from the FBI agents who were after him.

And then this.

It meant something. His imaginings were leading him somewhere. Not just to an inevitable sexual encounter with Sue and Mercedes – though that would certainly be pleasurable, for him *and* them – but something greater.

Play it out.

"What are you going to do?" he said to Raven.

The other man pursed his lips. Cocked his head as though thinking. "My view is that there are several ways this can go down. You can wait to be put in a naval brig when they pick us up, then transferred to death row when we get back, or...."

A long pause. Haeberle let it hang there for a moment. He remembered for a moment a game his mother had played: The Quiet Game. "Let's see who can be quiet fastest," she'd say to him and his brother when she was having one of her "headaches." Whoever won got a spoonful of brown sugar. Whoever lost got put in the closet for a few minutes or hours or days, depending on her mood.

Haeberle always won. The one time he spoke first –

(*accidentally Mommy it was an accident please don't put me away in the dark!*)

– he killed his brother and won by forfeit.

Mother hadn't given him his brown sugar. She just screamed. Which meant *she* lost the game. He put her body in the closet and ate all the brown sugar he could find.

But this Quiet Game was boring. He didn't know what the prize could possibly be, so why play?

"I'm waiting," he said.

"Well, the way I see it, whatever treasure's down there, it can best be retrieved and brought up by all of you. Many hands make light work and all that. But once aboard...." Raven spread his hands. Weak hands, the hands of a creature unborn and unreal. "It might be better if there were only two of us when the Navy got here. One of us, actually, since you would be hidden in the hold. Everyone else would be tragic collateral to the strange seismic activities of the last day."

Haeberle's head started to hurt with that last sentence. There were so many words, so many *big* words. And so many of them weren't needed.

Bastard. Trying to hurt me.

Kill you. Bastard.

"Or I could kill you," Haeberle said. Surprised that he was showing his hand like this. "Just take it all."

Raven nodded as though he had expected this. "You could. But then who would hide you? And if you killed *all* of us, the Navy or Coast Guard would tear this boat apart looking for evidence of what happened. And you'd have to just sit here waiting for them, because I don't think you're enough of a sailor to fix this boat, let alone get yourself back to shore."

"What if there's nothing down there? Just junk and ocean?"

Raven's eyes squinted to dead slits in his face. "That would be unfortunate for you. Let's hope it isn't so."

And Haeberle felt something unpleasant that crawled through him like an eel, cold and slimy and horrible.

I'll kill you.

TOUCHDOWN

~^~^~^~^~

Tim found the bottom. He found it by following the line, the pull of his BC, and the jungle drums that pounded ever louder in his ears.

He waited for a moment at the bottom of the anchor line, waiting for his pulse to quiet, waiting for those drums to fall back into the mists of his mind.

They didn't. Just kept pounding, *boom-boom-boom.*

I'm narced.

He'd expected it. At one-fifty *everyone* felt symptoms of nitrogen narcosis. Everyone felt the change in pressure not only as a giant hand clenching them, squeezing them, but as a subtle shift in the mind itself. The vision closed ever-so-slightly, black around the edges like an oil slick gathering around; a leviathan of the deep beginning the long, slow process of swallowing you.

Narced.

Boom-boom-boom.

Fish of every conceivable kind swam around him. But not the unnatural schools that had enveloped him on the way down. These were simply the fish drawn to a high-food-yield area. Coral drew in microorganisms, which in turn drew in larger fish, which were fed by larger fish in turn, and so on up the food chain.

Many of the most colorful fish in the world made coral their home. Clownfish were immune to the stinging nematocysts that coral used to paralyze prey, so they hid deep in the coral, finding refuge and safety there.

Parrotfish ate the coral and defecated the rock and stone they chipped off along with the live organisms.

It was a beautiful ecosystem. But here… it simply wasn't possible. There couldn't be coral like this, coral that would have taken decades, centuries, perhaps *millennia*. Not in a place that had been tossed up six hundred feet in a day. Even if it had existed on the floor and merely been shifted up, there would have been evidence of breakage, of destruction.

But there was no such thing. Even in the weak aureole created by his dive light, the coral looked healthy, established, permanent. The fish that darted among them were varied, gorgeous flashes of rainbow caught in the dark.

It was a gorgeous sight, a beautiful underwater jungle. To some, it was a meal: sharks were often plentiful around coral reefs.

He hoped to Heaven there weren't any here. Sharks – even the big ones – generally were inclined to leave people alone. But he thought of them as something akin to coyotes. One on one they probably weren't a threat. But the more there were, the more you started to look like a meal for the pack.

He forced himself to look away from the beauty that surrounded him, to search for the point where the anchor had caught. It had found a rocky outcropping, coral-encrusted and looking ancient as time itself. There was a curve in it that looked like the overgrown eye of a giant's needle.

Tim had a spool of nylon rope, and he used this to tie the anchor to the eye. Tying down was primary thing the first diver did: making sure the anchor was secure not only at the point it had caught on, but lashing it down to an additional hold point so there was no way it would loose and drift away, potentially stranding any divers.

The next order of business: letting the others know it was safe to come down.

As safe as it *could* be, at least.

Tim had two Styrofoam cups attached to his gear. They were attached to another spool, this one of fishing line. He let go of the cups and unreeled the line, letting the cups disappear above, swallowed by the darkness that still surrounded him.

Visibility was maybe ten feet here, thanks to his light. Without it he wouldn't be able to see his hand in front of his face.

The cups disappeared. They would pop to the surface in a few minutes. The others would see them and know Tim had secured the anchor. Time to dive.

Boom-boom-boom.

He looked at his dive computer. At this depth he had twenty minutes to look around. Twenty minutes before he had to begin the long climb back to the surface, stopping periodically at deco points. Twenty minutes of jungle drums and a vague sense of disconnect, as though his spirit held to his body only by the most tenuous of ties.

He was about to look up when something caught his eye. Not a flash, not even a glint. More the hint of such, the promise of a glimmer.

He leaned down. He was careful to touch nothing – he didn't want to disturb anything down here, not even in a place as impossible as this. He just waved a hand above, trying to stir away the surface sand. Silt whirled away. It revealed a thin rectangular shape, perhaps four inches long, two inches wide, a half-inch thick. Free of its burial plot it shone brightly in Tim's light and he started to tremble.

It was a gold bar.

Worn mostly smooth by years below, it still held traces of some kind of stamping. Wavy lines, some writing long-faded to illegibility.

A swastika.

Now Tim's trembles became shakes.

Nazi gold. Dammit, this is Nazi gold.

He looked around. Trying to make a shift in his mind. Trying to see something in the dim shapes around him. Trying to figure out if he stood on something natural, or if the coral had clung to something that had once held men.

There were still boats listed as missing on the roles of national maritime conflicts. Only twenty-five years previous a pair of divers had discovered an unknown U-boat a mere sixty miles off the coast of New Jersey. The U-boat had come close enough to just about see swimmers on the beach, and no one had even known about it until the 1990s.

So was it beyond the realm of possibility that this was a bar of gold from some still-missing transport ship?

Why here? Wouldn't a transport ship be going somewhere closer to Germany's territories?

He could barely make sense of the question. The drumbeat in his ears clouded his thinking, made answers a near-impossibility.

And then there was the thought that he was looking at thousands of dollars. More.

Gold.

Boom-boom-boom.

Gold.

Boom-boom.

Gold gold gold gold gold.

He reached for it.

Stopped himself.

Didn't touch. Didn't take.

He could always come back for it.

But not now. No reason to do so. And something about it felt... wrong.

Still, he wanted to look around. To see if there was more.

Boom-boom-boom.

He pulled a final spool of line to the front of his gear. Secured it to the anchor line.

And swam into the darkness. A single line trailing behind him. Darkness pressing in, drumbeats all around.

Boom-boom-boom.

He swam farther.

The anchor disappeared behind him.

GRACE

~^~^~^~^~

Mercedes Peterson had nothing.

Only a few years ago she had been rich – rich in friends, rich in family, rich in money, which to her was the least important of the three.

Now… the money was gone. The friends had somehow dried up when her bank balance dipped to nothing.

And family?

She felt tears pushing against the backs of her eyes. Insistent and persistent, the tears were always there, it seemed. Always waiting for the smallest excuse, the moment when they could push out and reduce her to the wreck she had been for so many weeks.

She had taken this trip because it was a chance to leave it all behind. Not a trip she could afford, not even one she felt she deserved.

But it was one she needed. An opportunity to stop being the Mercedes –

(*Don't say it, don't even think it!*)

– Peterson she had to be, and start being just Mercedes. Just a woman with no past, no stories. Only the present. Far from land, far from her reality. She was in the permanent now of each passing wave, the only ups and downs the gentle swells that rocked the boat.

That was the theory, at least. Not that it worked out in practice.

The one thing more people wish to run from than anything else is themselves. And that is exactly the one thing that gives no heed to time or distance. Self is always present, and since self is defined by the sum of past events, that means those past events are always present. The past transported by the time machine of experience, transmuted to present emotions, thoughts, actions.

She tried to be just Mercedes. And she failed miserably. The tears always pressing.

The only time she found relief was during the dives. In the water, the deep blue of the sea beneath what most people *thought of* as the sea... peace. Something like the bliss she imagined holy men and women felt when not merely communing with their gods, but being utterly at one with them.

But still, each dive came to an end. Each fall from Hell to a kind of grace ended when she first put her hand on the dive ladder, when she first climbed aboard the dive platform and the water drained from her wetsuit. Dry, she was herself again.

And that was the greatest tragedy of all.

Then... the coin. And suddenly she was able to look away from her past, to look beyond her present.

What if there was more?

What if there really *was* treasure?

She couldn't afford to hope. Couldn't afford the crushing pain of failure if the hope turned to ash.

But the hope came anyway.

That was why she was suiting up for a dive beyond anything she had ever attempted before.

She was falling to grace again. And perhaps – just perhaps – falling far enough that she could find a bit of that grace and bring it back up with her.

She could have her life back.

Something drew her out of herself for a moment. Jimmy J's voice, snapping out with a tone as close to agitation as she had ever heard. The kid was cute – she'd have gone for him once upon a time, back when she –

(*deserved*)

– was young enough for that sort of thing. And one of his more attractive qualities was his laid-back attitude to life. Just taking it as it came.

Which simply meant he hadn't experienced enough of it to know what it was really like. The simple passing of years would cure him of his relaxed manner quickly enough.

But for now he was innocent. And beautiful in the way that all innocents were.

Still, something was cracking through that innocence now. A seabed that leaped up to meet them. A friend gone deep below. And now....

"What are you *doing*?" he said.

Mercedes looked up. Saw Jimmy J looking at Geoffrey as the commodities trader – whatever the hell that was – came out of the salon.

She didn't like Geoffrey. She didn't think anyone on the boat did – probably including Geoffrey himself. He was the kind of man who viewed everything as a possible return on investment. Especially people. Everything went in the credit or debit column of his personal ledger, and if you weren't a credit you weren't worth knowing.

He was nice enough to Mercedes. At least, he was as nice as she suspected he was capable of. She knew why. Knew that she looked damn good in a bikini. She had worked hard enough for it, countless hours of Pilates and a million vertical miles on the Stairmaster.

Fat lot of good it did you.

But underneath that surface niceness, that shallow attempt at charm, he was just one more man. Just one more person willing to use, abuse, and lose her.

Now Geoffrey was flapping his finned feet as he crossed the deck, moving toward the dive platform.

"What are you *doing*?" Jimmy J demanded again, more insistently this time.

"You really think I'm going to let *him* find all the gold?" said Geoffrey, pointing at the twin Styrofoam cups that bobbed just off the port side of the ship.

"Are you nuts?" said Jimmy J. "He just barely –"

Splash. Geoffrey paused only long enough to throw a middle finger before disappearing into the water. Bubbles where he had gone down. Then nothing.

A moment later, Mercedes was ready as well. She headed toward the platform.

Mr. Raven was standing nearby, and she thought she saw him nod minutely. For a moment she couldn't figure what he was nodding at – not her, she was sure of it. Then Haeberle nodded back, his own nod not nearly so subtle. And he began pulling on the last of his gear.

She felt chilled. Haeberle gave her the creeps.

No. Not that. He scares you. Scares you silly.

True enough. The big man looked at her from time to time. That was bad. He smiled sometimes, too. That was much, much worse. The smile never went quite to his eyes. They were alive with a fire that reminded her of a wolf's, eyes reflecting the dying embers of a campfire, waiting for the fire to die, for that first moment of darkness when it could lunge into the camp and begin its bloody work.

No, Haeberle was not someone she wanted to share space with. Not *The Celeste*, not even the whole ocean.

But she had no choice.

She kept walking to the dive platform.

Sue and Cal were arguing. She liked them. Especially Sue. She was a woman, which was a huge point in her favor. Beyond that, she seemed genuinely sweet. Someone who sat with her at mealtimes, who chatted gently about nothing at all because she obviously sensed that nothing at all was the only thing Mercedes felt comfortable talking about.

Mercedes didn't even really contribute during their chats. Just listened, and that was nice. She could be there without having to figure out what to say, what deflections to use, what lies to spin.

"I'm going," Sue said to her father.

"Just... just wait a minute, can't you?"

"No. You may not care, but I need to know what happened."

Cal looked utterly stricken at that last. His face curled in a mix of surprise, pain, and regret.

Sue walked toward the platform. Mercedes gestured for her to jump first. Sue did. Bubbles. Bubbles.

Gone.

Mercedes jumped in after her.

Praying for her fall to grace.

Please, God, let this change things.

TANKED

~^~^~^~^~

Sue descended through the nothing-space of the sea, drifting in a controlled fall that took her rapidly from bright to night. She turned on her dive light. It was a Big Blue TL15000P: fifteen thousand lumens that cleaved the darkness like a white-hot knife. It was far more powerful a light than most divers carried, but she liked to see past the few feet that other dive lights illuminated.

That was why she saw the wreck when she was still fifty feet above it.

Her heart fluttered, batted to and fro by a complex set of emotions. Fear, grief, elation, uncertainty – they all battled for control of her soul.

Because the wreck wasn't Deb's boat. There was no question of that.

Even under the thick accretions of coral that had sprung up, and through the layers of fish that teemed through her light, she could see it was a large ship. No doubt at all. From up close it might be hard to tell, but from where she was she could see the gentle sweep of a keel, the broken extrusions that had once been forward and main batteries, pilot house and smokestacks.

The thing looked to be about two hundred feet long. About the size of a frigate or destroyer, and from the general outline she guessed it was old. She wasn't an expert by any means, and the coral and overgrowth was thick, all but obscuring parts of the boat. She thought it possible this was a World War II vessel, though how it had sunk or why it lay here undiscovered she couldn't begin to guess.

All this combined to let her know that she would find no answers about what had happened to Deb in this place. A terrible disappointment, given the almost overwhelming need she felt for some kind of closure. But at the same time, it felt good to see it *wasn't* Deb's ship. Because no matter how irrational it was, she could still hope for her sister to be alive until someone or something proved the contrary.

She could lie to herself. And knowing it was a lie didn't matter – not until she saw her sister's boat or her sister's body.

Sue let herself fall to where Tim had secured the anchor. She saw two lines leading in different directions: Tim, Geoffrey. She briefly considered following one of the lines in the hopes that it would lead to Tim. Rejected the idea almost as quickly as it came: she had no idea which line went to which person, and the last thing she wanted was to run into Geoffrey down here. She suspected that even without being able to speak he'd still be an insufferable prick.

She decided to surface. She wasn't a wreck diver; she knew this was risky business. And since this wasn't Deb's ship, since it had nothing to do with her there was no reason to –

Sue froze. Even the current seemed to die around her as everything went absolutely still. There was only the drumbeat of her pulse; the raspy, hollow sound of her breathing; the bouncing noise of bubbles rising past her with every exhalation. And then even those sounds disappeared. Faded from her consciousness.

There was only her. Her in the deep. Her in the bright white halo of her dive light.

Her... and *it*.

She swam as fast as she could to a nearby outcropping. The boat looked like it had settled at a forty-five degree angle, so everything canted madly below her. It was a disquieting feeling, following surfaces that refused to be vertical or horizontal but favored instead diagonal planes.

In the corner of what she assumed was the point where ship's deck met some extrusion – exhaust port, perhaps, or some other part of the ship unknown to her – she had seen something that made her blood run cold. Something that did not belong here. Not on a ship this old, not on a ship so thoroughly claimed by the deep.

She adjusted her buoyancy slightly, drifting down oh-so-slowly. Forcing herself not to touch it until she was practically standing on it.

Then she lifted it. The extra weight drove her down. Standing awkwardly on both deck and that other once-vertical surface. Her flippers touched softly, but even that impact was enough to cause long-dormant sand to billow in a great cloud that reached to her thighs. She suddenly couldn't see below her knees, and had the mad feeling that something would grab her.

Nothing did. Just her panic.

The tank had caught her eye because it was so obviously new. So obviously *not right*. Not for here.

She hefted it. It felt empty.

She turned it, spinning the cylinder in her hands.

Stopped.

Felt like screaming.

The drumbeat of her pulse came back. The pounding of nitrogen narcosis, the cottony feel that kept her from thinking straight engulfing her full force.

The tank had letters stenciled along the long axis. "NELSON CHEM."

And beside those letters –

(*oh no oh please oh please God no please don't let this be real please no no nonononoNO*)

– a few more. Smaller. Not stenciled, but written by hand with permanent marker.

"DEBI R."

The tank fell from her nerveless fingers. Disappeared in another cloud of sand that puffed up around it as it hit the bottom.

She looked around. Trying to see something else, anything else, that would help her know what had happened, that would help her understand how Deb had –

(*DIED!*)

– disappeared.

She saw nothing. Just fish and coral and the ship that ran off in all directions.

She began swimming. Drums pounding louder, louder, louder against the inside of her skull. Her head aching, her eyesight fading at the edges until she looked through a narrow tunnel of her own terror.

She only had one thing in mind. Only thought of finding answers. Finding evidence.

Finding Deb.

But behind that, something lurked. A thought so important it cried out to be noticed even as Sue kicked her way over the ship's deck.

She pushed it down. Not important. Nothing was important.

Only Deb. Only answers.

But the one thing remained. Below consciousness, below her reality. But there nonetheless. A pair of simple facts:

She had tied her line to the anchor line, but had forgotten to connect the other end to herself; she was floating free.

And she was caught in the current.

HATCH

~^~^~^~^~

Haeberle swam along the corner of a "V," two long structures that rose at an angle on either side of him. This thing didn't look much like a ship, didn't look like much of anything but hard and soft coral: a mix of rock-like outcroppings, leathery sheets that spread over as much as several feet, and anemone-like fingers spread into the current, swaying as they captured near-microscopic food and filtered them through some of nature's most rudimentary digestive systems.

He thought about turning back. But he didn't want to deal with that. He wasn't *afraid* of what Raven would do – he wasn't afraid of anything, anything at all, in this world of his own making – but he didn't want to deal with the hassle of it. Sometimes his id, or ego, or whatever part of his brain was responsible for all this, could be a whiny little bitch.

Thinking about his id and subconscious made him think of Cheyenne Shellabarger. She had been the first one to recognize the greatness in him. To understand how unique he was. That was the term she used when he was at the home, "unique." Scribbling away on her pad, furiously recording the presence of a God in her midst.

She had screamed when he took her, which he didn't understand. She had been so fascinated by him, all those hours talking to her, reclined on her comfortable couch, talking about his hopes and dreams – hopes and dreams which would inevitably come true.

But the screams stopped eventually. They always did.

He walked from her silent form, sated physically and mentally. *Id, ego, super-ego...* marvelous new places that had opened his eyes to his greatest power.

But the fact that those parts of him were in charge sometimes irritated him. Just a bit – not too smart to get mad at *yourself* – but still.... He really wasn't sure where he came up with people like Raven.

It would be fun when that man went silent. The way they all did, either because Haeberle left sight of them and they ceased to exist, or because he had the pleasure of *making* them be silent under the power of his own two hands.

He realized that he was drifting. Not in a current, but in the pleasant euphoria of his own thoughts. A small part of him remembered the words of warning that Tim –

(*bastard, idiot, imaginary* unfriend)

– had doled out. Remembered him talking about nitrogen narcosis and wondered if this might be what it felt like. He felt something pounding through him, sounding in time with his heartbeat.

Power. It must be.

At that moment, as if to confirm his thought, the glow of his dive light illuminated something. A twisted sheet, overgrown like everything else, but still recognizable as a door or a hatch of some kind. Twisted, rolled in on itself by some kind of impact.

And beside it: a dark space. A doorway.

Treasure.

The Deep

He dropped toward it....

Reached toward the darkness....

Treasure. Buried in the deep, caught in a dark coffin hundreds of feet long.

The drum-sound of thunder and lightning and *power* boomed louder in his ears, his mind, behind his eyes.

He felt the side of the doorway. Began orienting himself.

And paused.

Did something move in there?

He tried to pierce the blackness beyond the doorway, but could not. His light seemed to fail at the threshold, the line between teeming life and the black halls of a doomed ship.

His thoughts muddled. The beating in his head became louder, almost painful.

And something floated in front of him. Something big.

The shape terrified Haeberle. More so when it turned a single bright eye on him. The thing's gaze seared him, burned through his corneas and punched blazing holes in his mind.

A dark appendage reached out from behind that glowing gaze. Reached for *him*.

Haeberle screamed, a blast of bubbles escaping his regulator, looking like silvered jellyfish as they ran up and over his mask, obscuring his view.

There was only that bright eye. Only the silver of his screams.

144

Then the thing touched him.

Shook him.

Haeberle blinked. He was hearing a sound. Not him, something else.

He stopped the panic-screams, the terrified shaking of his head.

Focused on the monster.

Only it *wasn't* a monster –

(*why did I think it was a monster what's happening down here everything's strange Cheyenne nothing makes sense when I look hard enough so I just don't look*)

– it was that meddling sonofabitch, Tim.

The other diver had dropped between Haeberle and the hatch and was now calling around his regulator. A sound like "On't Oh" which Haeberle gradually realized was him screaming "Don't go."

As soon as Haeberle stopped moving, Tim held up his arm. There was an underwater slate on his forearm, a small piece of plastic with a pen that could write on it – the dry-erase board of the deep.

On the slate: "2 DANGEROUS INSIDE."

Haeberle stared at the slate in surprise. Shock.

Wrath.

How dare *he?*

How dare *anyone* tell him what to do? You did not tell the God of the world what to do. You just sat back and waited for him to work his wonders, his miracles, his givings and takings of pleasant agonies and final release.

Haeberle forgot about the writhing darkness. Forgot about the single moment when he had nearly admitted fear.

Because what *was* in there?

He decided to put Tim in his place. Not his final place – though that would come soon enough. Just his place in the order of commandment and obedience.

Haeberle gave orders. He did not take them.

He pounded with his fins. Two hard thrusts that pushed him past Tim, moving so suddenly the other man was left to gape in surprise.

In awe.

Haeberle was brave.

Haeberle feared nothing.

Haeberle swam into the ship.

SHARK

~^~^~^~^~

Mercedes had gone in a different direction. Not just in this place, but in her life. Her mother had told her it wouldn't end well, wouldn't end in dreams but in nightmares.

Mother had been right.

Of course, she didn't live to see it, to say "I told you so." Died of a sudden brain aneurysm, her skull filling so fast and full that she just slumped in the middle of Christmas dinner and when the doctors told Mercedes about the findings of the autopsy they shuddered and she pictured blood spewing out of her mother's eyes and ears as they cut in.

The children had nightmares for months. Waking up screaming in their small beds, clutching for Mother; shouting for Gramma Paula, please send her back, God, please send her back.

Mercedes held them. Held them close and felt at once incredibly loved and incredibly alone. She was a mother; she had children who called to her in the night. But she was a daughter now without parents of her own. Her father had died when she was only eight.

She was now the matriarch, the only remaining woman in the family.

And soon after, as though waiting for the passing of Mercedes' mother, Bill started screwing around.

Don't lie, Mercedes. That's when you found out about it. When he started is anyone's guess.

She pushed back the rest of the story. Thinking about how bad it had gotten after that was a good way to dissolve into tears. Not a good idea at one-hundred-fifty feet below sea level.

She concentrated on just swimming. Pumping her legs in slow, even motions that would maximize forward thrust while minimizing effort. She also pulled herself along on outcroppings below her, scaling a horizontal wall that she sensed *was* something special. She had dived reefs before – back when things were good she dove all the time – and this didn't feel like a natural growth.

Of course it's not natural. It wasn't even here *two days ago. This was open ocean.*

Another thing not to think about. No answers to what had happened here, no answers to how or why – just like every single yesterday she had experienced in the last months. No rhyme, no reason, just unrelenting attacks.

She pulled herself forward.

The motion disturbed the sand that had settled between corals. She tried not to disturb anything, tried not to touch the coral. Not only could it damage the coral itself, but there was no telling what lay below it – a bad cut was no fun when diving. Especially not when you couldn't surface until over an hour of decompression.

She shuddered as a chill swept over her. It had nothing to do with the cold of the water seeping into her wetsuit, chilling her to the bone. But the sudden realization of how far down she was, how far away – in time and space – she was from help… that chilled her soul.

Her hand plunged down. Pulled. She swam. Forward.

Collings

Move forward. Just move forward. Don't think about what's around you, don't think about the danger.

Move forward.

Blind motion. Her mantra in the last months.

She realized that her vision had darkened around the edges. One of the signs of the narcotic effect of nitrogen at this depth. The entire body reacting to a gas that grew poisonous below the ocean's surface. But she couldn't bring herself to worry about it. It just *was*. A part of her pointed out that this lack of worry was also a sign of narcosis – maybe a much worse one – but it was a small, faraway part.

Forward. Forward. Forward.

Flashes moved in and out of her field of vision. Fish, shimmering and bright in the lance of her dive light. Big ones, too – parrots and puffers and a few she had never seen and had no names for. Big, then bigger as she pulled along –

(*Forward. Forward.*)

– and got farther and farther from where she had tied onto the anchor line.

Something flashed into her sight. Grey, white on the bottom. A sleek body with a torpedo head. A shark.

It wasn't big – maybe only as big as her arm. But that was big enough for a nasty bite if it chose to take an interest in her.

Then it was gone.

Forward.

Another flashed into view. This one as big as her leg.

And another.

This one was nearly as big as she was. It would weigh far more than her. And as a predator in its element it could move faster, do more damage.

Gone.

Forward, Mercedes. Keep moving forward.

The next gray-white shape was huge. Coming right at her. It veered away at the last second, but the wake from its fin was enough to bat her back, to send her scrabbling for a grip on the coral below. She slipped.

Another shark came. Rushed her. Turned. Another blast of wake, a directed current that slammed her back. Then another shark. So many she couldn't see past them. A solid wall of gray and white.

She couldn't see *anything* but them. Coming at her, slashing through the water with teeth gaping, mouths so wide she could see into the dark maws beyond.

They kept circling. Their combined power creating whirlpools around her, pummeling her, pushing her. She clutched vainly for something to hold, looked vainly for somewhere to hide.

She knew what this was. They were testing her. Checking her out. Curious gazes, "flybys" to see if she was interesting.

One of the way sharks checked out what was interesting was by taking a bite of it.

If any of these sharks bit her, it would be a death sentence. She would have a choice between bleeding to death in the cold dark of the deep or surfacing so fast her blood would boil with the nitrogen bubbles.

Her fingers brushed against something. Clenched.

A hole. A sudden pit between coral, a dark ring that could only have been some kind of large porthole or window.

Was it large enough? It would be close.

Did she really *want* to go in there?

Another shark came. This one bumped into her.

She pulled herself into the dark. She would have to trust on her "go-home" line – the line that trailed from her to the anchor line – to lead her back. And hope that none of the sharks came in here after her.

She kicked her way in. But halfway through the hole, she bumped into something that stopped her. Not ahead, this was... behind? Her mind, fogged by depth and blanketed by terror, struggled to understand what was going on.

She felt fins batting against her legs. Bumps against her feet.

Push, push, push, but she *couldn't. Get. In.*

She started breathing even harder than she already was. Short, fast gasps that served not to energize but to drain her. She felt sluggish. Stupid. And if she wasn't careful, her air would –

Air!

She realized what was keeping her here, among the sharks that were now pushing constantly against her.

How long until they bite?

It was her ascent tanks. The air tanks she would switch to when she began her long trip to the top, two tanks she had slung in a side harness and that now kept her from getting into the hole.

She didn't think, just acted. Fumbled with the clips that bound the tanks to her. She would have to drop them. Leave them, and hope she could return to claim them after the sharks left.

If *they leave.*

Something nipped her leg. Not hard enough to qualify as a bite, but the pinch was accompanied by a small shake. A beginning to the bite and then to the frenzy that would follow.

Faster. Hurry. Faster!

She couldn't find the clips. Half in the ship, half out, and her arms couldn't bend around and find the clips.

She wiggled backward. Acutely aware that she was just presenting even more of herself to the sharks. Suddenly realizing that they wouldn't have to bite her: a nip to any of her air hoses could be catastrophic.

Back, Mercedes, get back, you worthless bitch!

It was Bill's voice that shouted at her. His words that almost ended her will to fight. She sagged for a moment, unaware of anything but the black edges seeping toward the center of her vision, the pound of her pulse.

Then a shark bit her.

This wasn't a nip, it was an actual bite. Fiery pain ran up her leg. Shocked her into action.

She found the rest of the clips and ties. Released the ascent tanks. They fell behind her, somewhere she couldn't see.

She wriggled her way into the porthole. Not sure how bad the bite to her leg was, not caring. She was in. She was away.

The darkness surrounded her.

And she was gone.

DANGERDANGERDANGER
~^~^~^~^~

After Mercedes disappeared, several things happened.

First, her go-home line caught on the rough edge of the aperture she had entered. It was a thick line, heavy gauge, strong.

It started to rasp back and forth. Started to fray.

Second, the sharks suddenly stopped moving. They floated motionless in the darkness. Each was aware of its brothers and sisters, hanging there in the silence of the deep.

Each was also aware of something else. Fingers reaching into rudimentary minds, pressing here, probing there. Touches that brought with them the basic impulses these predators could understand.

A moment before the sensations had been confusing. Each was herded in certain directions. Guided here with thoughts of *foodfoodfoodfoodfood*, then rocketing back with sensations of *dangerdangerdanger*.

None of them realized the way they were being used. Certainly not on a conscious level, and less so in the stimulus-response centers that were now being played so astutely. None understood that they had swam in controlled circles, that the strongest had been sent forth and turned away in very specific ways.

Ways that would drive them, and in so doing also drive the *other*. The strange creature that swam with even stranger fin-not-fin shapes. The thing that bubbled and made so much noise noise noise noise noise in the otherwise peaceful solemnity of the deep and the dark.

They drove it back

drove it back

drove it back

drove it back.

Foodfoodfoodfood and they raced at the thing, certain it was good, that it would satiate the sudden need in mind and emptiness in belly.

Then, mouths agape, they would hear the shriek of *dangerdangerdanger* and fling themselves away, turning on tail and rushing away until the cycle continued.

Then, suddenly, the strange creature had dropped away. Fallen into a hole that the creatures knew. This was a place darker than the ocean.

They hung there, motionless over the opening, but each knew that down there was *dangerdangerDANGER* greater than any they had ever known.

They hung. Fingers probed, tentacles tickled their minds.

Goodgoodgoodgood the sharks felt. *Gogogogogo*.

They shook themselves as one.

They swam away. To feed, to rest, to rut.

Away from the dark place.

Away from the *dangerdangerdangerDANGER* into which the strange fish had fallen.

DIAMOND

~^~^~^~^~

Geoffrey floated over crumbling bits of nothing and his head hurt and he wondered why the hell he was down here instead of in his nice office with its leather seats and air conditioning and his secretary with the amazing boobs. The pounding in his head was getting worse and worse, driving spikes into his mind, *boom-boom-boom.* All he could focus on was the pounding, all he could think of – aside from Jo of the Amazing Bazoombas – was *sonofabitch, bastard, sonofabitch, bastard.*

He was done. Tired. Thirsty. He usually brought along a squeeze bottle of Gatorade or something with a sport top to drink, but had forgotten this time. Drinking underwater was a tricky maneuver for idiot newbs, but Geoffrey was *not* an idiot newb. He had mastered the buying and selling of futures, the ability to be the short or the long of any deal and still make a killing; he could sure as hell manage squirting Mango Extremo into his mouth at fifty feet.

*But you're not at fifty, G-man. One-*hundred-*fifty.*

That voice pounded like his headache, and he wondered whose it was. Not his, that was sure. He was The Shiz, The Man, El Grande Macho. No way he was going to believe even for *one second* that this dive was beyond him.

So it must be that sonofabitchbastard Tim. Guy thought he knew everything. But what was he, really? A glorified swimming teacher. What did he know about putting together a portfolio, managing an ETF, predicting how far gold would go?

No, Tim was a twit and a bastard if there ever was one.

He might have been right about not going on this trip, though. Just not for the reasons he had his panties in a bunch about.

Geoffrey thought suddenly about Jo's panties. He hadn't seen them – yet. He bet they were amazing. And very small.

Geoffrey shook his head. His thoughts were all over the place. Was this the narcosis Sonofabitch Tim had been all over him about?

No. No way. That stuff probably affects lots of people, but I doubt it would get me this fast. Huh-uh.

Still, he thought it was probably time to go. His dive computer – which was a Suunto DX wristwatch style thirteen-hundred-dollar-top-of-the-line-you-sonofabitches-because-Daddy-deserves-the-*best* dive computer – said he had plenty of time left. But he was just... *bored.* Commodities were never boring. His life was never boring. Jo's fantastic chest muffins were *definitely* never boring.

But this, this was –

He froze. Stopped so suddenly that his right calf twinged from the speed at which he went from a leisurely kick to a stock-still hold.

What the...?

He had been swimming over a crumbled line of nothing. Just coral and little fishies and nothing else. But in front of him there was a huge pile of debris. Something that left no doubt in his mind that this was, in fact, a wreck. The structure itself was all but invisible, buried under the sea life that had slowly claimed it as its own. But something about the tilt, about the vertical lines where something had clearly shattered and come to rest in the perfectly straight layers and angles that nature abhorred... it all screamed "People Were Here."

The wreckage was a good six feet tall. It seemed to have appeared out of nowhere, though Geoffrey knew that was impossible. It had probably been there the whole time but he just hadn't noticed it because he was –

(*narced oh man I think it's real and I might be narced time to go G-man time to go*)

– thinking about Jo. Well, the *good parts* of Jo.

But here it was, piles of something that had collapsed in on itself under the power of whatever had killed this ship.

And between the piles: darknesses. Cracks and crevasses that eluded the light from his (best in class!) dive light.

And in the darkness – in one darkness in particular – a flash of light. A gleam.

Geoffrey remembered the coin that Raven –

(*no way to I call that douche nozzle* Mr.)

– had pulled from the stiff. The corpse had been thoroughly creepy, but there was nothing creepy about that gold piece. Geoffrey traded in gold all the time, and he had a nose for what was valuable, what was junk, what prices would go up, what would go down. That sonofabitch coin was pure value, nothing but rising profit in its future.

And it had glimmered. Gleamed the way something in the crack right in front of Geoffrey was gleaming now.

Sonofabitch, yes!

He reached for it... and a flurry of fish seemed to explode from nowhere. One second he was more or less alone, and the next he was in the eye of an underwater hurricane composed of silver fish the size of his arm. They flashed and flapped, spinning around him so close that he felt the ten thousand caresses of their ten thousand fins as they passed over and under and all around him.

He felt his breathing speed up. Panic. What was up? What was down?

A piece of his mind, about three levels below the part that engaged first in Jo's sweater stuffing and now focused on the less pleasant fact of impending panic, whispered at him to slow down. To control his breathing. Shallow breathing used up air that much faster, used up the oxygen that was the only thing between life and death down here. No matter how top of the line your dive computer was, it couldn't recalculate based on your breathing too fast underwater.

Darkness pushed at him. Surrounded him. The pounding in his head worsened. He felt his mouth go dry. Surrounded by water and he felt like his tongue was a damn crouton.

He hit the release valve on his BC and dropped, hoping irrationally that if he could get close to the ground – or to the deck of this wreck – that he could get below the fish. Like they were a fire and the first rule was to stop and drop.

That's two rules, G-man. Can't you count?

Shut up, man!

He fell downward, only certain that this *was* down because the bleed-off from his BC should have dropped him like a rock.

And sure enough, he hit the deck a second later. Literally. Felt the soft coral padding him. It'd probably kill them, but that was their fault for not being able to get out of the way.

The fish were gone.

Just like that. There, then not there.

He looked around, suddenly unsure if he had really seen all those fish. Maybe he had dreamed it. Maybe he *was* narced.

He was still breathing fast. Too fast. He tried to slow down, to take deep breaths. Couldn't. Panic was by its nature a force beyond control.

Geoffrey looked around wildly, not sure what he was even looking *for*, but unable to stop himself.

He looked into the crack. That deep dark place with the shining light of something. And before he could think about it, could think about the wisdom of putting his hand in a hole in the deep water, he reached in and grabbed for the glimmer.

He felt something hard. Round. Cold.

He pulled it out.

Opened his fist.

SONOFABITCHBASTARDBITCH!

It was a diamond. Not dirty, not crusted over with slimy sea life. Gleaming, beautiful, *perfect*.

And it was the size of a golf ball.

You've made it, G-man! Screw the trades, screw the job, screw Jo, I'm playing with the big boys from now on!

Then something darted out of the crack. The same place he had put forth his hand and drawn out his chance at riches beyond dream. But the thing that came out now wasn't dream… it was nightmare.

A green flash. The impression of a writhing hose.

Then pain.

The moray eel had to be six feet long. Thick as Geoffrey's neck, its mouth a permanently grimacing line of razor teeth.

That mouth had engulfed Geoffrey's hand. Those teeth were digging into him. It hurt. Oh sonofabitch it hurt.

Geoffrey screamed. A silver cloud enveloped him as the regulator popped out of his mouth. Then it faded away from his vision. Instead of silver he saw red: a cloud of blood floating around his hand. Mixing with the green of the eel, a bright tableau of pain.

Geoffrey kept screaming. Started whipping his hand back and forth, back and forth. The eel just ground down harder. More blood came.

Geoffrey's thoughts tumbled. Jo's boobs. The time he nearly lost it all on the market. And a random bit of trivia: the fact that morays clung to anchors in the rocks and crevasses they preferred. Their bite couldn't kill a man. Impossible.

But they could hold tight. Hold so long that a diver ran out of air.

Geoffrey shook his hand. Harder and harder and so hard he felt his shoulder ache with the force.

The eel held on.

Its eyes, unblinking and wide, seemed full of malevolent purpose. Hold, hold, hold.

Geoffrey realized he had stopped screaming. He needed to breathe, but his regulator was still floating around somewhere in front of him. Somewhere he couldn't concentrate on because he was dealing with the bastard eel.

I'm gonna die. Gonna die without ever seeing Jo's panties.

He yanked his hand harder. Harder. Couldn't even see it now: it was completely obscured by a shifting mass of blood.

And the eel held on.

QUESTIONS

~^~^~^~^~

Sue swam along the surface of the wreck, barely registering that everything below her was passing far faster than the rate she was actually swimming. She only thought of Debi.

Found her tank.

She's dead. No other story.

What if the tank went down without her?

She's been gone for weeks.

People have survived at sea for longer.

She swam, and then bled some air into her BC so she could swim a bit higher. Readjusted for neutral buoyancy at a height that allowed her a wider field of vision, allowed her to see more of the ship in the brightness of her dive light.

She kept swimming. Couldn't stop – on any level.

The more of the ship she passed over, the more convinced she became that this was a World War II vessel. A twist of metal that could have been the remains of a deck gun. A pile of wreckage that might have been a radar array.

Over it all was the near-deafening drum of her pulse. She had heard some technical divers refer to the sound one heard while deep air diving as "the jungle drums," and the name was apt. It wasn't just a pounding, it was a beat syncopated to the pounding of her heart, the arrhythmic bounce of air bubbles going by her ears. The jungle drums. One part of the mind calling out *Danger!* in a scream that could not be countered, only ignored.

When the drums pounded, the darkness at the edges of her eyesight seemed to pull in a bit closer. Then in the near-instant silences between drumbeats, it would retract. In, out, in, out. But she couldn't be sure if the ins and outs were the same in length, or if the darkness settled a bit farther each time it encroached. Territory taken from her consciousness that might never be replaced.

The ship ended.

The end was abrupt, a falling-away from ten feet below her to something far deeper. This was another risk of wreck diving: operating at one-hundred-fifty feet was the level at the *top* of the wreck. Following its contours might mean much deeper diving, depending on the size of the vessel.

This ship looked like it had been sheared in half.

Torpedo? Mine?

She had no way of knowing. All she knew was that the contours of the ship had revealed no more clues. Nothing but Debi's air tank.

She needed more.

She had to find out.

She went over the side.

Down.

TREASURES

~^~^~^~^~

Mercedes hadn't gone far. Not far at all.

First things first: her leg. As soon as she got far enough into the space into which she found herself, she shined her dive light on her leg. There were three small holes in the calf of her wetsuit, and red gleamed within them. Not as bad a bite as she had feared – something on a level she wouldn't even have worried about if it had happened on land. But here, under so much water, it seemed terribly important. It threatened to swallow her attention, to swallow *her* in a gaping mouth of panic that would chew her up and kill her with nothing but the sheer power of fear.

She forced herself to look away. Searching for something else to focus on.

Her surroundings.

The hole she had entered led to a corridor. Like everything else around here, the lines were wrong: floor and ceiling and walls had shifted on their axis to the point where it was difficult to figure out which was which. But the space itself was open enough. A long tunnel, dark and forbidding.

She almost went back out. Almost turned around and just left. But the thought of those sharks kept her inside. And moving forward. Because what if they came *in*? What if they smelled her wound? The wound wasn't bleeding enough that she could see anything beyond the line of the wetsuit, but sharks could smell a single drop of blood a quarter-mile away. Her? Bleeding on the other side of a doorway with no door to close behind her?

She pushed on into the tunnel.

Almost immediately she started to realize why wreck diving was a specialized skill; why so many people loved and feared it with such intensity. There was a thick coat of sand on the floor, looking like it had lain undisturbed for centuries.

(*How is that possible? This whole place moved six hundred feet just hours ago....*)

The sand stirred as she passed by, even the tiny wake she created with her flippers enough to fling it up into water above. And since there was no current here, nothing to push it away or down, it simply surged upward and hung in a fog-like mass in the corridor. It pushed higher and higher, and was soon hanging directly below her... and rising.

Nor was that the only problem. For some reason the water above her was changing as well. It seemed... *darker.* Cloudy, with some kind of invisible film that pervaded every part, every milliliter of water.

Oil.

She realized that was it. Realized in a sliver of her mind that had sheltered itself from her narcosis and was now shouting to be heard, shouting of danger and of dark and of things gone wrong.

Where? Where's oil coming from?

The answer came as she breathed out. Bubbles flinging up in quick surges. The oil must have come from some broken tank or pipe. And lighter than water, it had gathered at the ceiling of this bent and broken corridor. Found its way there and hung undisturbed until the bubbles from her regulator stirred them and pounded it into an expanding cloud, reaching down to foul the air and obscure her sight.

She froze. Heart beating, ears bursting with the *thop-thop-thop* of a pulse that wanted to explode out of her veins.

The oil just got worse. The sand continued *not* settling. She was caught on a horrible horizon between earth and a dark sky. Her dive light reflecting on the sand like headlights in the thickest fog, being swallowed by the darkness above.

And, somehow, through her muddled mind and the panic that burgeoned, she saw it.

It was some kind of chest. Sitting on a raised mound of sand that had gathered against the far end of the corridor – which she could make out as being collapsed. This was the end of the line… and like the end of the line on all true treasure hunts there was a pirate chest waiting. It even *looked* like a pirate chest, something out of *Pirates of the Caribbean* or some other "arrrrr, matey" kind of movie.

It was wood. Edges frayed with light damage, iron bands surrounding it in three places, giving it strength and an innate sense of age. It was nearly *elemental*, its risen position making it the dead king of this solitary place.

Narcosis had seized her fully. She was barely thinking, barely wondering what a pirate chest was doing here, in a place where the presence of oil clearly signaled a newer ship. Not the type of place to carry this chest anywhere at all, let alone just having it sitting there like –

(bait)

– a gift from God.

But here it is. Here's the answer, Mercedes. Here's what you wanted and what you still need.

(Don't! Don't go to it!)

The two parts of her mind screamed, but one of the screams was faint and distant and drowned out by the banging drums in her ears, the elemental feeling of providential opportunity that surged her forward, heedless of the new fogs of sand kicked up behind her.

She reached the chest. Felt it. It *felt* like a treasure chest. Solid, permanent. A fixture to be found in dark places after much trial; much suffering.

I've suffered. I've seen it all.

This is my ticket out.

(RUN!)

She pulled at the top of the chest. But of course –

(boom boom boom banging drums pounding head not thinking straight run please just leave it alone please run)

– it was locked. In the movies the chest just threw back its lid and exposed its inner riches to anyone who found it. But a *real* treasure chest? It would have to be locked.

She looked around for something to open it. Some tool she could use – a bit of metal or a length of pipe she could use as a crowbar to pry the thing open. To *make* it give up its hoard.

No such implement revealed itself. Only a rock, half-buried in the mountain of sand on which the chest perched.

She grabbed it.

Ow! What the –

She dropped the rock. As it fell it turned and she saw what had caused the pain. A red flare of feathers, attached to a ball-like foot, which in turn held to the rock. A sea urchin, all spines and danger for those that might eat it.

And a painful reminder that when seeking treasure there was always a guardian.

(*You're NOT MAKING SENSE. GET OUT.*)

The voice behind her thoughts almost got through. Nearly took control.

She looked at her hand. It was bleeding. Tight circles of red that oozed into the white/black of the tunnel's water. They stung like hell – some kind of venom.

(*RUN!*)

She picked up the rock – more carefully this time, and with her opposite hand – and turned it so the urchin pointed down.

Then she began slamming it against the front of the chest, where a lock was embedded in the wood. She couldn't swing from very far – the water resistance was too great to get much velocity or force – but when she came in close, she hit with a satisfying *thunk* that sounded like it came from all around her. Sound travels well underwater, but it is directionless.

A scream for help, for instance, can come from anywhere.

She hit the rock against the chest, and a satisfying puff of ooze came up. The urchin was crushed. She had vanquished the treasure's guardian.

A few more hits, and the lock crackled. A few after that it went *poing* as something inside it snapped.

She dropped the rock. It and the remains of the urchin tumbled out of sight below the clouds of sand that reached for her.

She opened the chest.

ALIEN

~ ^ ~ ^ ~ ^ ~ ^ ~

Geoffrey couldn't think. Nothing. Just the pain in his hand, the rush of bubbles around his ears, the steadily increasing thudding in his skull.

Pain pain pain pain pain pain pain....

It became the only thing in his universe. His hand, the eel that still held fast to him. The underlying, almost silent, knowledge that he was going to die here.

Black surrounded him. Narcosis and panic mixed to create a dark miasma that swallowed his thoughts, swallowed his vision, swallowed *him*.

He still couldn't breathe. The regulator spun out of reach, below his sight, below his ability to grab it or even understand where it was. He just knew the bubbles were everywhere – only parting to allow him the sight of the eel clamped on his hand. It had transformed in his panic-sight, his oxygen deprivation, to something more like dragon than eel. Something that held him so strongly there would never be an escape.

He was going to breathe in. He had to.

A hand slashed out. For a moment Geoffrey wondered where it had come from. He couldn't see through the darkness. Wondered if it was *his* hand.

But no. This wasn't his. He didn't own a crappy dive computer like that, did he? His was top of the line. That was a cheaper model.

And the hand held a knife Geoffrey had never seen. The knife slashed down. Cut the eel behind the head.

The eel didn't give. Didn't let go. Clamped down harder.

Geoffrey breathed in. Sucked water. It flooded his airway, dropped into his lungs. Salt that burned, burned, *burned.*

He couldn't make it stop. He gagged. Vomited the gasp of water he had just taken in.

The knife in the hand that did not belong to him –

(*where's it coming from and please let me breathe oh God I'm sorry just let me breathe*)

– cut down again. Another slashing blow.

The eel's head fell away from its body. Fell away from Geoffrey's bleeding hand.

Something spun him around. He would have screamed again, but he was too busy vomiting, inhaling, gagging. The thing in front of him was horrible. Huge eyes, tentacles.

(*tim it's tim*)

The voice didn't pierce the veil of panic. Nor did he understand why the thing in front of him was trying to push one of its tentacles into his mouth.

(*ALIEN TRYING TO TAKE ME OVER TRYING TO KILL ME*)

(*i'm dying*)

Geoffrey whipped his head around. Tried to avoid the thing's grasping tentacle. Vomiting. Now convulsing. His body curling into a bean, a pillbug, a nothing-shape.

(*AIR!*)

The word, the salvation it held, finally penetrated. He didn't know who this was, but the diver in front of him had air. Had the life that Geoffrey needed – damn well *deserved* to keep.

He grabbed at the face of the diver. Tried to pull the regulator out of his mouth. Never mind the octopus, the second-rate regulator hanging from the other guy's hand. He wanted the real thing.

Narcosis pushed him on. Spurred him to madness and beyond as he grabbed for the regulator.

The other diver pulled back. Fins pounding away. Pushing off the ground, flinging away from Geoffrey's grasping hands.

Geoffrey changed tacks. He grabbed for the thing in the other man's hand. The knife. Moved so fast the other guy didn't have a chance to react. Geffrey grabbed it.

Slashed.

CURRENT

~^~^~^~^~

Sue kept swimming. Swimming. Pushing forward.

She spotted movement out of the corner of her eye. Stopped. Turned.

Saw nothing.

Nothing but the coral on that side, bent over and waving gently.

She stared at it dully. Wondering why she watched so long, wondering why her brain was pinging so loud it had penetrated the fog in which she found herself until now.

Coral.

Beautiful.

Waving gently.

Waving....

She realized what she was looking at. Her heart immediately sped up, beating hard enough it felt like a hammer on the inside of her ribs. *Boom-boom-boom little pig little pig let me out.*

Her thoughts jumbled and threatened to spin away again. She frowned. Forced concentration.

The coral was bent.

Pushed.

By what?

The current.

And as she realized it she also noticed that she wasn't staring at the same growths she had been looking at a moment ago.

She was moving. Not kicking, not pulling the water with her hands.

But moving.

Caught. I'm caught.

She tried to judge how fast she was going. Not fast at all by terrestrial standards – maybe two miles per hour. But that was far faster than she could swim.

And – she realized for the first time – she didn't have an anchor line.

Beep. Beep. Beep. Beep.

The sound seemed to come from within her at first. Like an internal red alert that had gone off when she realized what kind of danger she was in.

But that wasn't it.

She looked around. Spun in place –

(*Still moving! Even spinning I'm still moving!*)

– and saw her dive computer.

Beep. Beep. Beep.

The words came to her. Jimmy J on deck, far above and safer than he had a right to be.

"*Some of you guys are using some DCs we had on board since yours weren't rated for this depth. They'll beep – loud – to let you know you have five minutes before you need to start back up. You go any later than that and you either run out of air down there or you have to come up too fast.*"

She looked at her dive computer.

One of the ones from *The Celeste*. Rated for deep dives. Beeping. Flashing. 4:46... 4:46... 4:45....

She spun, this time more purposefully, not even sure for a moment which way she had come from. Trying to get her bearings. Feeling the urgent passage of every second – every millisecond – that counted down her air before she began ascent.

I can still go up. Still got my air. Still got a chance.

And if you surface five miles away from the boat?

She forced herself to calm as much as possible, which was very little.

Booming, slamming, *pounding* in her ears. Thrumming of her pulse through every part of her.

The coral. Waving.

Caught in the current.

She turned until she was facing the opposite way to the direction the coral leaned. Began swimming.

Still falling behind. Falling back.

She dropped to the seabed. Began pulling herself as well as kicking. Now making headway, but only barely.

She didn't look at her dive computer. Didn't know what numbers it would show, but knew it didn't matter. No matter what they were, they would mean the same thing: *You're screwed.*

She pulled, kicked, pulled. An awkward lurch along the bottom.

And she knew she was going to die.

AIR

~^~^~^~^~

Mercedes' world seemed to be spinning.

What did I see? What was that? How was it?

She realized a moment later she had moved away from the chest. In following what she had seen –

(*impossible impossible I didn't I couldn't but how but please no I couldn't I didn't*)

– she had moved somewhere new and now had no idea of where she was. Inside this broken shell of a passage there were no landmarks, no nothing.

And what it was she saw?

How? HOW?

She didn't know.

Just focus on getting back. Did you go back into the first hall? The one with the chest?

She must have. But did she then change her course from the passage to another corridor? A room?

The sand had been disturbed to the point that she could see next to nothing.

Not even the walls.

Whether that meant she was, in fact, now in a room somewhere, or simply that the sand and oil had obscured her view of the walls in the very corridor that would lead her back out of the wreck and to her ascent tanks, she couldn't say. And she was hesitant to move in any direction.

The go-home line.

She grabbed at her waist. The line was still clipped there. Relief flooded her. She could do this. Could make it out.

And then what? Are you going to tell them? What it was you saw?

Later. First thing's first.

Bull. There's nothing but *what you saw.*

Images kept jamming their way into her sight.

The urchin.

The chest.

After the chest.

She pulled at the line. To follow it she would have to take in some slack. The tension would let her know which direction she should go.

And then what? Then what? THEN WHAT?

She pulled. Pulled. The slack remained, and soon she was frowning behind her mask.

What's going –

The line ran out. A ragged end was suddenly in her hand.

Beep. Beep. Beep.

She went cold. Her trip computer was telling her she needed to start up. And her main tank was smaller than the others – she had brought smaller tanks because she was a smaller person. Easier to haul, but less margin for error. She had calculated that she would run out of air when it was time to ascend. She needed to switch to her ascent tanks to make it back.

Five minutes. Not just to start her ascent, but to find her way out. To get to the other tanks that waited for her outside the hole she had entered through.

Beep. Beep. Beep.

She moved. No alternative. No chance to get out just sitting here in the blinding white of her light reflected back at her from all directions.

She swam.

The seconds counted down.

Her hands quested before her. Searching for something, anything, that would tell her where she was. The sand was so thick she couldn't even see them with her arms extended ahead of her this way.

Oh no oh on oh no....

The thought of what she had just seen actually left her for a moment. Survival pushed its way in. Took over.

Humans often devolve into simple animals when survival is at stake. No matter the riches, the wonders, the testaments to civilization or beauty or value that may stand before them, if the moment comes when their lives may end, that looming doom is all that matters. Past does not matter, only the present need for life and the possible futures shut away behind the promise of extinction.

Mercedes' right hand bumped into something. She was caught in currents of terror that pushed her forward so fast that when she hit it her fingers bent back painfully. Ached even when she pulled them back.

But the pain was a strange kind of bliss. She had found something. And any something was a source of hope in the dark brightness of shifting sands.

She pushed her hand down. Felt hard sand. That direction was down, which she hadn't even been sure of a moment ago. So she knew there was a wall – at least to her – in front of her, the "floor" below.

Where now?

She knew that staying in one place was doom. She had to move. Heads or tails or something in between, she had to choose a direction and hope it didn't lead her deeper into the ship.

Time ticking. Moments passing.

She turned, keeping that one hand – sore, the urchin stings still burning like knives against scorched skin – against the wall. She pulled forward. Hoping. Praying.

What did I see?

No matter how hard she tried, the feeling kept intruding.

She pulled breath in. Breath out. Tried to concentrate not on the events of a few minutes ago but instead on keeping her breathing regular.

Stretch the air. Take care and stretch your air, that's what the diving instructor said the first time I ever went in, that's what I've got to do now.

What was the instructor's name? What was her name? She was so beautiful, so assured, what was her name? Vannessa? Vannessa Something "L" I think.

What did I SEE?

Concentrate.

Pulling along. Moving carefully. Careful, she sensed even through the flurry of her thoughts, the intrusive fingers of panic tickling at her, was the only way out. The only chance at survival.

She realized it was getting harder to breathe. Thought at first that something was attacking her from within, some new thing that made even less sense than what she had seen.

Then realized it was nothing so massive or so irrational. She was simply running out of air.

A few more gasps.

Then nothing.

BAILOUT

~^~^~^~^~

Tim fluttered back, fins kicking like the wings of a panicked moth, trying to move away from the jabs and slashes Geoffrey was leveling at him. The other man's eyes were so wide with panic and narcosis that they seemed to take up the entirety of his mask. His pupils were black pits, only barely framed by the slightest bits of color. He was gone, totally narced, beyond reason.

Buddy diving was the rule in recreational diving. You stay with a friend, you keep him or her in your eyesight at all times. It could – and did – save a life if one or the other ran into trouble.

In the deep, though… things were different. Many deep divers eschewed a buddy. And Tim was finding out why. A diver panicked, a diver running short on or completely out of air, will not see another human nearby. He will see only air. A way out. A way to survive. Close friendships could dissolve, murder could be born.

Geoffrey cut again, and it was only the fact that his arm was slowed by the water's drag that allowed Tim to get away. Even so, the knife passed by so close that he nearly slashed one of Tim's hoses.

What do I do?

The smart money would be to run. To turn tail so that there was nothing Geoffrey could cut but Tim's flippers. He knew he could outswim the guy. Could leave him behind.

182

That would be the smart thing to do. And no one would blame him for it.

He didn't do it.

He waved at Geoffrey, screamed at him. Tried to shatter the panic and the drugging effect of the sea. Felt his own thoughts growing muddy and wondered how long before he made a mistake.

Then Geoffrey did something Tim didn't expect. He reached to his left. Moved something behind his back.

Two things happened: first, his tanks released, plummeting to the sea floor. Then, in the next instant there was a loud *hisssss* and Geoffrey rocketed straight up.

Tim knew what had happened in an instant: the guy had a bailout tank. A small cylinder attached to his back, ready to fill his BC up with enough air to cause massive buoyancy. Some recreational divers had them for emergency. Deep water divers didn't use them. Because a bailout tank could be accidentally triggered, sending the diver straight to the surface without deco stops. Death.

Geoffrey moved again as he shot upward. Blocks dumped away from him. His weights.

Tim lunged for the man. Grabbed at his rear fin.

It came off in his hands.

Then Geoffrey was moving beyond him.

Tim swam up. Knowing it was hopeless.

Knowing he had to try.

CARESSED

~^~^~^~^~

Air where's air need air need to breathe need need need needneedneedneed....

The thoughts fluttered through Geoffrey's brain. No cohesion to them. Needing air. Wondering what had happened. Wondering where he was. Darkness pressing in so completely that his life contracted to a small circle of brightness directly in front of him.

What's wrong with my dive light?

Sonofabitchbastard who sold it to me said it was the best.

LIAR!

Air air air need need need.

He felt himself start convulsing. Curving in, thrashing out. Bending side to side, the water in his lungs a tidal wave inside him.

The darkness around him encroached on his vision still further.

He was seeing things. The darkness moving. Reaching for him.

He felt something touch his leg.

Got me. It's got me air air need what's got me air what's touching me need need WHAT'S TOUCHING ME?

Something touched him again. The quivering caress of a lover.

What what what need need air air air air.

The pinpoint of light in front of his eyes flickered. Dark, light, dark, light. Strobes of lightning in the black sky of the deep.

Breaking my light's breaking why how it's supposed to be
—

What's touching me what's TOUCHING ME?
It's killing my light....

A fish darted out of the void. A shark. Five feet long. More.

Geoffrey managed to flinch, but it wasn't headed for him. Not directly. It veered at the last second. A course correction that brought it to Geoffrey's shoulder. The creature bumped him. He felt something yank.

The light disappeared.

Ate it he ate my light.

Air air need.

The air was gone.

The light was gone.

Geoffrey felt himself stop convulsing. Felt his body loosen. Muscles limp.

Something fell from his hand. Knife.

A moment later his other hand opened. Something else fell. Swallowed instantly by the formless dark all around.

His last thought: *My diamond. Something's touching me. Where's my diamond? Sonofabi* —

FLOAT

~^~^~^~^~

Mercedes wanted to panic. Wanted to thrash and shriek into the nothing of the sandy world that was her only existence.

But she didn't. Her mind slipped to the one thing that was always razor sharp. Always a thought that cut her deep, made her mind feel like it was being hacked to painful pieces.

She thought of what she had lost. Not Bill. Better that the bastard was gone.

No, it was all the rest. Especially....

She shook her head. The momentary jabs from her past sharpened her, brought her back to herself.

What did that dive instructor say? The pretty one?

Long as there's air, there's hope.

But I'm out of air.

No. No, please, no.

As if to taunt her, a single bubble appeared before her mask. Probably caught under her mask when she last exhaled. A thing sent from Hell – or maybe from Bill, they were much the same – to let her know what was forever out of her grasp.

Just like everything else I ever loved. Floated away and gone.

Floated.

An idea began to tickle her brain. Not one of the lightbulb variety, where all the lights go on and you scream "Eureka!" No, she was too deep in terror for that. But it was a candle. An ember of hope.

What is it?

Floated.

What?

Float.

And she knew. She kicked up – somehow remembering to keep her hand on the wall since it would do no good to survive this moment and then get lost in the next.

Her head hit the ceiling. Hard. Her vision spun and she almost inhaled. Didn't. But it was hard, so hard not to. She wanted to breathe. Desperate. Knew that in the next second she would inhale no matter what.

She shined her light. Not in front of her, into the dense murk she had created for herself. She looked *up*.

Sand.

More sand.

Silver.

She leaned back. Ripped off her mask and tilted her head back. She kicked up slightly until her face was pressed against the ceiling. Until she was *kissing* it.

Then she opened her mouth. Crossed mental fingers and... inhaled.

Air. Sweet, sweet air. The air that she had breathed out with every breath in, escaping from her regulator and bubbling upward where it was trapped against the ceiling in bubble-pockets that looked like silver in her light. Each had more CO_2 than normal tank air, but still enough oxygen to survive.

She took in one breath. One breath of the air that had escaped from her regulator before her tank ran dry. She crawled along the ceiling. Inhaling, then shining her light to look for more silver. More precious than any silver you could find on land, this was a silver that bought her a single breath each time she found it – a single moment of existence.

Not just because she was breathing again. But because the bubbles marked the way she had come. Breadcrumbs leading her back home, back to the tanks she had left at the opening to this place.

The terror, the muddled feelings, the pain in her hand, even the shock at what she had seen in this place… it all faded. She existed only to follow the trail.

Then it ran out.

She couldn't see more. No more air. Nothing. Just sand floating in the murk.

Again, she forced herself to hang still, to let her thoughts work. It was hard. The air she'd breathed for what felt like an eternity was barely enough to keep going. She was already feeling the loss in her lungs. Panic burgeoned.

Where'd it go? Where did the air go? Where –

She felt like hitting herself. She pushed out a hand. Felt a wall.

No, not a wall. *The* wall.

She dropped along its length. Felt wall, wall, wall… and then nothing.

She followed the void. Pushed forward.

Pushed her head out of the hole through which she had come.

Her ascent tanks were there. She couldn't see them well, not without the mask she still held in her hand, but there was a dark blur in the spot she remembered putting the tanks.

She pushed out of the hole, lungs burning so much she felt like all the air bubbles had been some kind of dream; surely it had been hours since her last breath?

She got to the tanks. Switched over from her dry one to these by feel. Air flooded her regulator.

She breathed in, and it was the most exquisite sensation she had ever experienced. Oxygen blasting in, rejuvenating her not only physically, but mentally and emotionally. For one blessed instant the fog that had accompanied her throughout the entirety of this dive was gone; blown away by that first puff of air.

It settled back in again, along with the pounding in her ears and the beast trapped in her ribcage. But none were so terrifying, none so daunting.

She had air. She could make it.

She put her mask back on. It was full of water, of course, so she held the top and leaned her head back. Inhaled through the regulator, then blew out steadily through her nose. Repeated the process several times, and each time the water level in her mask dropped as the air pressure forced it out. Soon she was blinking seawater free from her eyes and lashes, focusing once more on her surroundings.

The joy that she had felt with the first breath was something incomparable. An emotion so powerful she didn't know if she'd ever match it. Still, what she saw next made her feel like dancing, right there at fifteen stories below the surface.

Her go-home line.

She grabbed it. Started to pull/swim her way to the anchor line. She was using up her ascent air, but if she got to the anchor line fast enough, she might just make it.

But what did I see down here?

How was it even possible?

NOTHING

~^~^~^~^~^~

Tim pounded his way up. Feeling his legs burn like he had swum miles and miles – though he knew it was only ten or fifteen feet. But he had thrashed so hard, whipped his legs and feet so fast, that the burn of overexertion had prickled its way in almost immediately.

Geoffrey was a globe above him. A small brightness that diminished in size and intensity with every passing moment.

Tim stopped kicking. Heard something in the background: the distant *beep beep beep* of his dive computer.

Five minutes.

He hung where he was, torn. He wanted with everything he was to go after Geoffrey. To grab him and rescue him from his fatal ascent. But he knew that there was no way for him to catch up. Even if he had had his own bailout tank and felt like committing an extremely painful suicide by rocketing his way after the man, there was no way he could catch up. Not now.

Not ever.

He turned. His go-home line still trailed after. Still led the way – appropriately – home. Or what had seemed like a home before all this began. Now, with people dying and the deep spewing impossibilities up, everything seemed alien. He was no longer in a place of comfort, a place he understood. He drifted in strange currents.

He held the go-home line. Tugged it. Began to follow it to the anchor.

There was nothing else he could do.

ONE

~^~^~^~^~

Many creatures moved in this place. The reef – the impossible, inexplicable reef – housed many fish, many coral, and a few beings that did not belong to the deep.

Yet.

Among all the life, there were many things dead. Rocks and sand and things once above the waves that now lay below.

And an eel. Mottled green, the color of flesh long-rotted. Its body swayed like a thick seaweed in the current. Its head rested nearby, wedged between seabed and a rock.

Gradually the body of the eel settled. Its tail still disappeared into the crevice from which it had sprung, but its body drifted down, touched the seabed very near to where its head was anchored.

The body twitched. An observer would have wondered if the body had somehow been touched by electricity. A current that stiffened the creature. Lengthened it suddenly. It lurched up, standing nearly vertically in the water.

The head moved, too. The skin around its mouth tightened, exposing needle-teeth and a dark throat. The mouth opened wide, then snapped shut as though attempting to capture some unseen prey.

The body swept down. Not in the current, moving against the water's movement as it bent in a graceful arc that brought it near the head once again.

Strands reached from the body. Red and stringy, looking like thin tendon and gristle lined with tiny spines that promised pain. The fleshy lines snaked across the distance between head and trunk. Punched into the short stump behind the eel's head.

They retracted. Pulling back toward the body, drawing the head with them.

The head and body pulled together. Not perfectly: the head hung off the body at a grotesque angle. But the eyes moved, the mouth opened and closed in a semblance of life.

The eel reached upward again. Body straightening. And if there had been any observers, they might have seen that the eel had been eviscerated. Its body hollow as an abandoned shell on the beach.

The eel that was not really an eel at all – not anymore – swayed. Waited to act should action be necessary.

Waited. Alive-not-alive and waiting for the moment it would be needed, as it had been needed when it bit down on the man, when it pulled and pulled from hoped-for light to inevitable dark.

It had failed then. But that was, in the end, all right. Because the man had been claimed. He was One as the not-eel was One.

As all would soon be One.

194

HOPE

~^~^~^~^~

Tim made it to the anchor line just as Mercedes and Haeberle approached. Mercedes' eyes were huge behind her mask, but there was no time to begin a cumbersome conversation. Up top there would be time to ask each person what they had experienced. Time aplenty, since the Navy was so far off.

Time for recounting… and recriminations.

There would be no search for Geoffrey. And Tim felt a pang, repeating the image of the fin coming off in his hand, a permanent loop that he suspected would haunt him until he died. Geoffrey was a jerk. A terrible passenger and a prize prick. But he was human, he deserved better than to die alone and in pain.

Haeberle looked calm. Creepy as always, but ready to ascend.

Tim looked at them. At their lines. Those plus the one that led to his own gear made three. One more led up and away at a diagonal angle: Geoffrey's. His body hanging in the nowhere, dragged up by his bailout tank, and out by the underwater current. A grisly image: the picture of a corpse in the dark. But it was also good news in that Geoffrey's body would not be lost. He could be retrieved. His relatives and friends – if he had any – could properly grieve and have the closure that helped that grief.

And there was one more line. Hanging motionless in the water, a spool hanging off the anchor-line but not leading to anything.

Oh, no.

He turned to Haeberle and Mercedes. He wrote, "Sue?" on his slate and showed it to both of them.

Haeberle shook his head and then without a backward glance began his ascent.

Tim looked to Mercedes. She shook her head, then motioned at his slate. He rubbed it clean and handed her the pen. She wrote on it: "HOW I HELP?"

Tim shook his head and pointed up. Then rubbed the slate again and wrote: "GO up. I Look."

Mercedes hesitated. Then shook her head and pointed at his dive computer. The meaning was clear: there wasn't air enough to spend time here. Not without risking decompression sickness.

Tim knew that. He also knew that he had lost Geoffrey and was not about to come up with another body floating in the depths.

Especially not Sue.

Mercedes was still hanging there. Not moving, just waiting, and he noticed that she had switched over to her ascent tanks. He gestured up with as much ferocity as he could manage.

Mercedes' shoulders slumped. She began to swim up.

Two people were going up. Two that had a reasonable chance of making it to the boat.

Now... Sue. Where was she? He was keenly aware of the fact that he had to ascend, should have done so a few seconds ago. But he also knew he would die down here rather than leave her behind. Because it was his job. And because –

(*face it*)

– Sue meant more to him than the other passengers. Maybe a lot more.

But where to find her? Her go-home line wasn't attached, and he had no way of knowing where to go.

He looked around, hoping he would see her nearby. Knowing that hope was a ridiculous one, unable to stop it from surging through him in desperate waves.

No, no Sue. No fish, either. Which seemed strange given how plentiful – freakishly so – they had been on this dive.

It was just him and the coral. And that was what gave him his only chance. The current that made them dance, acting like blades of grass dropped on a golf course, giving him his only hint as to where to go.

He oriented himself. Pushed away from the anchor line. Into the current.

Hoping.

SHELL

~^~^~^~^~

Sue was still engaged in the strange combination of swimming and crawling, still trying to outrun the current.

And still knowing that it was a ridiculous attempt. There was no way she could get to the anchor line in time – even assuming she was going in the right direction, which was doubtful.

Something batted her side. She kept moving forward. Didn't have time to look or energy to spare. Just forward, forward.

The sensation returned. On the other side now.

This time she did look. Turned her head to look back while continuing her imitation of an insane crab.

Fish. Two. About the size of her arm, each ran at her, slammed into with the force of a light punch, then turned back far enough to get up some speed and come at her again.

She didn't understand that. It wasn't like fish that size to go after strange intruders.

What...?

Before she could complete the thought, three more fish joined the original two. Then three more.

And then the shaft of her light, the halo that surrounded her, darkened suddenly as a *thousand* fish came at her. They flitted against her body and each individual touch was barely tangible to her beneath her gear and her wetsuit. But together....

She rocked with the force of the blows. Pummeled this way and that.

Something big came into sight. A snub-nosed shark, somehow managing to look both ponderous and sleek, powerful in the way that only predators could be. It hit her shoulder and neck, then she felt its skin rasp its way to her face. Her mask went sideways, the edges grinding into her cheeks and the bridge of her nose as it fell away from its proper position. Seawater flooded her vision, stung her eyes. Everything had already been a blur of motion and movement as the fish descended en masse, but now there was even less to see, each individual fish becoming nothing but a speck in her vision.

Something huge came at her.

Sue reared back, her hands flinging themselves in front of her, an automatic reaction. Punching a shark in the nose or gills might dissuade it from attacking, she knew. But she also knew with utter clarity that doing so while being attacked was all but impossible. Humans, supreme on the land above, were nearly helpless in this place they were not designed to be.

The frenzied waves of sea life thickened around her, obscuring even the huge shape that loomed.

The thing hit her.

She twisted, fighting in a panic. Felt something wrap itself around her. She pushed on it, trying to force it away from her, to throw it away or at least throw away its tanks –

Tanks?

She realized in that moment what she had been struggling against, and relief flooded over her as thoroughly as the water in which she swam.

Tim.

It was him. She couldn't see the other diver with any clarity, but she knew to a certainty that it was him. There was no one else that could have come looking for her, no one else that could have found her.

She wrapped her arms around him. Felt him pulling her, knew he must be yanking them both along his go-home line.

The fish were still everywhere. Surrounding her so completely there was no way she could have seen anything even with her mask on. Just bodies swarming, pummeling at them from every direction.

Then, just as suddenly as they had come, the fish parted. Like the cleaving of the Red Sea for Moses, they split apart, creating a narrow corridor with Tim's go-home line in the middle. She had time to wonder at the event, a split-second to think that perhaps whatever was causing the fish to swarm this way was in fact trying to *help* them.

That's crazy. That would mean something's doing this. On purpose.

No. No way.

Then a form drifted down into the same corridor through which she and Tim were moving. It drifted oddly, a black blot with what looked to her like dozens of tentacles extending from its body.

Then she heard the scream. Realized it was Tim. A shriek that, even under uncounted tons of water, thousands of pounds of pressure, could be mistaken for nothing but perfect terror.

He kept pulling, though. Kept yanking them along. Toward the anchor line… toward the black form.

And then they were close. So close that even she, with eyes burning and half-closed against the saltwater, could make it out.

Geoffrey.

His face was a mass of red and purple, bruises from capillaries that must have burst by the thousands. One eye was rolled back so far it was only white. The other seemed to have burst. As though something inside him inflated to the point where the pressure popped his eye like a bung from a barrel. Something had burrowed into his cheek, some kind of fish that had been goaded to insane aggression and now had its tail outside Geoffrey's cheek, its head deep in the man's mouth.

She couldn't understand what the tentacles were, though. What it was she had seen that had made him appear so alien.

Then she saw. Saw and, like Tim, shrieked. The scream rang clear and clean through the water, and the fish all around them seemed to back off. As though they had heard the sound and feared it. Or perhaps feared the dark form that had wrung the noise from her lips.

The tentacles were Geoffrey's innards. Something had slit him open from neck to groin. Some of his intestines remained partially attached to their moorings within, floating like the many legs of a nightmare arachnid.

Most of him, though, most of what should have been inside him – heart, lungs, spleen, the vast majority of his GI tract – was just gone. Ripped away so perfectly and completely that what was left was just a hollow shell.

Just like that diver. Just like the first one. The one we found. Just like we're going to be. Oh no, no-no-no, just like us.

Geoffrey bobbed toward them. At first she thought he was swimming toward them –

(no how's that possible how can he move like that what's he doing what's he going to do to us?)

– then she realized Geoffrey – his body – was simply pushing toward them because they were headed into the current, and he had no motor function to combat the water's pull. Just swaying like a large leaf in a gentle breeze, moving toward them.

What am I going to do if he touches me? I'll go crazy. I'll lose it and that'll be it.

He bobbed toward them. And now she realized that Tim was kicking, angling them slightly *up*. Toward Geoffrey.

"What are you doing?" she wanted to scream. But she gagged back the words. They would have come out as meaningless garble around her regulator. Beyond that, she thought if she started screaming things like that – even if she was the only one who understood what she was saying – she would spiral into a panic from which she could never emerge.

In the next moment she realized what Tim was doing. He let go of his own go-home line long enough to push Geoffrey's corpse out of the way, then grab the line that trailed from its center. He slashed it with a knife that seemed to appear in his hand by magic, then looped the loose end through his gear.

He was going to bring Geoffrey's body. Wasn't going to let him stay here, but was going to bring him up.

Sue was torn. Admiration for Tim's dedication and care warred with the very real desire to grab Tim's knife and use it to cut Geoffrey free. Not only was he disgusting, horrifying, he was also slowing them down. Too much?

She didn't know.

Tim pulled them. A moment later she reached out and pulled as well. They engaged in something like a three-legged race: each unwilling to let go of the other, each using their free hand to pull in syncopated movements that dragged them forward.

They arrived at the anchor. A sight both mundane and more magical than anything Sue had ever seen before.

Tim didn't spend time untying from the line. He just slashed his own go-home line and started pulling up. Pulling fast, then faster. She couldn't keep up with the motion of his arms, and their progress became a continuous, lurching ascent.

He's panicking. He's lost control.

He won't stop at the deco points.

She shook him. Hard. He didn't stop, kept going up.

She flicked the front of his mask.

Tim jerked back, his motion that of someone who's been stung on the nose. She knew her tap couldn't possibly have hurt him, but knew as well that it would have startled the crap out of him, coming out of nowhere the way it did.

That was what she wanted. What he needed.

Tim flailed for a moment. Let go of the anchor line, and that seemed to remind him where he was and what he was doing. He leaped forward, grabbing the line and then just hanging there. He looked around – left, right, up, down – with the jerky motions of a cornered fox in a hunt.

Nothing. They had climbed far enough that their lights no longer illuminated the wreck below. No fish. No nothing.

She felt his body slacken. Some of the terrified tension left his muscles, and with that she realized that every part of her ached with the pain of unremitting tension that had flexed every muscle she had into a tight ball.

Tim looked at his dive computer. Wrote on his slate. "THANK U." She nodded, and he wrote, "DECO POINT IN 10." She nodded.

They were going to make it.

Unless something else happened.

She looked at Geoffrey's corpse. Still dangling from Tim by a line that stretched seven or eight feet away. A few of the entrails drifted close enough that she could have reached out and touched their flailing ends.

Geoffrey rotated in the current. Stared at them through one white eye.

She looked away. But knew he was still there.

Still watching.

BODY

~^~^~^~^~

At the second deco point Tim finally allowed himself to think about what had just happened.

What's with the fish? What's going on down here?

It seemed that Geoffrey had run out of air. But why? He should have had plenty left to go on, or at least enough that attacking Tim the way he had would have made no sense.

Narced. Narced beyond belief.

That had to be it. Tim had heard tales of people completely losing it underwater for no reason at all. Just the influence of gases that had once been inert suddenly influencing their minds in strange and unpredictable ways.

And Sue?

That was easy, too: she was obsessed with finding her sister. Focused enough on that one goal that she was willing to go into danger without thought for safety protocols.

Mercedes?

He remembered the way she had looked when he saw her at the anchor line: eyes wide, lips pinched and white around the regulator. What had happened to *her*?

What had she seen that scared her so badly she looked like she was halfway to the grave? Like her soul was escaping even as she watched, and she was helpless to do anything about it.

He didn't know. Nor did he understand the strange motion of the fish: here one moment, gone the next; normal foraging and swimming, then sudden schools that turned ten thousand fish into one malicious monstrosity.

What's happening?

Something tugged on his line. Geoffrey had floated up, hanging ten feet above them. Tim didn't look at the body. He couldn't. Couldn't handle seeing the wreck that the man had become.

Just like the first diver they found.

Sue suddenly twitched.

Then the twitching turned into a tremor. The tremor to a series of shivers.

Tim looked at her. She popped out her regulator and sliced a hand against her throat.

He understood the motion instantly: *No air left.*

He looked at his dive computer automatically. Plenty of air left for him. Enough to make it to the top. Barely.

What had happened with her?

She must have been hyperventilating the whole time they swam through the fish. That plus the exertion of swimming against the current must have depleted her tanks. At one-hundred-fifty feet, the pressure was over four times higher than at sea level. That meant air pressed out of the tanks at four times normal density, breaths took up four times more pressure to equalize the internal pressure of the lungs against the massive force bearing down on them. A natural event that no one had any control over.

It also meant that panic used up air at a tremendous rate. And Sue's tanks were smaller than his: fine for a woman her size, unless she just burned through them because of panic and exertion.

He didn't think beyond that. Just pushed his octopus at her. She didn't take the spare regulator. Shook her head.

He didn't understand. Pushed the octopus at her again.

She grabbed his wrist. The slate. Wrote, "I breathe we both die."

Tim knew she was right. The dive computer confirmed it, but even without that he would have known it.

Still he tossed a thumbs up at her. Wrote, "I got this," on his slate. Another thumbs up.

She took the octopus. Bubbles began escaping her mouth as she inhaled, exhaled, inhaled, exhaled.

He smiled around his regulator. Crossed his eyes at her. She smiled back.

But she looked pinched. Not just afraid, but exhausted. She was running on fumes. They both were.

Literally.

In spite of his cheery outward appearance, Tim felt a fist in the center of his gut, clenching around his insides and drawing everything tight.

He didn't have enough air to get them to the surface. Not nearly enough.

But he knew someone who did.

He motioned to Sue to close her eyes by squinching his own eyes shut and then pointing to her. He had to repeat the motion a few times before she got what he wanted.

She shook her head. *No way.*

He shrugged. Nodded. She was tough. Willing even after the events of the past minutes to risk whatever was coming.

And, in truth, he was glad. The idea of having her close her eyes had filled him with revulsion and a creeping kind of dread. If her eyes were closed it was something like her being absent. If they were open she was with him – not just physically, but mentally. He was glad of that. Glad to have her near, glad to have her support.

He pulled on the line that trailed from Geoffrey's grisly corpse. Sue looked stricken. Also confused. Geoffrey's tanks were gone, and she clearly didn't know what could be done with the body.

Tim did.

He hoped.

SURFACED

~^~^~^~^~

Jimmy J watched the area off the aft deck and the dive platform anxiously.

It's been plenty of time. Plenty of time for them to go and then come back.

So where are they?

He had no answer. Swells lapped against the rear of the boat. He felt something akin to motion sickness, a nauseating sensation that spread from deep within him and tightened both heart and throat.

He realized he was terrified.

Too long. Been too long.

And thinking that, he had to admit that his friend's death wasn't the only thing he was worried about. His arm hurt. A lot. He had awakened that morning scratching at the spot where he had been jabbed by something on the corpse they found yesterday.

Only yesterday? It seems like forever ago.

He went to the head right after waking and took off the Everlast Boxing sweatshirt he'd worn to sleep for the past seven years since Tim gave it to him. Looked at his arm. And had to bite back his gorge.

It was a yellowed, pus-encrusted mass. Reddened skin, dark veins surging to the surface.

What the hell?

He didn't know what it was; had never heard of anything like this. He felt the skin, certain it would be hot as an oven, burning up with infection.

It was cool. Not clammy, not cold, just cool. So no infection fever. But still, there was Serious Wrongness happening.

He didn't tell anyone. Who would care? Who would be able to do anything about it? Medical attention was still several days away, and there were very seriously crazed things happening today.

He kept the Everlast sweater on. Long sleeves protecting him from the gruesome sight of his arm, protecting Tim from worrying the way he knew only Tim could do.

There was nothing that could be done. Just ignore it and move on. He used up the whole tube of antibiotic ointment in the first aid kit, but other than that... just pretending life was normal.

People have an almost infinite ability to ignore problems and forge on as though nothing is wrong. The most problem-averse ostrich could take lessons.

Something bobbed to the surface, jerking Jimmy J back to the present. He shouted with joy, pumping his fist.

"Who is it?" said Cal. "Is it Sue?" The older man had been holding the same vigil Jimmy J had been engaged in. He stepped forward, nearly running to the dive platform.

Then he reared back.

Screamed.

When Jimmy J saw why, he screamed, too.

HELD

~^~^~^~^~

Out of air.

Tim took one last draw, and at the same moment Sue felt her air go thin, and disappear.

Nothing.

And they were still deep enough that they couldn't surface without bending. No rescue ship for a few days, which meant no way to get into a hyperbaric chamber and decompress properly.

Dead.

Tim looked at her. He smiled a strange, melancholy grin. Shrugged. The gesture seemed to say, *There are worse ways to go.*

But she knew he was wrong. Knew that drowning was one of the worst possible deaths. Maybe two minutes of convulsions, vomiting, agony. Body spewing forth waste and finally succumbing to a dark, lonely death.

Tim took her in his arms. It was awkward with all their gear, the kind of motion that should have been ridiculous. But it wasn't. It calmed her. Made her think that maybe there were ways to go. Worse than just hanging here in the deep, hanging –

Hanging.

She shoved Tim away. Looked at him, then gestured toward his vest. He shook his head. Didn't understand. A small bubble leaked out of the corner of his mouth. Maybe a second of breath lost.

They had to move quickly.

FASTER

~^~^~^~^~

"Faster!" Cal shouted. He felt like weeping.

Not Sue. Already lost Deb. Not Sue, too. God, please save her, I don't know what I'll do without her, please please please.

Jimmy J didn't answer. Just kept reeling line, hand over hand.

"Faster!" Cal shouted again. Then, in a whisper, "Faster." His voice sounded empty.

Bereft of hope.

BC

~^~^~^~^~

Tim watched what Sue was doing, and after only a few seconds he understood and mimicked her.

Sue had grabbed the release valve of her BC. Put it to her mouth.

The buoyancy compensator was basically a balloon that could float a diver up or down.

And how did it do this?

Up: filling with air.

Down: *letting air out.*

Tim shoved the release valve of his own BC into his mouth. Twisted.

Air.

He forced himself to breathe shallow. To sip at it rather than gulp.

He still hadn't gotten his answer from Jimmy J. Didn't know if his friend had even gotten the message in the first place, or how long it would take for him to figure out what Tim needed.

He looked at Sue. She was grinning around her own release valve. Mouth closed slightly as she inhaled.

Tim popped the release valve out of his mouth. Said, "I love you," as clearly as he could.

Sue looked suddenly startled, and he realized how weird that probably sounded. He had meant it only as his most effusive thanks, but she looked – what, worried? –

that he might have meant something else. Something ridiculously intimate and even desperate.

Maybe you did *mean it that way. A little.*

For a moment he felt like he was out of air again. Lightheaded and gripped by a sudden conviction that Sue was going to swim away. Like she'd rather die than deal with his unwanted and overenthusiastic declaration of affection.

She smiled.

Winked.

He didn't know if that meant she had taken his statement the right way. Or even what the right way *was*.

But he felt good.

We're going to make it.

Tim smiled back at Sue. The both of them now hanging fifty feet below the surface, grinning like fools and so close to each other he could practically feel her against him.

Yeah. There were worse ways to go.

His BC ran dry. He began sinking. That was a problem: he didn't want to fall back the way he'd come. Sue was lower, too, moving down a bit as her air bladders emptied.

He grabbed her with one hand. The anchor line with the other. Holding her. Out of air.

Worse ways to go.

Something hit him on the back of the head.

AFFECTIONS

~^~^~^~^~

"I love you."

It actually came out more like "By of you," but Sue understood it. Even spoken underwater on shallow breath, it was clear enough.

She'd had men tell her that before. Some of them saw the words as a shortcut to Sexville. Others actually meant it. Either way, they were always awful words. A loaded gun held to her head.

"I love you." Three words, but there was always more unsaid. "Are you gonna get naked or what?" "I think we should be exclusive." "Let's move in together." And, worst of all, "Do *you* love *me*?"

"I love you" always signaled the end. Of whatever the guy had or hoped to have with her.

So when Tim said it, she should have felt that way. More, since she barely knew him.

But she didn't. The words made her feel... *good*. A strange sensation, hanging in the middle of nothing, sucking fumes and only seconds from suffocation.

But she liked it.

She grinned at him. He grinned back.

Felt good.

And she saw something drop toward them. A dark blur at first, then a semblance of shape, a promise from above.

It headed straight for Tim. She moved to warn him, but before the motion was even half-begun, it hit him in the back of the head.

He lurched toward her. Arms going around her reflexively. She could barely feel it through her suit and her gear and the numbness of a body too long immersed in cold, cold water.

So why does it make me feel like a bear hug?

She didn't have time to answer that question – though she suspected she knew. She had to grab the pair of air tanks that had fallen from above. Gifts from God – or Jimmy J.

Tim had reeled in Geoffrey's body, then let go of it after writing "SEND AIR" across the corpse's forehead, just above the white orb of his remaining eye.

Then he wrote it on each cheek, and on Geoffrey's hands and on the light blue arms of his wetsuit. Then let it go.

The corpse still wore its BC, and was still positively buoyant. It floated up. But slowly – so slowly Sue didn't know if it would reach the surface in time. And even if it did, what if it was dragged away by the ocean's current? The current wasn't as stiff here as it had been at the bottom, but it was still definitely present. What if the body went to a side of the boat where no one was watching?

What if this was hopeless?

But just as she and Tim ran out of the last of their air – the air each had in their BCs, pumped in there from their tanks in order to buoy them up and float them to the surface – a pair of tanks fell down to them.

And now they had air. They had time.
They were going to make it.

CALLED

~^~^~^~^~

Sue's head broke the surface, and before her mouth was even above the water she had ripped out her regulator. An instant later she sucked in a great, gasping breath of air.

It tasted better than the best meal. Better than the most expensive wine. It was an ecstatic experience the likes of which could only be felt by someone who has faced a forward rush by the Grim Reaper and somehow managed to sidestep that final charge.

A spray of water signaled Tim breaking the surface and following her lead beat for beat.

They laughed. Another good feeling. He hugged her.

Perhaps the best feeling of all.

Sue looked around. They had come up about six feet off the dive platform. It looked like afternoon, and that was an almost jarring realization.

Shouldn't it be later? Didn't we stay down there longer... like forever?

But no. Same day. Just a few hours that had felt like that many lifetimes and more.

They paddled to the dive platform. Her father was already waiting for her, his hand reaching down to help her up. Jimmy J helped Tim, wincing for some reason as Tim's hand went up the younger man's arm.

Mercedes, she was glad to see, was already there. Taking off her gear.

Haeberle was there, too. She was less glad to see that. Tried to be happy – he was a human being, he deserved a measure of joy at the fact that he had survived – but utterly failed.

"You okay, Sue?" said Cal. "I was so worried when the others came up without you."

"I'm okay."

"You hurt? Did you –"

"I'm okay!"

The words came out harsher than she expected. More an attack than a response. She hadn't meant to do it, but just as suddenly as her elation had been born, it died. Yes, she had made it. Yes, she had come back home.

But she'd seen Debi's tank.

Is that all that's left of her?

She saw something beyond her father. A lump covered by a tarp. Geoffrey's body, certainly.

Did that happen to Deb? Was she torn apart, ripped open, one blank eye staring into death for eternity?

Cal seemed to be thinking along the same lines. "Did you...." He gulped. Licked dry lips. "Did you find anything?"

She knew what he really meant. Not "Did you find *anything*?" but "Did you find *Debi*?"

"No. Yes." She sighed and shrugged out of her tanks. "I found a tank with her name on it."

Her father looked down. Staring at his feet or perhaps beyond them – trying to find his daughter's body through the boat and the intervening tons of water. An impossible challenge, but it was an impossible moment. Facing the very real likelihood that his daughter was gone.

Sue felt numb all of a sudden. Elation at her survival gone, burgeoning grief fled. She just stood there, motionless and unsure what to do next.

She heard Tim, speaking to Mercedes and Haeberle. "You guys okay?"

Mercedes nodded. She looked exhausted. But beyond that there was a strange sense of... something. Sue couldn't put her finger on it.

Something happened to her down there.

But what?

"Yeah," said Mercedes.

"Fine," said Haeberle.

"What did you find?" said another voice. Mr. Raven, stepping out of the salon. Somehow it didn't surprise her that while her father and Jimmy J watched anxiously for the divers' return, Mr. Raven had been relaxing in solitude.

"Nothing," said Haeberle. "Just sand and fish."

Mr. Raven took a breath that somehow communicated not merely irritation at the answer, but at the entire universe. Like he was convinced he'd won some cosmic lottery but the payment check kept bouncing.

He turned to Mercedes. "What about you?"

"Same." She swallowed visibly, then looked away. "There was a trunk or a chest or something, but...." She gulped again. "It was empty."

She's lying.

What did she see?

Mr. Raven looked like he was thinking exactly the same thing as Sue. He stared at Mercedes, waiting for more.

She didn't say anything.

"What happened to Geoffrey?" said Jimmy J. Sue almost answered, but realized he was talking to Tim.

Tim was stripping off his gear. He glanced at the tarp on the deck. "He panicked. Got bitten by an eel and beelined for daylight."

Jimmy J gaped. "You are crapping me."

Tim shook his head.

Mr. Raven looked at the sky. "Well, it's too late for us to go again today." He looked at the group. "So we'll rest up for tomorrow's dive."

"Go again?" Tim's voice rose to a high spike. "Did you not see what happened?" He pointed to where Geoffrey's body lay. "We already lost one person."

Mr. Raven shrugged. "You said he panicked. The rest of the divers seem better-equipped, so –"

"*No!*" Tim flung his arms in the air. "We can't do this again. It's too dangerous!"

Mr. Raven's mouth firmed into a bloodless line. "This is still my ship, Tim. Besides… what if the others *want* to go?"

Haeberle spoke up almost immediately, only pausing for a strangely pregnant glance at Mr. Raven. "I'm going again."

The next voice came forward almost as fast, though from a surprising source. "Me, too," said Mercedes. That was a shock: Mercedes was a good diver, but this was a

221

whole new level for her. And her face was white, pinched, drawn. She looked like she'd seen –

(*a ghost?*)

– something terrible down there. Some terrifying revelation that amounted to a look in her own empty grave.

And now she was stepping deep into the hole.

Sue's father shook his head. Stepped to her and put a hand on her shoulder. "Not us. It's too –"

A voice interrupted him. "I'm going." And it actually took a heartbeat for Sue to realize it had been her.

After what just happened?

You know what happened to Deb. There's no reason to go.

But I don't *know. Not really.*

And she realized she was never going to win this argument with herself. Realized, too, that she didn't care what its outcome was. She was going – the need was strange, fundamental, nearly primordial. An urging from some long-forgotten part of her, a siren that called only to the deep parts that operated on levels that consisted solely of pleasure/pain, stimulus/response.

This wasn't about Debi. Not anymore.

What is *it about, then? What am I trying to do?*

(*Where am I? What's happened to me?*)

The final sounds of reason were just echoes in her mind, fading shadows of themselves. There was suddenly only a drive to return, to explore, to –

(*die*)

– find whatever was down there. And then....

And then....

Her father was talking, she realized. And she wondered how long he had been doing so, how long she had disappeared into a circle of confusion caused by her own actions.

"... You just can't be serious," he said. "You found her tank, what more –"

Again the words came without her conscious choice. "We still don't know. Not for sure. I *have to know.*"

Lies. It wasn't about Deb.

What is it about?

A sliver of her mind was screaming. The part that realized the call to return to the deep was new. Even before the first time she went down, the call to explore what lay below hadn't been this powerful.

Now, though....

"There," said Mr. Raven. His voice was gentle, as though he were linked to her, knew that she was in a fragile place and didn't want to shift her from her current determination. "That settles it. We recharge the tanks, get some rest. Another big day tomorrow."

He turned toward the salon, then stopped and swiveled back to face Jimmy J. "So sorry, Jimmy. You're the only one who didn't get a chance to go. Would you like to try and go today?"

Jimmy suddenly looked like he *did* want to. More than anything. Like what lay below was, for him, everything that made life worth living. Then he winced and his hand went to his arm. "I think I better sit this one out. A bit sore. But I'll take point tomorrow." He looked at Tim. "You deserve a rest, that's for sure."

Tim didn't say anything. Sue wondered what he was feeling, if he felt the same –

(*pull*)

– desire to go into the water again.

His expression was dark. He looked concerned. Afraid.

Of what? What's there to be afraid of?

That thin piece of her mind cried out again. *Danger, death, only death will find you down there.*

The rest of her brain shouted louder. Shouted of answers, and reunions, and the most basic and important of joys.

She was called.

And she would answer.

SHIFT

~^~^~^~^~

Night.

The boat is silent. Or nearly so.

The darkness outside seems to have pervaded everything. A seeping sickness that, once contracted, cannot be healed.

Silence. Repose save a few small pockets of motion. Like rats hiding behind baseboards. Cringing, waiting for inevitable destruction.

Hunted.

The ship creaks. A shifting that signals nothing save the shift of the hull, microscopic expansions and contractions endemic to any vessel.

There are two bodies where one used to lay. A bundle of arms and legs, trunks and heads. The one who was found first now covered by the grisly blanket of another corpse. Both hidden from view by a dark tarp.

Death. Only death.

Then something shifts under the tarp.

Motion.

It is night, and the boat is silent.

Or nearly so.

GOD

~^~^~^~^~

Haeberle sat in the corner of the salon. Watching.

At the table, Jimmy J, Cal, and Raven played a game of poker. Jimmy J was winning, slapping down cards over and over and screaming, "Eat *that* cheese, bitches!" every time he did so. Cal and Raven would grimace, toss in their own cards, then watch Jimmy J rake in whatever chips had accumulated.

In another corner: Mercedes. She was staring at nothing. Looking like she was lost in thought, though of course that was impossible. Since Haeberle was the only one who was really alive, he was the only one who could really think, really hope or dream or love or hate.

But she *looked* amazing, in spite of her non-reality. Sitting there in a t-shirt that showed off her curves and a pair of cutoff jeans shorts that were so short the pockets showed against her upper thighs.

Soon. She was almost ready, almost *ripe*.

He felt a grin stretch across his face. Did not stop it. It was good to indulge. Good to revel in the fear of his imagined creatures.

Mercedes caught him looking. He grinned even wider. Showing as many teeth as possible. *Gramma, what big* teeth *you have.*

And he knew how that story would end for this woman.

Mercedes looked away. Looked at her feet. And that was right, too. Subjects *should* remain with eyes cast down

226

when confronted by the overwhelming reality of their God.

There was a noise beside him. Tim came up the stairs. Looking irritated, vaguely uncertain. He caught Haeberle's look, the leering smile he was lavishing on Mercedes.

Haeberle cranked the smile a little wider. Keeping Tim in the corner of his vision, but ignoring him to all appearances.

Tim frowned.

Haeberle: just that smile. Even bigger now, because he wasn't just fantasizing about the inevitable moment when Mercedes threw herself at him, but at the image of taking her while killing Tim at the same time. Sex and violence intertwined into a beautiful tapestry of sensation, of joy.

Tim left the room.

Haeberle kept watching Mercedes. She kept looking away.

And that was right. For he was a king, a God, and something greater than both.

TOGETHER

~^~^~^~^~

Tim found Sue sitting on the edge of the dive platform. Her feet dangled off the side, hanging only inches from the water. Tim wanted to tell her not to do that, wanted to remind her about the fish and the strange ways they had acted.

What if something worse happened?

But he held his peace. Everyone was acting strangely – except Haeberle, who had started out weird and so was functioning on more or less the same level he always had.

But Sue? Insisting on going again? And Mercedes? That didn't make sense. It didn't add up to come so close to death the way they both had said they had during the telling of what had happened to each –

(*But they didn't really tell us. They left things out, especially Mercedes.*)

– and then to hunger to return. Even the most driven daredevils and adrenaline-junkies would wait. Would cool off. Would dive in a different place – a place that made sense.

The ocean floor rising.

The fish swarming.

What happened to Geoffrey.

None of it – *none* – made any sense.

He remained silent. Just went and stood behind her a moment. Sue didn't say anything, didn't indicate she wanted to be alone with her thoughts, so he sat next to her.

"You going to warn me not to go again?"

Yes. "No. I already said what I have to say. You're a big girl."

"You going to ask why?"

He shook his head. "You'll either tell me or you won't. I'll take what you give."

He was painfully aware how the last part of that could be taken. And couldn't bring himself to care too much, because it was true on every level.

And that was *him* acting crazy. Because he barely knew this woman, this captivating person. Just the conversations they'd had over the past days, the shared experience below.

Maybe that was it. Maybe it was the look at death that drew him so strongly to her. When staring at mortality, we all feel the urge to cling to others. To not go gentle into that dark night, and if the dark night must be entered, not to go alone. We hold each other at arm's length so often in life, where the greatest tragedy is that love is so often felt but so rarely expressed. But when night falls, we reach out – some of us for the first time – and quest for the saving touch of a beloved.

So maybe that was what had happened. And maybe that was enough. Relationships had certainly started with less.

They lapsed into a comfortable silence. Another rarity for Tim: most people needed to fill up empty spaces with nothings, with unimportant proofs of their own existence. They filled display cases with nick-nacks that represented memories they owned, they filled rooms with furniture that expressed who they were and how real their lives, and they filled silences with empty speech to keep at bay the creeping fear that they did not matter to anyone or anything.

Sue... silence. Not cold, but warm. The silence of a friend who knows you are there, and who knows you care. He suspected she would sit like this with almost anyone. An inclusive mentality, the willingness to extend personal space to more than the few people she really knew.

Rare.

Beautiful.

Something flashed in the edges of the boat's lights. A silvery splash that could have been the motion of a swell, could have been something else.

The comfort of the moment disappeared.

"I've never seen fish act like that," he said. "You?"

"Not like that. I was in the middle of a school of tuna once. Couldn't tell up from down. Scary, but wonderful, too. Like I was in the midst of this big dance, this natural thing that no one ever gets to see. When it was over I was sad." She licked her –

(*lovely*)

– lips and continued, "That's not how I felt today."

"No," he agreed. "That didn't feel natural at all."

They fell silent again. But not the convivial silence of good friends. Instead it was the hush of tiny creatures in the dark, knowing the wolves are out in force.

And hungry.

TARP

~^~^~^~^~

The tarp that had covered one corpse for a day, and now shielded two from view…

… was moved aside.

HISTORY

~^~^~^~^~

Tim moved a bit closer to Sue, and she didn't mind a bit. It was cold – not merely the cold of a night on the open sea, but the deeper chill of things unknown, and perhaps unknowable.

"Where'd you learn to dive?" he said. A nothing question, a question that took her mind away from the unpleasantness of now and back to the good feelings of a bright then.

"My mom. She did underwater photography and she taught me and my sister to swim as soon as we could walk. I do photography now, too."

"She must be proud."

"She would be, if she was alive."

"I'm sorry."

Sue shrugged. A motion that she knew said less "It's okay" than "I hurt." "She went out on a trip looking to photo a whale shark, some other exotic fish. Captain came back without her. Said she just went out in the morning and never came back." She turned to Tim. Took in his expression, drank in his calm. "I can't let that happen again," she said. "I can't let another person disappear. I've got to find her, or at least find out for sure what happened to her."

He smiled, and in the smile she saw clearly the question, "Why isn't finding her tank enough?" But he didn't say that. He let the question rest – perhaps not dead, but at least asleep for the time being – and said instead, "What was Debi doing here?"

Sue hadn't told anyone about Debi's work. Not sure how they would react. And she still wasn't – but she took a blind step. A move in faith that she hoped wouldn't push Tim away. Because a lot of people who worked on the waves held them in esteem, in reverence.

Not Debi. She would be anathema to those types.

"She worked for a chemical company. The kind of outfit that strips everything of value out of earth, air, and sea. We... disagreed about the fundamental value of the ocean. She just saw it as a place that could be mined. Literally."

Tim frowned. She said, "Did you know there's sixteen trillion dollars' worth of platinum in the world's seawater?"

Tim looked bemused. It was a cute expression. "I knew there was gold, but...."

"Gold, platinum, uranium. Riches untold."

"But it's all too expensive to get out," he said. "I think I read that somewhere. Isn't it harder than mining an asteroid would be?"

She nodded. "Yes. Until now. Apparently Nelson Chem – that's the company Debi worked for – found an agent that bonds with the heavier metals in seawater, then creates some kind of gel around them as part of the process and floats them to the surface of the sea."

"But?" said Tim.

She grimaced. "But from what Debi told me, it kills pretty much everything within a mile of the sea-mining."

She laughed. "That's what she called it: sea-mining. Like she was just digging in a dead mountain."

Tim gawked at her. "That's insane. Why would anyone do something like that?" he said, gesturing at the ocean.

She shrugged. "Money. The fact that the ocean dies a bit at a time isn't nearly as important as the fact that pockets get lined."

"I take it you and she were at odds over this?" said Tim.

"Yeah."

"I get that."

"But I still love her."

"I bet you do."

Tim and Sue turned toward the source of the last words spoken. The comfortable feeling they had held between them fled as she saw who stood behind them.

Haeberle wasn't looking at them. He stared at the starry sky, a strange expression on his face.

He rubbed his arms. The motion was familiar for some reason, though at first Sue couldn't understand what was familiar *about* it.

Jimmy J. That's how he rubs his arm.

She frowned, wondering why the motion suddenly scared her.

"You need something, Haeberle?" said Tim. His voice was hard, all flat planes and sharp edges.

Haeberle smiled dreamily. "That's the question, isn't it?" Sue looked at Tim, and his expression mirrored the one

234

on her own face: an uneven mix of confusion and concern. Haeberle sounded odd. Even for him. Tones that rose and fell like those of a sleepwalker, speaking to those not present.

The man turned to them. Captured Tim with his gaze. "You ever wonder what's down there?" he said. "*Really* down there?"

"Sure. All the time."

"Not me. Not until today." Haeberle chuckled, the laugh catching in his throat and emerging rough and lacerated. "That being narced is something else. I liked it. Made me feel... light. Like I was me for the first time ever."

Sue didn't respond. Tim was silent. But there was something new in the air. A tension that went beyond the "normal" discomfort Haeberle always brought to the table.

"You didn't tell me about the visions, though."

Tim frowned at this. "Visions? I don't –"

"A woman," said Haeberle. He spoke as though he hadn't heard Tim's words. Or as though they just didn't matter. "Beautiful. Swimming away from me. I followed her – she wanted me, I know she did. Made me horny as hell. But she was too fast for me." Now he turned his eyes to Sue. She had heard of being undressed with someone's eyes – had even experienced it on several uncomfortable occasions – but this was the first time she ever felt *violated*. "Too fast for me," whispered Haeberle. A smile crawled over his face. He kept staring at her. "The fast ones are the most heartbreaking, don't you think?"

And he left. Just turned on his heel and went to the salon door and went in. He nearly collided with Mercedes, who was coming out as he went in. She limped a bit, her leg bound in a white strip of gauze that covered the shallow shark bites she had surfaced with.

"Well, that was a first-class ticket to Creepyville," said Sue.

"Agreed," said Tim. "I don't think you should be alone with that guy." He broadened his gaze to include Mercedes, who was holding herself for warmth in the chill sea air. But she didn't go in the salon, and Sue couldn't blame her. "I don't think *either* of you should be alone with him," Tim continued.

"You either," said Sue. "I don't get the sense he's what you'd call a discriminating psycho."

Tim laughed. Visibly trying to lighten the darkness that seemed to accompany Haeberle and settle wherever he went. "What about you, Mercedes?" he said.

The other woman almost jumped. Sue had the impression that the woman was trying to hide – not from sight, but simply from the awareness of those around her. A chameleon who had been birthed in some kind of pain.

"What do you mean?" said Mercedes.

Sue gestured at her before Tim could answer. Beckoning for the woman to join them. Tim was on her left, so Sue patted the spot on her right.

"Why are you going down?" Tim clarified. "It's not a good idea – for *any* of us. I get why Haeberle's going – he wants treasure, and apparently he's got a girlfriend waiting for him down there. And Sue's got her sister. But you?"

236

Mercedes' next words surprised Sue: "I wasn't even supposed to be here." She laughed. No happiness in the sound, just a hollow sense of loss.

"What do you mean?" said Tim. "You booked with us a year ago."

"I know. And six months after that I found out my husband's been banging some whore from his office. Three months later he proclaims his intention to keep the kids. So I wasn't about to come here. Too much time away – from the courts, from the kids he already has believing *I'm* the one at fault." Mercedes' eyes glimmered. She wiped them, but the shine remained. Tears tracked down her cheeks. "But the court ruled in his favor last week. He gets the kids. He gets to keep his money. He gets to keep his whore."

"That's bullshit!" The words surprised Sue, even though they came from her own mouth. She knew that she was only hearing one side of the story, but she didn't think Mercedes was lying. There was too much grief, too much pain for her to be the culpable party in the dispute she described.

Mercedes laughed that empty laugh again. "That's the court system: the one who has the trickiest accountant proves he hasn't *really* got ten million in overseas accounts, and the one with the best lawyer convinces the court it's not even worth the time to look and why *shouldn't* the kids live with him?" She shook her head. Her fists balled at her sides, but Sue didn't get the sense she was angry. It was more as though she was holding on with her last strength to the sense of self she had once enjoyed.

"I guess I figured I might as well come on the dive," she continued. "Since it was pretty much the only thing I still have in my name. And something about what happened the other day... I wanted to believe in a treasure. I know it's silly, but what if there was more gold? Enough to take back with me, enough for *me* to be the one with the better attorney?" Now her fists *did* seem angry. The rage on her face clear as she said, "I'd like to see him on the losing side for once in his life. And I'd like to hire someone to break the whore's fingers and pop her fake tits." She closed her eyes. "I'm joking about that last part. I think."

"Why?" said Tim. "It's what I'd want to do. Though I guess if my spouse cheated on me with a whore with fake tits I'd be living a whole different lifestyle. So who knows?"

He smiled, trying to jolly Mercedes out of her funk. It seemed to work, if only a little. And the small kindness made him all the more endearing. Sue thought he wasn't just interesting, not just an object of infatuation. Tim was....

She searched for a word. Finally came up with *good*. Nothing fancy, nothing ornate. Just a basic quality that spoke of someone who treated others well, who was careful to leave the world a better place than he found it.

Yeah, that was Tim. Good.

"You still have those kids, you know," he continued. "And this dive isn't worth dying for." He threw a sidelong glance at Sue. "For either of you."

A pregnant silence. Mercedes didn't break it. Neither did Sue, though she knew Tim was hoping they would both say they'd changed their minds.

But they couldn't.

Why not? Why can't I just let this go? Just drop it, you know she's dead, you know there's no chance so –

The thought cut off as hard and fast as if she had been knocked unconscious. The line of questions ran into a wall that prevented further thought. Prevented her from talking herself out of this –

(*insane*)

– quest to find Debi's remains or other concrete proof of her death.

For a single instant, a moment so fast it barely existed, Sue wondered why she couldn't even contemplate not going back. Like she had become a fish on a hook, a dumb creature that knew it was being pulled inexorably toward something, but had no understanding of why or how to slip the barb.

Tim sighed. "I guess we're going again tomorrow, then."

"You don't have to –" Sue began. Knowing he wouldn't let her finish, because he could not even contemplate what she would have said.

"You remember what happened to you today?" He threw a quick smile her way. "Who else is going to keep you out of trouble?" He puffed out his chest in a mockery of macho posturing. "Besides, I'm the dive leader. This kind of danger is what makes me so attractive to the ladies and earns me glory and the big bucks."

"Well, the first one, at least," said Sue. She blushed as she said it, then blushed more when she saw that *Tim* was blushing. Another thing about him that was tremendously attractive: he apparently didn't know how good-looking he was. Not in the sense that he had movie star looks or the dimples of a leading man. No, he was attractive in the way that truly good people can be: attractive because he would never hurt you, but would make it his mission to protect you and keep you happy.

It was a nice moment. Mercedes sat next to them, and the three shared a silence that allowed Sue to hear the lap of the waves and enjoy the thought of Tim watching out for *her*.

"Mercedes?" she said. "Did you find anything down there? Really?"

After the dive, all the divers – except Haeberle, of course, who had refused – had shared their adventures. Had told what happened to them. Mercedes mentioned finding an empty storage chest of some kind, told of running out of air and almost becoming lost in the wreck. But Sue had gotten the feeling that the other woman was holding something back.

Mercedes didn't answer at first. Just stared into the water. Then, apparently, she decided. She turned to Sue. "I –"

A thud cut her off. Then the distinctive crack of broken glass.

A splash.

Something had been tossed overboard.

Or some*one* had fallen off the boat.

BREAKAGE

~^~^~^~^~

One good thing about what had happened today: it had taken Mercedes' mind off the rest of her life. At least a little. Hard to think of a philandering husband and his slut of a mistress or even your estranged kids when –

No. Don't think of it. It wasn't real. Couldn't *have been real.*

Still, she couldn't help but think of it. Couldn't help but see again the forms she had spotted down there. Not floating. Not swimming. Almost like they were *walking* toward her. Like they –

(No. It's not true. Can't be true.)

– had gone out to play and found her in some underwater hideaway.

No.

She tried to hide from her thoughts, tried to take shelter in the obvious interest that Tim and Sue were taking in each other. It would have been cute to watch if it hadn't been in the middle of… all *this.*

Then the crash. The smash of glass broken.

Like Sue and Tim, Mercedes leaped to her feet. Mercedes ran with Sue to the starboard side, while Tim rushed to port.

"Sounded like something went over!" shouted Tim.

"I can't see anything!" Mercedes answered.

"Me either," said Sue.

A new voice joined theirs: Cal. Sounding confused and maybe a bit sleepy, like he'd been drowsing in the salon when this – whatever it was – happened. "What was that?" he said. "What –"

His voice was slashed to silence by a near-rabid shout. Mr. Raven's voice, rising to an ugly screech as he screamed, "Who the hell broke this?"

Mercedes felt herself carried along with Sue, Tim, and Cal back into the salon. Mr. Raven was standing on the stairs that led to the wheelhouse, Haeberle was looking out the portside window. Shattered from the inside. Wind and cool air blew through the empty square.

"Who did this?" Mr. Raven demanded again.

"Beats me," said Cal. "I just finished in the head and came out to see Sue."

Mr. Raven swung a baleful gaze at Mercedes, Sue, and Tim. Mercedes felt like wilting.

"Don't look at us," said Tim.

"We were outside," added Sue. "Sounded like something went overboard."

"Something big," added Mercedes, wishing she hadn't spoken almost immediately after the words left her mouth. The look Mr. Raven levied at her made her feel small, useless. The kind of look that Bill had always used on her.

"*Mark?*" said Mr. Raven, looking at Haeberle. He emphasized the word like it had more meaning than a simple name. And Haeberle bristled like he agreed. And didn't like the meaning it held.

"I was with you," he said to Mr. Raven. "Not a single damn clue what this is."

Tim was looking around, scanning each face in turn before saying, "Where's Jimmy J?"

"Not upstairs," said Mr. Raven.

"He must be below," added Cal.

"Why didn't he come up?" asked Tim.

Mercedes barely heard any of the words. She was staring at the wrecked window, gripped suddenly by an awful thought.

What if it followed me? What if the things I saw... what if they were real?

What if they're here?

CORRUPTION

~^~^~^~^~

Different reasons for looking for Jimmy J. Tim could tell that Mr. Raven had it in his head that the young crewmember had somehow caused the broken window.

Tim was just worried.

More than that. Scared.

He suddenly realized that Jimmy J – normally so gregarious, so outgoing – had disappeared downstairs well before dinner. Not like him at all.

He had said he was fine... but "fine" was also code for "terrible," depending on who said it and under what circumstances.

Tim went down the stairs, followed closely by Sue, Mr. Raven, Cal. The others trailed in a caravan behind him. Weird that they would all come on the search for Jimmy J.

Or maybe not. Maybe they all felt like him. Like something was dreadfully wrong. Even more so than an ocean floor rising, more so than insane fish.

The berths were in a square room, lined on the sides in rows that allowed ten bunks to be squashed into the tight space. Or it *would* have ten bunks normally. But in the far corner only the lower bunk hung from the wall. Above it, in the space that bunk ten should have occupied, was a hammock. Jimmy J slept there, saying he preferred it to the cots that were old enough they were mostly springs half-hidden by a thin coating of mattress.

"Besides," he always said, "the hammock makes me feel like a pirate."

But now, looking at it, Tim didn't feel like he was looking at a friend's quirk. The edges of the hammock had drawn in on themselves, covering –

(*whatever's in there*)

– Jimmy J's form completely.

No, not a pirate hammock. He looked like he had woven a chrysalis around himself. A strange larva unknown and perhaps unknowable.

"Jimmy J?" said Tim. He realized he was standing just inside the door, and realized also that he was frozen in place. "Jimmy J, you okay?"

Mr. Raven got impatient. He shoved past Tim. "Jimmy, did you punch a hole in my ship again?" he said. He walked quickly to the hammock. "If you did, so help me –"

He threw back the closest edge of the hammock.

Tim heard someone gasp behind him. He thought it was Cal. Couldn't tell for sure. Someone else cursed.

Me. It was me.

What the hell happened to him?

Jimmy J was staring straight up. Eyes riveted on the ceiling – or perhaps something beyond. His mouth lay open, so wide it almost dragged against his chest. Drool oozed over the corner of his mouth, creating a shiny track down his cheek, following the line of his jaw, then disappearing behind his neck.

His arm – the arm Tim had noticed him favoring all day – was a mass of weeping pustules. Gross and diseased, the flesh yellowed and translucent in the few areas where skin was visible below the oozing sores.

The rest of him was nothing but black veins, dark scabs. They went all the way to his chin, even following the curve of his neck so they were just below his face.

Corruption.

A perversion of flesh.

And obviously dead.

"What could have done that?" Sue.

Mr. Raven snorted. "More important, why would he want to break a window in my boat?"

Tim's mouth fell open nearly as far as Jimmy J's. He shot a glare at Mr. Raven.

But Mr. Raven didn't notice. Or didn't appear to.

And then Mercedes screamed.

GONE

~^~^~^~^~

Cal had hated every single moment of this damn trip.

Bad enough that he was revisiting the place his daughter had died. Now this. Oceans shifting, bodies literally piling up, and worst of all it seemed that being here was having exactly the opposite effect he had hoped it would have.

He and Sue had drifted apart over the years, he knew. And he knew that was his fault, at least in part. He had married again when Sue was in her teens, and that had turned out to be a nightmare. No wicked stepmother in a Disney movie could have been more cruel to the girls than she was. And not only had he not seen it, he hadn't believed it when Sue came to him. Had told her she was wrong, that she was trying to break him and Shallyn apart, that she would *never get her real mother back so stop acting like a baby*.

He saw it eventually, of course. Saw how she snapped at the girls when she thought he wasn't looking, noticed that she never wanted to do anything as a family.

But it was too late. By then Sue had decided he was as much to blame for her situation as Shallyn was. And she was probably right.

She moved out the day after she graduated from high school. Asked him to cosign a lease for her, but after that he didn't hear from her for more than a year. Debi kept in contact with her, of course – they had always been friends – but other than second-hand reports he might as well have only had one daughter.

Then he got Debi the job. He knew the head of Nelson Chem – he'd represented Deanna Nelson and Nelson Chemical itself in dozens of litigations and administrative hearings with the EPA over the years. He knew all Nelson's dealings, all their projects, all their dirty laundry.

So when he asked Deanna to take a look at Debi's resume she didn't hesitate.

And, of course, that just made things worse for him and Sue. Both his girls had taken to diving like they were born to it, but where Debi viewed it as an adventure and – eventually – as a skill that made her uniquely valuable to Nelson Chemical – Sue seemed to think diving was almost... sacred. Time in the waves was her sacrament, the water her church.

Nelson Chemical, with its close relation with "evil polluters" and companies that regularly showed up on Greenpeace's "Worst Of" lists, was an abomination. And so of course Debi's working with them was immediately an act of evil the magnitude of the Nazi invasion of Poland... and was one more huge black mark against Cal.

And if she knew what Nelson Chem was really *doing?*

He thought of that often. Thought of telling her. And just as quickly realized that would be a permanent end to their relationship.

Still, with every move she made to distance herself from him, he tried to respect her. Tried not to give any indication he resented Sue's choices or blamed her for their estrangement. But he still loved her. He sent letters asking for forgiveness and got back only curt notes with "Thank you" or "Hope you are well" – often scrawled on the backs of the very letters he had written.

It wasn't until Debi was lost that she actually let him in. Because she wanted to go to the area where she had disappeared. Wanted to look for herself.

And didn't have the money to do it.

He was glad to pay. Not because he thought Debi was alive, not because he thought the trip was a good idea – he thought it was terrible, thought it was just going to prevent any possibility of closure – but because it was a chance. A possible reconciliation.

And it had seemed to work, a little. She had talked to him more on this trip than she had in the entire time since she left home. Had shared – almost shared – a drink with him.

She hadn't treated him like a father. But she had treated him like he was human. That was a start.

But now… all this. Not just the strangeness of the ocean itself, but the more tangible presence of corpses, the danger of deep diving. And Jimmy J.

What's wrong with him? What could do this to a person?

Cal wasn't a doctor, but he was reasonably well-read. And he'd never seen or heard of anything like whatever it was the young man was afflicted with. From the looks on the faces around him, no one else had any clue what had happened, either.

Then Mercedes screamed.

He was closer to her than anyone else. Whipped around and saw her staring into the storage area where they had stacked the bodies of Geoffrey and the Nelson Chem employee.

What now?

He took the four or five steps to her in one single lunge.

Stared.

Blinked.

Stared.

"It was open," Mercedes said. Her voice came out choked, strained. "Just a little, but I peeked in, I don't know why, I just did, I...." Her voice finally pinched away to nothing.

And easy to see why: the bodies were gone. The tarp that had covered them lay on the floor, crumpled into a twisted mass as though it had been tossed aside hurriedly, as though someone hadn't been able to wait for a chance to cast their eyes on the grisly scene below.

"Where'd they go?" said Haeberle. Another huge problem with this dive. Cal had seen the way he looked at Sue, and Mercedes, too. Like they were something he wanted to own.

Not own. Something worse. Like he's a malicious boy with a fragile toy. Like he wants to break *them.*

"All right," said Mr. Raven as he joined them in the doorway. "Which one of you is doing this? Do you think this is funny?"

"No one is laughing, Mr. Raven," said Tim. He, at least, was one of the bright spots of the dive. Sue clearly liked him, and Cal could tell the feeling was mutual. From what he could tell, Tim was a good guy, warm and kind. The sort of person who would be good for his daughter.

Cal looked closer at the mussed tarp. It seemed to shine in light of the single bulb that illuminated the galley storage room. And when he noticed that he saw something else he'd missed in the shock of seeing that the bodies had disappeared.

Streaks. Smears of some dark, oily substance that seemed to ripple in the light. It was all over the floor, all over the tarp.

Cal leaned in to look at it.

"Don't touch it," said Sue. He felt a thrill of happiness at that. It was the first time she had shown a real interest in him, shown that his wellbeing was something that mattered.

He smiled at her. "Not about to." But he leaned in a bit closer. Sniffed.

"What does it smell like?" said Mr. Raven.

Cal shrugged. "Like everything else on the boat: the sea."

But there was something under that smell. Something he couldn't identify. Something he suspected he'd never smelled before. But at the same time it was familiar on a deep level, the place where we stop being human and start being wild creatures. Where we divide everything into good and bad, safety or danger.

This smell said danger. Said it loud.

BLAME

~^~^~^~^~

Sue watched Tim and her father move Jimmy J's body – still wrapped in the hammock – to the galley storage. No one wanted to put him in there, but there was no better space.

She noted how both men avoided those black streaks.

What are *they?*

One more question without answer. One more thing that seemed likely only to cause difficulty, danger.

Pain.

When the body had been lowered, Sue's father stood and cracked his back. Tim didn't stand. He lowered himself to a crate near the body and simply sat there, bowed down and looking wrecked.

"Pity," said Mr. Raven. "He was a good diver. Cheap, too." Then he left. So did Mercedes, Haeberle (small blessing, that), and Sue's father.

Sue waited a moment. She didn't want to interrupt Tim, but she also didn't want him to suffer alone. Some people crawl into holes when they are in pain, but only half of them do it so they can be alone. The others are hoping to be rescued. Praying for contact that will bring them a bit closer to the light.

She didn't know which kind of grieving Tim was doing. But hoped she could help.

"You okay?" she finally said.

252

"Not even close." He was silent for a long time. But he didn't tell her to leave, so she didn't go. "He got this job because of me," he said after another minute. "Went on a day-dive, one of those trips rich ladies buy as birthday presents for their grandkids." He chuckled, a gasping laugh that sounded like it was fighting with tears. "Didn't know jack about diving, but he fell in love with it. Got certified, worked hard. Ended up right back here with me." Another one of those gasping laughs. "Bet he wishes he'd stayed away."

"You can't blame yourself," said Sue.

"Like you don't blame yourself for your sister?"

That hurt. Sue knew she was carrying around blame for what had happened to Debi. Like if she'd stayed closer she could have kept her away from whatever happened to her. Like she could have made a difference.

Most people hurry to take blame for things they cannot control. Sue was no different. And knowing that Debi had taken her own path, made her own choices – it just didn't matter. On some basic level Sue was convinced that her sister's death was her fault.

And having Tim say it – even speaking from a place of reckless grief – was a slap to her face. It was irrational, it was ridiculous, but hearing her mad quest put into such plain, simple terms... it enraged her. Not because she was angry at him, but because she was angry at herself. So, like all good members of the family *hominidae*, she lashed out.

"I'll leave you alone," she said.

And she did.

FIGHT

~^~^~^~^~

The day was gone, and the lights were on in the salon when Tim finally came up from his vigil over Jimmy J.

The lights in the salon were dimmer than he remembered. He wondered if that meant that something in the wiring had fizzled at the same time the engine crapped out.

Great.

The rest of the guests were in the salon. Haeberle sat alone in a corner, looking unabashedly at a *Playboy*, grunting in satisfaction or pleasure as he turned the pages. Not even trying to pretend he was reading the articles.

Mercedes stared out the broken window. She scratched absently at her hand. Back and forth, back and forth, like she was doing a yoga move, some kind of ritualistic repetition that might bring a measure of order and calm to the situation.

Sue and Cal sat at the dinner table, each holding a beer. They sat slightly apart, as though unwilling to be too close, but there was something pleasing about seeing them together.

Tim sat with them. Next to Sue.

"Sorry," he said.

"Don't worry about it," she answered. He believed she meant it.

"You don't have another one of those, do you?" he said, gesturing at the beers.

Sue reached under the table. Brought out a beer. Handed it to him. "Nice and warm," she said.

"Fridge isn't much good at the moment," added Cal.

They drank as one. Like a silent toast for Jimmy J.

"Two more days to go," said Sue. She sipped at her drink again, then said, "At least we won't be bored."

It took a moment for Tim to understand what she was saying. When he did, he couldn't help but answer in something approaching a yell. "You're not seriously going back down?"

"I still haven't found what I came for," she said.

Tim's world was spinning. How could she *possibly*...? "Are you shitting me?" he said. "Three dead bodies, two of which disappear, and two of them dying of God-only-knows-what, and you want to *dive* tomorrow? Forget the fact that it's insane, how about just plain disrespectful?"

He looked around the room, searching for some support from the others. Haeberle was the first to meet his gaze, and his grin said clearly that he intended to go down again. Mercedes just scratched her hand and looked away: the affirmative of someone who wanted as little confrontation as possible.

Tim shook his head. "No way. I won't let you guys go."

Haeberle's grin disappeared. He stood and moved to the table. Towering over Tim. He would have towered even if Tim had been standing, but with Tim seated he completely *loomed*, like a skyscraper next to a cottage.

"How you plan on stopping me, Timmy?"

Tim didn't back down. He rose to his feet. Coming almost to Haeberle's clavicle.

"However I have to, you idiot. If it means I have to break your legs to save your life, then fine – *uff*."

The air exploded from Tim's lungs as Haeberle rammed into him. No warning, just a quick lunge, a body check that sent Tim painfully into the table. He heard Sue and Cal both scream in chorus. He felt hands between him and Haeberle. Figured it must be Cal trying to stop the fight.

A fist slammed into the side of his head. Tim saw stars, but managed to slam his own fist into Haeberle's midsection. Not a tremendously hard punch – his angle was bad for that – but he must have tagged Haeberle's liver, because the big man gagged. Still, he didn't stop. He punched Tim again. Another blow to the temple. This time he didn't see stars, he saw darkness. Not unconscious, but someone had coated his eyeballs with thick black paint.

He thought for a moment of the black sludge where the bodies had been. Thought crazily that this was what he was seeing now. That he had contracted a case of whatever had carried the bodies away.

No. Doesn't make sense. Get back to the fight. Get back –

Another hit rocked him. He felt his grasp on consciousness slipping. Only dark and his breathing like torn cloth and the siren –

Siren?

He felt the weight come off him. His sight slowly returned – black and white at first, then color bleeding into everything.

The siren kept sounding.

Mr. Raven stood in the narrow stairway that led to the wheelhouse, holding a megaphone above his head. Pressing a button so hard his thumb was white. The siren came from the speaker, a loud *wha-wha-wha* that shifted to a higher tone, then went back to the original siren.

When he was satisfied that no one was going to keep fighting, Mr. Raven lowered the megaphone. The siren clipped off. "What is the meaning of this, children?" he asked.

Haeberle, still holding Tim's shirt with one massive hand, said, "This asshole thinks he can stop us from diving."

Tim managed to pick himself up off the table. Threw Haeberle's hand aside. Tried to, at least; the guy didn't let go but kept his hand knotted in Tim's shirt. "And *this* asshole thinks –"

Mr. Raven put the megaphone to his lips. "Never mind," he said through it, the words deafening in the small space. "I'm sorry I asked." He lowered the megaphone again, then looked around the room. "You know, I think Tim is right. No dives tomorrow."

Sue and Mercedes started to protest. Haeberle said nothing, just stood quietly, which Tim thought strange. The big man had been ready to pound him into a soggy blot on the table, but when Mr. Raven spoke, he acquiesced.

What's up between those two?

Mr. Raven raised a hand to cut off the protestations of the two women. "Now, now, we can come back again as soon as we put into port and fix *The Celeste*. I'll even foot the bill for the return trip." He smiled, and Tim got the impression he was trying for "sincere." He only managed "weaselly" and Tim thought for perhaps the thousandth time that Mr. Raven might not actually be human – just something pretending to be. Something all about the moment, the buck he could make, the convenience or inconvenience that things brought him.

"It's the least I can do after all that's happened," said Mr. Raven.

The lights flickered. Went out. No one moved. Mr. Raven was a black smudge in the darkness. "No diving in conditions like this. Agreed?"

No one contradicted him. "Fantastic. Someone's finally making sense," said Tim.

"Sure," Haeberle added. "Sure thing, Mr. Raven."

He finally let go of Tim. Moved belowdecks.

Mr. Raven left, too. And Tim once again wondered what – if anything – was going on between them.

Wondered... and, for the first time, feared.

DOC

~^~^~^~^~

Sue and Cal were asleep in one set of bunks, Haeberle snored away on another berth.

Mercedes did not sleep. Could not. She felt a lump below her mattress and thought briefly of the story of the princess and the pea. Only she was no princess, and this was definitely no pea she lay on.

She heard a rasp below her: Tim, turning the pages of the book he was reading by flashlight. She had seen the book before she got into her berth: some horror thing about a family that got trapped in their own house. And she wondered how he could read anything scary in a situation like this.

His berth hadn't been below hers originally. Nor had Cal and Sue shared a bunk set. But the passengers who had originally spread out had, without words, gathered together. Only Haeberle slept apart, seemingly unconcerned by all that had happened. He gave her that look of his, that *hungry* look, as he climbed into his bed.

She hoped they were never alone together. She sensed it would be dangerous.

Tim turned another page.

She felt what was under the mattress.

Came to a decision.

He'll think you're crazy.

Maybe that's okay. Maybe it would be better if I imagined this.

She leaned over the side of her bunk. "Tim," she whispered.

He started, his body twitching in surprise. He looked up, a sheepish grin on his face. "Yeah, Mercedes?" he said. His voice was kind. Always kind, always concerned.

She knew it was his job, knew he was being paid to attend to them. Still, she sensed he would have spoken to her this way even with no money at all on the line for him. He was, she believed, kind.

So there are still a few kind men left.

"You asked what I saw down there. Why I wanted to go back down."

"Uh-huh," he said.

She pulled it out from under her mattress. The thing she had touched; the treasure she had brought up from below. She handed it down to him.

"I found it in the wreck."

Tim took it. Turned it over in his hands with a vague curiosity. "What is it?" he said.

"A Doc McStuffins doll."

(*Hands. Small hands, reaching for her. Calling her.*)

"Weird," he said. Still looking at the doll. Slightly warped, dirty from where it had rested. One eye –

(*not one eye the* same *eye*)

– scratched nearly to the point of being indistinguishable. But intact – surprisingly so. "I got the feeling the ship was pretty old. World War II."

"Me, too."

"Do you know if these dolls were around in the forties?"

"No. No way. Feel the plastic, too. It's new."

(*And not knowing if they felt through the dark for the doll, or for her. Not knowing which would be worse... or better.*)

"Maybe fell off the ship that Sue's sister was on."

Mercedes shook her head. "And got into a locked chest, *inside* the wreck?"

Tim fell silent. Turned the doll over in his hands a few times, then handed it back to her. He was visibly –

(*frightened*)

(*Hands searching. Reaching for her.*)

– disconcerted. "Weird," he said.

"No," she answered. "The weird thing is that my daughter had this exact doll. And its eye got scratched up when she and my son got into a big fight about six months ago.

They stared at each other. Then Mercedes leaned back onto her bed, cradling the doll in her hands.

Tell him the other thing. The thing that makes it not just weird, but terrifying.

No.

"What do you... what do you think is happening?" asked Tim.

"I don't know," she said. Then, before she could think about it too much, she added, "But the other thing that happened...."

"Yeah?"

No. Don't. Don't. DON'T.

"I thought I saw my kids down there. Reaching for me from deeper in the boat. Barely saw them through the sand and oil I'd stirred up, but...." She couldn't finish.

"Narcosis," said Tim. But his voice was hushed. Low. She didn't think he'd be doing any more scary reading tonight.

"Yeah," she said. Even though –

(*it was real*)

– she didn't remember feeling narced when it happened. More joyous. More like if she followed them she'd find the answers to everything. To happiness, to a return to the way it had been.

She hadn't followed. But it had been hard. So hard.

She held the doll above her face. "Do you know what's going on, Doc?" she whispered. So low there was no way Tim could hear her.

After a time – she couldn't tell how long – she heard Tim shut his book. Roll over.

He didn't turn his light off.

CARGO

~^~^~^~^~

All was quiet.

Only the bounce of the waves, the gentle shifting of gear.

Mr. Raven slept, as he always did, in the pilot's chair in the wheelhouse.

Sue, Cal, and Tim slept fitfully belowdecks. Haeberle slept the deep sleep of the innocent and the insane.

Mercedes dragged something onto the deck.

Her hand was a black mass, oozing, capturing the glint of starlight on its slick flesh.

She pulled her cargo fully out of the salon.

Jimmy J's body. Still wrapped in the forever-cocoon of his hammock.

She yanked the bundle to the edge of the dive platform. Stopping every few feet and cocking a head as if listening for the others to come and stop her. Or perhaps listening to something darker, and deeper, and farther away.

When she got her prize to the edge of the dive platform she waited. Looked up at the stars. Panting with the effort.

She scratched at hand and arm. Flesh peeled off in ragged strips. She did not notice.

A moment later, something emerged from the darkness below the water. Tendrils like those that had bound eel's head to eel's body in a gruesome sewing that none of the beings aboard the ship had seen.

Mercedes did not appear worried. Did not even appear to notice what was happening. She just scratched, and scratched, and peeled rotting flesh from her body.

The tendrils writhed. Searched. Found the hammock. They pierced it. Pushed deep.

The hammock moved. Perhaps the tendrils. Perhaps the gift it held.

Then the tendrils yanked. Pulled Jimmy J – what had been him, once upon a time – into the deep.

Mercedes scratched, scratched, scratched. Flesh falling to the dive platform at her feet.

More tendrils appeared. They curled around the shreds of skin and drew them off the platform as well.

Mercedes turned.

Went to the ladder that led to the wheelhouse. Climbed.

Mr. Raven snored in his chair. She ignored him.

Headed for the ship's controls.

SPLASH

~^~^~^~^~

Tim's eyes fluttered. Then snapped fully open when he heard the splash.

He sat up so fast he banged his head on the bunk above his. Swiveled and shot his feet over the edge of his berth, then stood. Looked around. Mercedes was still asleep on her bunk, her arm tangled up in a blanket that looked strangely like a snake trying to swallow her.

Cal and Sue were blinking, apparently awakened by the noise as well. Sue had already swiveled and put her feet on the cold floor. "What?" she mumbled.

Tim looked at the last bunk. The empty bunk.

Haeberle's bunk.

He rushed out of the room, past the storage room –

(*Was that open last night?*)

– and up the stairs to the salon. Then out to the deck, where….

"You sonofabitch! You *knew* he was going to do this!"

Mr. Raven didn't turn from where he stood at the edge of the dive platform. But his words shot back like nails: piercing, nearly overcome with a sharp rage. "Of course I did, you fool. But it was easier to appear to give in than to fight you."

He turned now. Pointed. Tim wasn't sure what he was pointing *at*, but then realized: Geoffrey's fishing gear. Not fully stowed, just shoved off to the side of the deck.

"The hook is set when you let out slack, not when you pull," he said with a smirk.

Tim growled. Ran for the salon. The rest of the group were just coming up the stairs. Cal and Sue looked askance, but neither they nor Mercedes, who trailed behind in a long-sleeve blouse that looked oddly over-formal here and with hands buried deep in her pockets, said a thing.

Tim ran to the front deck. Then back through a moment later, holding his gear in a massive bundle.

"Want some treasure for yourself?" said Mr. Raven.

Tim threw him the angriest look he could muster. "No, I just don't want another person dying on my watch."

He geared up as fast as he could, which didn't seem fast at the best of times. Not with the one-hundred-plus pounds of gear needed for a deep dive. No, not fast at all.

Slow, slow, slow.

(Just let him go.)

The tiny voice at the back of his mind urged him to just stop. Haeberle was bound and determined to go down, wasn't he? He was an adult, correct?

And he was scary. Damn scary. A fuse about to burn to its nub and ignite some explosive fury that Tim didn't want to be around to see.

(So just... let him go.)

He growled and shouldered the last of his gear. Then flapped his way to the dive platform.

"Don't you want to know what he's doing? Where he's going?" asked Mr. Raven casually.

Tim stopped. Trying to ignore his own whispered entreaties to just stay put and let this play out.

No. No one else dies. No one.

"I printed more bottom profiles last night." Mr. Raven licked his lips. An expression the eerie mirror of Haeberle's playing across his face. "There are *more ships below us*. I'm certain of it. Haeberle took an extra length of line down, and he's letting the current take him beyond the first wreck, to see what he can find." Mr. Raven coughed delicately. "I suggest you do the same. We could all come out of this rich as barons."

He produced a spool of cable. Extra-long: enough for Tim to let go searching on his own.

Tim took it. He had no intention of treasure hunting. But maybe this would help him find Haeberle.

He clipped the spool securely to him. Shoved the regulator in his mouth.

Stepped off the platform.

Fell.

No fish this time.

He was utterly alone.

SEIZE

~^~^~^~^~

Sue watched as the bubbles that Tim trailed slowly dissipated. Spread so far by the intervening water that the swells ate them and spat them out in bits too small to discern.

"Anyone want breakfast while we wait for our intrepid treasure hunters?" asked Mr. Raven. "We have three kinds of dry cereal aboard. My favorite, of course, is Cap'n Crunch."

Sue looked at her father. "I'm going after him." She moved away from the dive platform, toward where her own gear was stowed.

"Sue, don't." Cal looked pained. "You don't have to fight every fight."

She threw a look over her shoulder. Suddenly disgusted. The attempts at closeness melted away. "And you don't have to give up every time."

She took another step. Then Mercedes positioned herself in front of her. The other woman put a hand on Sue's shoulder.

"Don't," she whispered. "There are things down there. Bad things."

That was weird enough that it actually stopped Sue. Cut off her forward momentum as surely as if it had never existed. "What do you mean?" she asked.

"I... I...." Mercedes looked like she was fighting herself. Struggling to find the words.

268

Then, suddenly, her eyes rolled so far back in her head that only whites showed. Colorless orbs that were utterly alien in appearance.

Mercedes fell.

Her body curled in on itself, then thrashed back. Repeated the motion.

She was having a seizure.

DARK

~^~^~^~^~

Tim fell. It seemed like the darkness was greater this time. Reaching for him, wanting to not just surround, but to utterly *possess* him.

He dropped past the spot that had held the reserve tank yesterday... gone now.

Dropped past the strobe. Dark. Battery spent.

He hit his light. Wondered if it would even turn on down here.

Why think that?

An image of a child's doll played before his eyes in the instant before the light clicked on. One good eye, one ruined. He suspected that when the light *did* switch on, it would illuminate a thousand of those dolls, reaching for him in the darkness.

But the light showed nothing. Just the empty silence of a dead place.

He continued down.

MESS

~ ^ ~ ^ ~ ^ ~ ^ ~

Cal reached Mercedes first. Grabbed her and tried to remember what the hell you *did* for someone who was having a seizure.

Hold them? Let them go? Jam something in their mouth?

Nothing sounded right. Nothing sounded good. But he had to do something. Sue was wrong – he didn't always just sit back and let life happen. If he had, then maybe Debi would have found her own job. A different job.

Maybe she'd still be alive.

That was his own burden to bear. Forever heavy, never relenting.

What do I do? What can I do?

Her blouse had ridden up on her arms, and they were whipping back and forth so fast they were nothing but a blur.

Cal grabbed her arms. The skin was wet. Loose. He couldn't hold.

The skin sloughed off in his hands.

Cal screamed. Shrieked and looked at his own palms, which were suddenly covered in the wrecked flesh of another person.

Sue was there a moment later. She didn't hesitate. Just flipped the other woman over and lay across Mercedes' chest, pinning her to the deck.

"What's going on?" shouted Mr. Raven. "What's happening?"

"I don't know!" screamed Sue.

Cal ripped his gaze away from the slime, the gore, that coated his hands, and looked at Mercedes. Sue had her pinned, his daughter laying perpendicular to the other woman. Her face was practically rubbing up against the deck as she bore down as hard as she could.

That was why she couldn't see. If she had seen, she would scream and jump off Mercedes, would jump away as fast as she could.

No. She wouldn't. You would, but not her. Maybe she's right about you.

Something was writhing under the bare skin visible at Mercedes' throat, just above the neckline of her blouse. Dark lines that moved back and forth, giving the impression of plant tendrils reaching for sun, for sustenance.

But what's there to eat up there? In her head?

Cal's thoughts pinwheeled through his mind, unmoored and tossed in the madness of the moment.

The tendrils disappeared. Though whether they had died or withdrawn to her trunk or simply drawn deeper into her throat, below sight, Cal couldn't tell. Whatever they *had* done, it triggered a new reaction. Mercedes' body clenched, her entire frame rising as her back arched and her head and feet became the only points of contact with the deck.

Then she fell back. Slack. Loose.

"She alive?" said Cal. Proud of himself for managing the words, for not crying or screaming or puking or any of the thousand other things he wanted to do that *weren't* asking a coherent question.

Sue felt Mercedes' throat. She did it quickly. If she'd moved a bit more slowly Cal would have screamed for her to stay away stay *away* from the other woman's throat.

Things. Moving things. Under the skin. What does that?

Does it matter? It's wrong, bad, evil.

"I think she's alive," said Sue.

"Let's get her off the deck," said Mr. Raven. Cal was surprised: not only had he utterly forgotten the other man was still there, but this sounded like an uncharacteristically kind move. Then he saw the other man gazing at the peels of skin, red ribbons curling wetly over the deck. "This is very messy. Maybe we can put her with Jimmy J."

Sue glared at him. "Get on the horn to the Navy," she said.

Mr. Raven glared right back, though not with anger. More exasperation, like he was a teacher staring down a stunningly stupid pupil. "I told you. They're three days away."

Sue rose quickly. Stepped into his space and jammed a finger against his breastbone. "That was before people started *dying*. Before someone went into a coma. Maybe they can send a helicopter or something."

Mr. Raven looked at the spot off the dive platform where Tim – and probably Haeberle – had disappeared. Cal could see him calculating the probability of taking home whatever the men found.

It was too much. The gobbets of flesh on his hands, the terror of what he had seen under Mercedes' skin – and now he couldn't even count on the captain of the ship to act in a rational manner.

"*Move your ass!*" he screamed. And by heaven if Raven didn't move he'd pound him to a bloody smear right beside the "messy" woman at his feet.

Raven looked like he was still considering. Cal stepped toward him. He was a big man, stood head-and-shoulders taller than the boat's owner. When he got within arm's reach of the other man, Raven shrunk within himself. Turned.

Headed up the ladder to call the Navy.

Cal followed. Because he didn't trust this guy.

After what he'd just seen, the madness he'd just witnessed, he didn't trust anyone but Sue. Not even himself.

Did I see that? Really see that?

But he knew he had. And he suspected that he might see worse. Soon.

RADIO

~^~^~^~^~

Two thoughts tossed around in Raven's mind. Only two:

How can I get my treasure?

How dare *that bastard order me around?* Me!

But as often as he turned them in his mind, he failed to come up with satisfactory answers. His only options lay with Haeberle; with the hope that the man come back with something worth all this hassle.

And that he be willing to finish what needed to be finished.

Of course, Raven had no intention of permitting that psycho to keep *anything* he found. He couldn't turn him over to the authorities – he'd talk too much. But surely there would be a moment. An instant when Raven could stab him, or poison him, or just push him overboard and leave him behind.

But all that went out the window if the Navy showed up too soon.

What do I do? What do I do?

A third question, encapsulating the previous two. And still no answer. Not with Cal following him into the wheelhouse, watching as he went to the radio, pulled the mic off its clip….

And salvation came. Something Raven wouldn't have thought of, but was entirely perfect.

He waved the mic, trailing a spiral cord that went not to the radio but to a ragged edge that had been cut away from the main part of the radio. And the radio itself, now that he noticed, had been sabotaged. The knobs popped off, the screen scratched and in portions completely broken through.

He nearly laughed.

He didn't know how it had happened. Maybe Haeberle. Maybe someone else –

Though who else would do this? Why?

It didn't matter. The world was, perhaps, finally turning his way.

TANGLE

~^~^~^~^~

Tim stopped at the line that trailed into the darkness, heading down the current to some dark place. Somewhere that only Haeberle was willing to go, driven by whatever hopes or fears would push someone into waters so deep, a place so dangerous and unknown.

And what else was down here? What else would he see? Would he find his own doll? Would children from some woman's past reach out to him?

He forced the thoughts from his mind. It was hard, though, with the drumbeat of narcosis pounding clarity from him, pushing sanity to a faraway place that could not be found this deep in the ocean.

He tied his line near Haeberle's. Then bled some air into his BC so he was floating just above it. He let go of the anchor line. Kicked once.

Then the current had him.

It was fast. Faster than he remembered, faster than it had been, he was sure. Like an underwater river had moved here in the single day since he had been in the area.

Why not? The entire ocean floor *moved up, why not a measly current?*

He was moving with it. Fast, then too fast. A sudden surge caught his fin, spun him without warning. Nothing he could do about it. He turned, turned. Trying to right himself.

Tangling in his own go-home line.

The drums got louder in his ears, only now they weren't just empty beats, they screamed *you'll die, you'll die, you'll die* in time with his heart. The shriek pushed rationality from his mind. Narced, unable to think.

You'll die, you'll die, you'll die.

He caught glimpses, spinning on three axes. The brightness of his light, leading at times only to a dark horizon, at times flashing over the wreck as he continued to spin his way over it.

Catching movement. Shifting in the dark/not-dark of the empty portholes and doorways of the wreck, visible in quick slices as he turned and twisted and tried to regain control.

Part of him screamed. Not because he was tangled, not because he might drown. Because he was seeing something *wrong*. The movements in the ship were in the shadows, just barely too dark to see. But they weren't fish, weren't human. Nothing that could possibly be here. An intruder, something that had pushed its way into this place… and wanted to push its way into *him*, too. He could feel it.

He realized Haeberle's line was dropping. Either because Tim was ascending, or because Haeberle had dropped a bit more toward the ship.

He panicked. Now the drums said *you'll get bent, you'll get bent, you'll get bent.*

He tried to right himself. Tried to pull himself free of loops of his line, curled around arms and legs.

Failed.

CONTAGION

~^~^~^~^~^~

Sue had Mercedes' head in her lap. Not sure what she hoped to accomplish by that, but she hesitated to move her too much, even though her pulse had strengthened and stabilized.

Still, it seemed wrong to just leave her laying on the hard deck. She hadn't seemed to hit her head on anything, so Sue didn't think there were spinal injuries. Surely lifting her head a little, so she'd be more comfortable, wouldn't hurt anything.

She heard the clank of feet on metal rungs and looked over to see Mr. Raven coming down the ladder that led to the wheelhouse. Her father descended as well, his face a grim, stiff mask.

"What did they say?" she asked.

"Someone's destroyed the radio," said Mr. Raven. For some reason it looked like he was trying hard not to smile.

"What?" She nearly shouted. "Who would do that?"

The almost-smile disappeared from Mr. Raven's features. Replaced by a challenging scowl. "How the hell should I know?"

No one spoke. No one moved. The sun burned down on them.

Two more days. Two days until help comes.

She looked at Mercedes. "Let's get her inside. Out of the sun."

Suddenly she felt something shift under her hands. Pulled back the neck of Mercedes' blouse. She didn't want to touch the hands or arms, with their skin peeled off and wet muscle oozing dark pus beneath. But here…

… safe?

No. It was worse. Nothing could have prepared her for the motion beneath Mercedes' skin. The black lines like discolored veins. Only these veins *moved*. Swished back and forth like reeds in a wind.

She kicked back. Heard Mr. Raven scream in rage and disgust. "What the hell is that? Is it contagious? Get her away! What if it's contagious?"

And as she watched, the lines disappeared.

Her father stepped forward. And, surprisingly, stepped up. He took Mercedes' shoulders. "Let's get her inside."

"Are you *insane*?" demanded Mr. Raven. "What if we can catch something?"

"If she's contagious," said Sue's father, "then it jumped from Jimmy J to her in a single day… and we've already caught it."

He waited.

Sue took Mercedes' legs.

Together, they moved her inside.

CENTER

~^~^~^~^~

One... more... pull....

There!

Tim had spun out of control for what felt like miles, what felt like hours. But neither could have been true, because he was tangled, so he couldn't have been moving far, if at all. Still, it took a long forever for him to realize that he would never be able to simply swim his way out of the knot he had found himself at the center of.

He switched tactics. Pulling on the nearest loop, around his leg. It tightened against his other leg.

How long is this taking me?

When will I run out of air?

He tried another loop. Pulled. Felt no corresponding pain in his other extremities. He worked it off his leg. Felt himself slam out a few feet as the current took up the slack he had created.

One down. How many to go?

He forced himself not to think of what would happen, what he might face if he ran out of air and couldn't start his ascent.

Pull. Find. Unloop. Pull. Find.

Forever.

He finally loosed the last loop. The spool at his side started unwinding again.

And he saw Haeberle.

A good twenty feet below him, the glow of the other man's light joining with the one on Tim's shoulder to form a ghostly hourglass in the dark.

And between Haeberle's light and his own, the two combined to create a greater light, a broader range of vision. Allowed Tim to see....

How many are there?

Wrecks. The one they had explored already, which he could now see was a World War II destroyer. And beyond that, the bow of a galleon that looked like it had been old when the 1700s rolled around. The curving edges of a submarine.

Something that looked like a yacht or a research vessel. The name *Evermore* on its hull, with a logo and the words Nelson Chemical below it.

More. Ships of all shapes and sizes, as far as their lights could illuminate. The only thing they had in common was that they pointed toward a single point, like enormous spokes of a rotting wagon wheel.

In the center there was nothing. No wrecks, no life. Only a strange radiance, a blossom of blue-purple like the world's most intense black light, something on the outer edge of humanity's capability to visually apprehend. The black light reached fingers into the deep, casting all into purples and white-blues that made everything seem even more dead than it already was. Tiny specks of sediment stirred by the current, perhaps dead plant and animal matter so small it normally passed beneath notice, caught the strange light and reflected, refracted it. The place at the center of the ships was not merely a blossoming flower of alien light, but a flower in a snowstorm. A blizzard that whirled in a tight circle, a snow globe of impossible proportions.

Haeberle stood at the leading edge of the black light. His light waving rhythmically back and forth as he leaned forward, back, forward, back. Almost touching the blizzard, nearly a part of the storm.

Tim swam for him. Grabbed his arm.

Haeberle kept weaving. Didn't seem to even notice Tim.

Tim pulled him again. And now Haeberle *did* notice. His eyes widened behind his mask. With fear or lust or greed or some other ugly emotion so potent and so deep that it frightened Tim.

Haeberle shook him away. Tim grabbed for him again, but Haeberle was swimming for the black light, for the sepulchral bloom in the center of this graveyard.

Tim grabbed his foot, just before the other man touched the leading edge of the snow globe. Haeberle kicked at him, but he refused to let go. He started to haul both of them back, winding his go-home line around his arm and drawing them toward the anchor line an inch at a time.

Haeberle kicked at him again. Tim barely avoided getting a heel to the face, and realized belatedly that this wasn't going to work. He wasn't going to be able to get them both back to the anchor by pulling them like this.

He stopped, just hung motionless for a moment. The current had died here, as though once drawing them into the center it could dissipate.

Tim suddenly remembered the fish. The currents he had experienced before.

Were they all for this? All to draw us here?

He didn't know. It was crazy, but even narced it felt like a reality. Or maybe it was *because* he was narced. Maybe only someone in the half-haze of narcosis would see this and think something –

(*old alien alive maleficent corrupt*)

– had drawn them here with a purpose.

Haeberle kicked out once more. This time he connected. Hit Tim on the back of the head. Not hard enough to daze him, but enough to drive home the fact that he had to do something, fast.

He pushed forward. A quick pump of his fins that drove him up Haeberle's length. Then, before the other man could grab him or try to strike him again, Tim looped his go-home line over the man's wrist. Then a quick twist around his trailing leg.

Haeberle didn't know what was happening, that was clear. He started kicking violently, trying to get away. But that just gave Tim an easier target as he continued to foul the other man on the line. Soon Haeberle was at the center of a knot rivaling that of an amateur fisherman casting his first line.

Tim let out about ten feet of line. Enough to be out of reach, but not so much that Haeberle would be out of his sight. He swam around the still-thrashing man, then grabbed the trailing edge of the go-home line. Began pulling them both back to the anchor, hand over hand.

The current picked up again. Hard. Pulling debris at them. Bits of flotsam. Small animals that had been noticeably absent when Tim was moving *toward* the center of the wrecks.

Then the fish came. Schools. Thousands, millions. Mismatched creatures – silver and yellow and blue and a hundred thousand colors stolen from a hundred thousand rainbows. Species that did not belong together, that should be fighting or fleeing or feeding, but all focused instead on *him*.

That's crazy.

That's impossible.

It's true.

And he knew it was. Knew he had to get out of here, because whatever was at the center of the boats was –

(*hungry*)

– evil, and meant him only harm.

Haeberle was a dead weight. A drag that caused Tim to breathe harder, faster, deeper. He knew his air was getting low enough he would have to go up soon – or not at all.

He kept pulling.

He got to the anchor line.

Tim clipped onto the anchor line.

And just as he did, an explosion threw him sideways, and the water pulsed like it had passed through a sonic boom.

BONES

~^~^~^~^~

They lay Mercedes on one of the lower berths. The table in the salon was too small, the chairs and benches absolutely *not* designed to hold an unconscious human of any size.

So they ported her down the stairs, past the cracked-open door to the galley storage. Then into the cabin, to the bunk Mercedes had slept on last night.

Was she going through this all night? Sue wondered. Did she just not tell us for some reason?

That would be lunacy.

But things were hardly sane right now, were they?

She and her father got Mercedes in the berth, and she tried not to notice the strips of flesh that peeled their way across the sheets and blanket as she and her father placed the unconscious woman there. She caught a glimpse of Mr. Raven's face, scrunched in a scowl of pure disgust.

She felt like punching him.

They had barely gotten Mercedes settled when something boomed. It was like the previous explosions, only it seemed even louder this time. Maybe that was just because they were all below the water line, closer to wherever it was coming from, but the sound nearly deafened Sue.

Then she forgot about the pain in her ears as the entire cabin tilted sideways. She saw Mr. Raven slam into a wall that had abruptly shifted from "beside" to "below."

Sue felt arms grab her. Felt her father hold her as they both tumbled to the side. Heard him "oof" as he slammed into one of the berths with both his weight and hers driving him down.

She saw, as the world tilted, Mercedes slam limply sideways and up. The crunch of bone breaking as she hit the bunk above hers.

Then she was lost in a new sound. The creak of wood, the shriek of joints.

The sound of a boat under strain it had not been designed to withstand.

The sound of a boat breaking apart.

She felt water on her feet.

TRUST

~^~^~^~^~

The anchor line whipped around like a snake, jerking Tim and Haeberle with bruising force. Even with the water's drag, even under all the pressure down here, Tim felt himself tossed like a leaf in a hurricane.

What's going on?

The ship. Something wrong above.

The thoughts flitted in and out of his mind, tiny fish disappearing in a black reef of pain, fear, confusion, narcosis.

Then, as fast as they came, the surges of current that had batted at him dissipated and disappeared completely.

He looked at Haeberle. The guy had lost his regulator, and Tim swam over and put it back in his mouth. Haeberle's eyes had changed. No longer dazed, hypnotized. Whatever had just happened had shaken him out of his mindless state, his empty need to flee to the darkness where…

… where the explosion came from.

Tim knew it was true. Didn't know *how*, but sensed that he had been close to something of great power. And great malevolence.

He looked Haeberle in the eye. Trying to gauge if the man was going to fight him or not. Realized that he was hearing a beeping. He checked his dive computer. It said he had a couple minutes left before his ascent time.

Tim checked Haeberle's DC; noted he was into the time he should ascend.

He wrote on his wrist slate: "Don't fight me or we BOTH DIE."

Haeberle nodded. He pointed his chin at the closest of the cords that Tim had bound him in. Clearly motioning to be let loose.

Tim thought about it.

Thought about how hard it would be to drag Haeberle all the way up.

Then thought about how much harder it would be if the guy went batshit crazy again and tried to escape or fight him.

He wrote on his slate. "Sorry. Cant trust U."

He began his ascent, trailing Haeberle behind him like bizarre bait on the world's shortest fishing line.

And tried not to think about what lay below, or what they might find above.

FUN

~^~^~^~^~

The higher they went, the more it seemed like what had just happened was simply a dream.

And if it's my *dream, inside this big dream I'm already dreaming, does that make it a dream in a dream, or a dream of a dream?*

A good question, but one that Haeberle couldn't seem to focus on. He was too busy remembering....

Not the boom. Not the smashing, pounding feel of water pulling in all directions at once. No, that was... unreal. Didn't seem like anything at all. Just that dream.

What was real, though... what was real about the dive was nothing short of amazing. Bliss.

He hung loose at the end of the line that Tim had wrapped around him, and was strangely content. This was his world, he understood that now on a level he had never attained before. Understood it from the subatomic particles that created him, the God of this world, to the extension of Himself that created all around him.

Especially what he had found below. A dream *of* a dream, a dream *in* a dream. And at the same time more real than anything he had experienced.

He remembered dropping to the bottom. Tying on. The pulse of his heartbeat, the beat of narcosis merely a pleasant background to his actions. Syncopation provided by him and for him – as, indeed, all creation *was* by and of him.

Then swimming over the wrecks. To the center. To....

He shivered. Ecstasy so great he felt like he might just lose control of his body right here.

He looked up. Saw Tim.

And something else. Something dark that hung motionless against the light of the sun that broke through the surface of the water. The anchor line led to its center.

The ship.

But the outline was wrong somehow. Instead of being a sleek wedge designed to cut through the water, it had odd bulges, strange outcroppings.

Tim swam/pulled them both closer. Then stopped suddenly. And Haeberle saw why.

The ship had capsized. Up became down, down up.

Tim looked at Haeberle, his eyes telling of his fear, asking, "Do you think everyone's okay?"

Haeberle grinned. Tim would probably take that as encouragement – the guy was dumber than most of the creations in Haeberle's world – but it was really just security. Of *course* the people would be all right.

If they were *dead*, who would there be to play with?

Her. She *would still be there. Waiting.*

The dream of/in dream intruded. Hands beckoning, beauty waiting.

Haeberle felt himself grow aroused.

His smile grew wider.

Tim pulled him up. Drawing him close as he kicked his way around the side of the capsized boat.

There would be plenty of people left. Of course there would.

He surfaced a moment after Tim. His stupid creation had already spit his regulator out, and now Tim shouted, "Hey!"

A face appeared over the top of the boat – what had been the hull until just recently.

Sue. A pretty piece of meat, a toy just waiting for Haeberle's pleasure.

He saw Tim's face and almost laughed. What kind of fool would think she was interested in him when *Haeberle* was around?

Still, there was no mistaking the relief in Tim's voice when he said, "Thank God, you're alive."

For a moment Haeberle imagined – it *must* have been imagination – that Sue was actually glad to see Tim.

No. Just me. Just waiting for my touch.

Well, you'll have to wait, little girl, little ripe peach. Someone else –

(hands reaching, body ready, mine just mine just MINE)

– will receive my ministrations first.

But your time will come. It will come.

Cal's face poked into view as well. Then Raven.

Prick. Can't wait to kill you. Right in front of the treasure you hoped to have, I'll slit your throat and then maybe take my time... enjoying the corpse.

All of them – Sue, Cal, and Raven – sported bruises and bumps and cuts. Lucky –

(Blessed. *By me.*)

– to be alive, but it was clear they hadn't come through the pounding of *The Celeste* unscathed.

He thought Sue's abrasions made her, if possible, even more lovely.

So ripe, so ready. You'll have to wait.

But soon.

Sue reached a hand toward them. So did Cal. Tim pushed Haeberle toward the older man, then let Sue help him out of the water.

Getting Haeberle out was harder. He could have helped a bit, he supposed, but it was fun watching Cal grunt and turn beet red as he struggled with the bigger man's mass.

He smiled.

This will be… so. Much. Fun.

EYES

~^~^~^~^~

Cal barely managed to pull Haeberle out of the drink.

And when he saw the man's eyes, even through the droplet-coated mask he still wore, he nearly dropped him in and let him sink.

Only an innate sense of right and wrong kept him from doing it. That and the fact that Tim would undoubtedly just dive in after the guy, gaining nothing.

So, yeah, if Tim hadn't been here, Cal would have dropped him in the drink.

Because of Haeberle's eyes. They were pinned on Sue, watching her every movement. And the look wasn't just ugly – it was so evil, so *wicked*, that Cal in that moment absolutely knew the man wanted something dire for his daughter. Something as deep and powerful and utterly dark as the sea far below them.

He wouldn't let that happen. He couldn't lose another daughter.

She was all he had left.

RAFT

~^~^~^~^~

Sue got Tim up to the hull of the boat. Knowing what he was seeing: her, her father, Mr. Raven. Mercedes, still unconscious and shuddering as whatever strange *thing* inside her wove its way through her internal organs. All in shock, all looking as wet and bedraggled as they could be.

Movement as Mercedes shivered. Sue had marveled that her father managed to get the dead weight out of the cabin before it flooded. Marveled, and admired.

But there was also a small portion – so tiny she could almost deny its existence – that wished he hadn't.

Mercedes scared her. Whatever had happened to her, whatever made those thin black filaments dance below her skin… was it as bad as capsizing? Was it worse?

But that was a ridiculous question. It *was* the capsizing. Whatever was doing this to Mercedes was the reason they had gone down in the first place, the reason the seabed had changed… it was *everything.* All of it tied together in a gruesome bow, covering a present that she feared would end them.

"Why aren't you all in the life raft?" asked Tim after he had shed his gear.

Mr. Raven answered, his voice heavy with sarcasm. "Because we all got hit with idiot sticks." He waved at the ocean, as if to say it wasn't his fault they were here, so nothing else could be his fault, either. "We've been a bit busy here. And none of us have scuba gear on, so we couldn't dive without risking getting trapped."

Sue looked askance at Tim. He sighed. "The life raft is stowed in the storage room. Not the place I would have picked," he added, with a meaningful glance at Mr. Raven. "But no matter where it was, it's likely that no one could have gotten to it, I guess. It was made for circumstances other than sudden capsizing."

Mr. Raven smirked, then turned to a rope he had managed to snare off the side of the boat. He had tied it to the propeller and tossed it over, and now drew it up. There were a series of knots in it. He looked at them.

"I was right," he said. "We're definitely sinking."

"Can someone goddam untie me?" said Haeberle suddenly. But the angry words weren't matched by his tone, which was strange and dreamy. He sounded stoned.

"Why's he tied up?" said Sue's father.

Tim shrugged. "He didn't want to come back up." He turned to Haeberle. "Why *didn't* you want to come up?"

In that same strange voice, Haeberle said, "I don't know why this asshole tied me up in the first place." He looked at Tim, his eyes hooded by half-shut lids. "Didn't you see her?" he asked.

"Her?" Tim looked baffled. "Her who?"

"The woman." The dreamy look on Haeberle's face somehow managed to intensify. It gave Sue the creeps. "The same one I saw last time I went down. But this time she was naked, man. Waiting. Real dish, real ripe peach. She was between the boats. Calling me. Calling...." His voice wafted away on the gentle breeze that blew over the sea. "She wanted me," he said suddenly. "I could tell." He turned his head toward Mercedes, who still shivered, arms still wet and sticky beneath their shed skin. "I can always tell when they want me."

Sue felt dirty in a way she had never felt before. Not even if Haeberle had looked at *her* that way, not even then could she have managed the sick feeling that swept through her. She suspected – *knew* – that it didn't matter to him that Mercedes was unconscious and grossly maimed.

He would enjoy whatever he was thinking of doing all the more.

A wave hit the boat. Not the gentle, slapping waves that were normal –

(*Yeah, but normal took a time-out some time ago, Sue.*)

– but a rolling surge that sent everyone lurching across the hull of the boat.

Mercedes started to slide toward the water. Sue didn't think, just jumped. A leap that carried her forward and down like she was the world's biggest penguin slipping across the ice.

She caught Mercedes' leg. Wondering if the skin would pull off in her hands. If the woman would shred to pieces below her palms.

She didn't. Her flesh held.

A moment later, Sue's father was there as well. Grabbing Mercedes' other leg, pulling as hard as he could, hauling her up to the boat's keel again.

She saw Mr. Raven as they both pulled. He didn't move to help them, just watched it all with an expression of severest distaste, his every muscle saying "Why me?" loud and clear.

"Well," he said, "we can't stay here." He turned to Tim, who was sitting quietly, still burdened by the many pounds of gear he had taken with him after Haeberle. "You're going to have to go under and get the emergency life raft."

Tim sighed. But he didn't even appear to think about it. Just nodded.

"It's probably a two-person job. I'll need help," said Tim.

"Well, obviously I'm not going," said Mr. Raven. "So that leaves –"

"I'll go," said Sue's father. She looked at him sharply. She hadn't expected that. When they had left on this trip he had made it extremely clear that he had no intention of diving with her; that he considered it a waste of time. But he was stepping up now. And not just that, but.... "And you stay," he said to Tim. "I'll take Haeberle."

Tim's jaw all but fell right out of his head. Sue knew what he was feeling. Who would *volunteer* for a job with that guy? He was obviously unhinged, giving her a more serious case of the willies every time she talked to him.

"I don't think that's a good –" Tim said. But Sue's father cut him off.

"Listen. We need the emergency raft. We need two people to get it. I'm not about to let my daughter go down there and get it –"

That riled her a bit. She knew he was coming from a good place, but still. "Please, I –"

He ignored her. Steamrolled her speech. "– and I'm not about to let this scumbag stay up here with her, either," he said, with a cursory gesture at Haeberle. The nutball just grinned at him. "So that means he goes down, and so do I. You look out for everyone up here," he said, and looked hard at Tim. Sue knew what her father was really saying to him: *Look out for my daughter*.

For a moment, she felt like things might be all right between her and her father. Maybe not today, maybe not tomorrow. But he wasn't bad. He worried about her, he had helped her come here even though he never believed in the trip. He had even come *with* her, for crying out loud.

Tim wasn't giving up. "I can go with him. I –"

Sue's father would have none of it. "You need to off-gas and rest. You're so tired you can barely move."

Tim appeared to think about this. Then he nodded. Started stripping off his gear. "There's enough air in the tank for another ten minutes or so," he said.

Sue's father nodded. "That should be fine. Just tell me where to go."

"Galley storage."

Sue saw surprise flit across her father's face. Tim shrugged. "Yeah."

He glanced meaningfully at Mr. Raven, who glared. Sue wondered what kind of cost-cutting could have motivated him to put it down there. It probably meant he could fit another paying fare onboard or something. She resolved to punch the man in the nose if and when they got out of this.

"Well, it is what it is," said Sue's father. "Will the life raft hold us all?"

This time Tim glanced at Mr. Raven. "Sure. It should."

And Sue knew Tim was lying. Lying, and planning to be the one who would n't stay in it. Because Mr. Raven had cheaped out on buying a raft big enough for everyone.

She also noticed Haeberle. He grew suddenly alert, suddenly tense.

He knows, too. Knows, and intends to be in the raft when it's ready to go.

No matter what.

The boat chose that moment to shift. Sue already had a grip on Mercedes, but even so the dead weight of the woman nearly dragged her off the side.

"Better than this thing, at least," said Tim.

Sue's father moved to Tim. Began helping him shed his gear.

"Dad?" she said.

Her dad started. She wondered why. Then realized: she hadn't called him that – hadn't called him "Dad" – in years.

And she suddenly realized that it wasn't he who had stolen their relationship. That it wasn't he who had ripped them apart. He had always been there, ready to help at a moment's notice.

It was her. All her.

"Be careful," she said.

And he beamed. So happy for that simple, basic, *human* expression of concern.

She felt shame burn within her. Painful but also cleansing. Like with this moment bridging the gap between them they might be able to build a relationship again.

Her dad winked. Warmth flowed into her. Her dad was going to save them.

Then she looked at Haeberle. Saw his grin, that wolf-grin, shark-grin. The look of a creature about to feed.

The good feelings drained from her. Fear replaced them. Not just for herself, but for Tim and her dad and *everyone* in the man's range.

He was, she realized belatedly, not... *right*. Everyone else was terrified, total fear lurking just below calm surfaces. And what lurked below the smiling surface of Haeberle's expression?

She didn't know.

She *feared* knowing.

BETRAYAL

~^~^~^~^~

Things were getting fun.

The woman under the water had been a promise. A pledge of future pleasures, and a reassurance that no matter what happened, this universe would bend itself to Haeberle's will. The laws of physics were nothing next to the desires of a God.

He had no doubt that he could survive without the raft. But why should he? When there was a pleasant way to float along and wait for the Navy vessel? They knew he was a criminal, it was true, but he had no doubt that life would present a way for him to sidestep incarceration, just as it had when the first Haeberle presented himself.

Besides, the raft would present the perfect opportunity to spend some quality time with Sue and Mercedes. Yes, that meant that Tim and Cal and Mr. Raven would have to die, but there really hadn't been much chance of their making it through all this. They were weak, they were boring, and above all they were his to play with.

Just as Sue and Mercedes were his. Sue especially. Mercedes seemed a bit… broken. Maybe he'd just dump her over the side of the raft and watch her sink. That would be almost as fun as using her up.

Yeah. He'd do that.

But first things first. Get the raft. And if it was light enough, he figured there was no reason that Cal had to come back up with him. He still had the knife he'd tried to use on Tim down below. It would work on Cal just fine.

They swam under the boat. The water below had shifted into an obstacle course of tangled lines, clotted masses of debris.

Cal looked at Haeberle. Haeberle gestured: "After you."

Cal shook his head, looking a bit exasperated, which made no sense to Haeberle because after all, he'd only been polite.

He decided to cut the other man somewhere painful. Maybe the stomach.

Cal swam carefully to the salon door. It looked strange, hanging above the wheelhouse instead of situated below as it always had been. Vertigo gripped Haeberle. Surprising because he hadn't known he could be affected by something like that.

Tangled lines draped across the open doorway to the salon. Cal drew a knife from a sheath on his thigh – must have gotten it from Tim when they shifted gear – and began slashing away at the spider web in front of them.

Haeberle joined in. He saw Cal look at his knife. Saw the other man's worry.

He had to keep himself from laughing around his regulator.

When the way was more or less clear, the two men swam into the salon. Again, Haeberle was struck by a sense of wrongness, a weightlessness that he imagined must be similar to an outer space adventure. A deck of playing cards had exploded and hung in "midair." His *Playboy* flapped gently in unseen currents. He kind of wanted to look at it, kind of wondered if it would be as sexy underwater as it was dry.

But Cal was already moving. Kicking his way to the stairs that led "up" to the space belowdecks. Pulling himself along the stairs.

Haeberle followed. Still holding his knife.

Into the galley storage.

It was a wreck. Food, boxes, cans. Some of the boxes and cans had ruptured, creating strange clouds of gunk in the water. Haeberle looked through it all, peering about for the raft while Cal did the same.

He suddenly realized that Jimmy J's body wasn't here. Wondered where it was.

And then knew. It was below. With *her*. How it had gotten there, he wasn't sure. But things were strange, and delicious in a way he'd never known. And he was sure that after he killed Cal in here and the others above, he'd find out the answers to everything.

So. Much. Fun.

Cal suddenly kicked up toward the floor of the galley storage. Haeberle followed, and both broke into an air bubble trapped there.

Stuck in one of the metal racks was a yellow bundle with the letters "EMRGCY RFT" stenciled in red on its side. Cal grabbed it and started pulling it toward him.

Haeberle spit out his regulator. "How heavy is it?"

Cal spit out his, too. "Not too heavy. Mostly awkward. Here, grab this –"

Then he froze. And Haeberle knew he saw his doom. Cal turned to him. Leaving the raft behind. "This raft is probably on the small side," he said. His voice quivered. "I've seen the way you look at Sue. The way you act around her."

And Haeberle felt something pinch him. He looked down.

Red clouded the water around him. He looked up at Cal. The older man continued. "I know you were planning on getting her alone, one way or another."

Cal moved, and the knife embedded in Haeberle's gut dragged its way up to his breastbone. The water was suddenly alive with writhing eels.

Not eels. My guts. My guts....

He felt himself start to drift. Not in the water, but in the world. Felt the universe start to bleach of color. "It wasn't," he murmured. "Wasn't... wasn't supposed to...."

"You're not touching her," said Cal. He twisted the knife. Fire erupted in Haeberle's center. "Or anyone else."

Cal pulled the knife free.

This can't happen.

"You'll all die," said Haeberle. "If you kill me, this all ends. You'll all –"

Cal buried the knife in Haeberle's neck, cutting off the words. But the thoughts continued.

They'll all die if I do. Doesn't he know that? Can't he see that? Can't he... see...?

He saw Cal yank the knife free. Saw the other man cut himself, a thin gash on his cheek.

Then saw nothing.

Don't they know? Don't...?

Then he was gone.

DESPAIR

~^~^~^~^~

They watched the water where Cal and Haeberle had disappeared, and Raven wondered why the universe hated him so much. It wasn't fair. It just wasn't *fair*. Wasn't he nice to people? Didn't he pay taxes every year? And here God was being such an absolute prick in return.

A hand broke the surface. Tim immediately leaned out as far as he could without falling off the boat himself. Grabbed the hand. Hauled it toward him.

It was Cal. Tim pulled him onto the hull of the boat, which was much easier to do than it would have been only an hour before – the vessel had sunk noticeably in that time.

Cal had a large bundle under one arm. The life raft.

Tim looked around. "Where's Haeberle?"

At the same time, Sue asked, "What happened to you, Dad?"

She sounded horrified, and for a moment Raven couldn't see why. Then he realized that blood was streaming off a long cut on Cal's face.

The older man was breathless. "He tried to… tried to… kill me…."

Tim looked white. Sue didn't. She looked like she had half-expected that to happen – which marked her as the smarter of the two. No surprise there, Raven mused. Tim had always been a soft-hearted moron, surpassed in stupidity only by Jimmy J. Perhaps.

"Where is he?" asked Tim.

"Dead," said Cal. "Dead, I...." He trembled. Couldn't finish the sentence. He fell into spastic shudders, post-traumatic shock wracking his frame.

But something about it struck Raven as wrong. Forced.

He suddenly knew it hadn't happened that way.

So what *had* happened?

Sue held her father. Cradled him against her breast. And that was when Raven knew.

Old bastard did *kill Haeberle. But he moved first.*

It was fair; Raven couldn't really blame him for doing it. But it was damned inconvenient. Just one more "Screw you" from the Man Upstairs.

Not that you had any chance of treasure at this point.

"He's dead?" said Tim. Still looking shocked.

"I didn't have a choice. Didn't...." He turned his head into his daughter's embrace. Shaking, shaking.

Damn. The guy's good. Probably a hell of a lawyer.

Tim watched a moment, clearly unsure how to react to this last turn of events. Then turned to the life raft. There was a red pull tab on the side of the bundle. He yanked it.

There was an explosive hiss, and the thing unfolded – but only partway. It turned into a limp yellow slug, then even that flattened out. Slug became tapeworm, and then it was just a mass of useless plastic on the hull.

"Why is it doing that?" Raven heard his voice. Heard the pitch rising to a sharp point.

Are you laughing, God? Because this isn't funny anymore.

Tim pawed through the folds of the plastic, then finally pulled a length of yellow away from the rest of the raft.

A hole. A good three feet across, shredding its way through the separate chambers that were supposed to guarantee the life raft would remain afloat even if part of it were punctured.

"What are we going to do?" said Raven. His voice kept climbing, rising with every word. "We can't just wait here. Can't just stay here! We'll *die!*"

Tim looked disconsolate, just running his hands along the edges of the gaping hole, shaking his head. "We don't have much choice."

And then a sound came to them. Not the sea, not the creak of the boat as it settled deeper and deeper into the water.

Mercedes.

MOVEMENT
~^~^~^~^~

A body in the water. A loose form, drifting in blood and intestines and the offal that flooded from it in the last instants of life.

It floats.

Floats.

Floats.

There is always movement in the deep. Deep rivers, unseen currents waiting to capture the jetsam and the creatures unlucky enough to fall under their influence. Or even just the Brownian motion of the one point three billion cubic kilometers that comprise the world's oceans.

There is always motion.

Even among the dead.

The body floats, but it floats in motion. It floats in movement.

And, eventually, it floats *with* movement.

Black threads appear at the edges of its open eyes. Covering the whites, the irises, the dilated pupils until the orbs have become a black field. The hands grow strange, organic gloves of writhing fibrils.

The body moves.

It floats toward the door of the small room in which it had hung. But an observer – any who would have had the strength to stay, the stupid courage required to not swim away screaming into the water – would have noted that the body did not seem to be swimming. It moved as

310

though being drawn through the water. Tugged in the direction of the door. Then through the hall. The stairs. The salon.

And down.

Down.

Down.

YOU

~^~^~^~^~

Mercedes moaned, and Tim had a moment of hope that she might come out of whatever coma held her, but after that one sound she fell silent and still again. He took his BC from Cal, stripped it of all its gear, and then used it to shield her face from the sun as much as possible.

Beyond that there was almost nothing that could be done. He dove over the bow of the boat at one point, not bothering to put on the tanks. Just hoping to see where the life jackets were stowed on the foredeck. But the area around the compartment where they were held was in the middle of a tangle of rope and detritus. Getting in there would be impossible. Suicidal. It couldn't have been more perfectly blocked if someone had tried to block it.

Some*thing.*

He came back with a few regulators. Useless without tanks to breathe *from,* but he grabbed them as something he *could* grab, as though to do nothing, to come back empty-handed, would be to admit death.

Some*thing.*

That thought kept coming back to him as the sun lowered, as night fell. The look of the tangle, the visions that Haeberle and Mercedes had had, the ships with that dark hole at their center.

Some*thing.*

Night came.

Sue crawled over and sat next to him. Her father and Mr. Raven leaned against the boat's rudder, both of them silent, either keeping their own counsel or simply asleep.

"They're not going to find us, are they?" said Sue.

He smiled. "Of course they are." A lie.

"We're going to sink before they get here."

He didn't say anything this time. Didn't want to lie to her again. And he was just too tired to pretend at hope.

"What did you find down there?" she said a moment later.

It took Tim a moment to understand what she was saying. The time on the boat, the time from when he had surfaced with Haeberle to now, had stretched out to an eternity. Thinking of ways to get through this, coming up with nothing. He hadn't even seen anything that they could use to float on when the boat went down – it all seemed one mass, one creature with tentacles fastened securely to its trunk.

"Well?"

"I, uh…." Then he remembered. *Oh, yeah. I went down to get Haeberle. And what else was there?* "Ships," he said. He felt tired. More than just the effects of the dive, it was everything that had happened over the past few days. He felt stretched out and emptied.

"More than one?"

"Lots," he said. "Some looked hundreds of years old, some were brand new." He said it quickly, as though hoping if he said it fast enough she wouldn't ask what he knew was coming next. But that was as ridiculous as any hope of rescue. They were going to die out here. They were going to die, and he was going to have to answer to her.

"Was...," she began. "Did you see...." She couldn't finish.

He was tempted to feign ignorance. To ignore the question until she dropped it or managed to finish it. But he knew that would only stretch things out, and would be cruel.

He nodded. "One of the boats had a Nelson Chemical logo on the side." He looked back at the ocean, the small waves lapping a bit closer to their feet with every passing second, the boat settling deeper and deeper. "I'm sorry."

She didn't answer at first. Just looked out into the darkness with him. Something clicked behind them. A light flared. The gloom brightened around them for a moment, then darkness surrounded them again as the light clicked off.

Probably Cal, Tim thought, checking on Mercedes.

"It's okay," said Sue. "I knew that's what the end would be. I just wanted to find it. Just had to *know*. So we found her tanks, found her boat." He felt her shrug beside him. "Now I know."

The boat groaned. Tim heard bubbling on one side. Felt his stomach drop.

"What's happening?" said Sue.

"We're sinking."

"No, not just that. I mean –"

"I know what you mean." The empty feeling intensified. Tim felt like everything he had ever experienced, everything he'd ever done, was pouring out of him. He was empty. He was nothing. Already a corpse, just waiting for the official word.

"There was something else down there," he said. "All the ships were.... They were pointed toward the center. Toward something in the center."

"What?"

Behind them, something scraped against the fiberglass hull. He thought it was just Cal or Mr. Raven shifting, but then Mercedes moaned and he realized it was her. She'd been doing that since he and Haeberle surfaced, periodically giving out a groan and thrashing around for a moment or two before settling down into her coma again.

It was deeply disconcerting, making it seem like she wasn't really comatose but rather in some deep sleep; dreaming the mother of all nightmares.

"Do you think what was down there has something to do with Mercedes and Jimmy J and the bodies that disappeared?" said Sue.

Tim frowned. She wouldn't see the expression, but she seemed to sense him reaching for words because she didn't push for an answer. Just waited.

"My dad used to take me fishing," he said. "Just off the pier at first, then he took me out for deep water fishing."

"I'm not sure what –"

"Do you know what the main difference is between fishing off the side of the pier and trying to catch big fish way offshore?"

He heard the rustle of Sue's clothes: a shake of the head, he guessed. "The boat, I guess."

"No. It's the bait. In deep water you use a small fish to catch a bigger one. And live bait is always the best."

"So?"

"So I can't help thinking.... We find a body with some gold, just enough to get us moving down to a shallow spot that shouldn't exist. And then we come back, and Haeberle has seen some woman that's got his creep-factor red-lining, Mercedes brings back a doll that belongs to her children."

"What do you mean, 'a doll that belongs to her children'?"

Tim recounted the conversation he and Mercedes had had: of the doll, the children she saw somewhere farther in the ship – a place he would have bet was closer to that strange spot between the ships.

"And you?" he continued. "You see something that belongs to your sister. Everyone saw what they wanted to see."

"You didn't."

He laughed. "I don't want anything."

She laughed back. "You must want something."

"You." The word popped out before he could stop it, and he no longer felt empty. Instead he felt like he would very much like to follow the foot he had swallowed with his leg, his body, his head, and then disappear into a tiny black hole of embarrassment.

She was silent.

Then he felt her hand. Holding his.

And for a moment, an exquisite, infinite moment, he was almost glad he had come on this trip.

BREATH

~^~^~^~^~

It felt wonderful to hold his hand. But Sue couldn't ignore Tim's words.

At least, not for too long. She allowed herself a few wonderful seconds just to feel his fingers threaded through hers, to feel his pulse in time with hers. They were both sweaty, both coated with salt from the sea and the air. Both tired, both afraid.

Both together.

Then the moment ended. Whatever curtain had drawn itself between them and the fear she felt pulled away once more. She thought of his last words.

Everyone saw what they wanted to see.

"You think those things were bait?" she said.

"Yeah," he said. "When I went down to find Haeberle...." She actually heard him gulp. "There was something down there. I could feel it. Something pulling us in, catching us, picking us off one at a time."

"But –

(*but that's crazy but that's impossible but that's too terrifying to be real*)

– you didn't see anything. Just that light."

Like that isn't weird enough.

"No, I mean, we all saw things we wanted, we all saw weird things. But not you. Why not you?"

"Yeah, I've been thinking about that. And the only thing I can think of is that I didn't touch anything down there. Mercedes touched the chest, you touched the tank. I thought I saw Geoffrey holding something, and heaven only knows what Haeberle did down there." He shrugged. "Or maybe it's because of what I said, because there's not anything I want. Not down there."

He sounded so hesitant, so much the opposite of when he had blurted out that he wanted her before, that she had to laugh. "Is this you asking me out on a date? Because you're terrible at it."

"Maybe. If we survive. You like fishing?"

She laughed harder. "Not much. I could be persuaded to do a nice steak dinner, though."

"I think he's right," said her dad. The sudden sound startled her so badly she probably would have slid right off the side of the boat if Tim hadn't caught hold of her arm.

"Geez, Dad!"

"Sorry. Didn't mean to scare you or eavesdrop." He settled down beside her. "Not a lot of room up here. And there's a little less every minute."

"I've been thinking about that, too," said Tim. He paused, waiting so long that Sue almost asked him what he meant by that. "I think I can get another life raft," he finally said.

"There's another one on this thing?" said her dad. "Why didn't we –"

Tim shook his head. "Not on this boat. But...." He drifted off, and she got the distinct impression that he didn't want to finish his sentence. Then he continued speaking, and she understood why. "But there are a lot of boats right below us. One in particular that should have something we can use."

It took a moment for that to sink in.

Another to realize that if Tim did what he was implying, she'd never get her steak dinner.

Because what he was implying was suicide.

She shook her head. "No, we can't. *You* can't. It's –"

A gasp. The sound was low, barely loud enough to make its way through the minute gaps in her words. But it did manage to penetrate, and it cut her off instantly. The sound was a mix of horror and revulsion, the sound of someone viewing something utterly wrong, completely *evil.*

Sue turned with the others. Tim shouted, a small cry, and her father cursed quietly under his breath.

Mr. Raven had turned on the dive light that had been attached to Tim's buoyancy compensator. Shone it toward them. But not *at* them. Instead, he aimed the light at the form that stood right behind them.

At Mercedes.

But it was barely recognizable as the woman. Her arms, bereft of flesh, now wore a thick coat of black tissue. The new flesh rippled and writhed, made of thousands of snake-like strands that twined together to form a semblance of skin.

The plaits reached out from under the neck of her blouse as well, crawling up her neck and chin, reaching tendrils into her gaping mouth. Forcing their way in.

Sue felt like vomiting as she saw the things, each pulsing grotesquely, like they were breathing or perhaps *eating*, push blindly into the other woman's mouth.

Mercedes' eyes were completely black. Either covered by the horrible strands, or eaten away and replaced completely by them.

Mercedes' mouth opened, wider and wider, to admit more and more of the things. As it did, she started to jitter, to dance in place. She looked like she was having a grand mal seizure. But she didn't fall. No matter how hard she shuddered, no matter how much her muscles clenched and then loosened, she remained standing.

Sue thought, insanely, of Pinocchio. A puppet held aloft by strings at first, before becoming enchanted and able to walk without them holding him up.

In the next moment Mercedes' strings seemed to be cut. She slumped.

But not completely. Her arms remained high, as though she were being supported by invisible rescuers who had her arms over their shoulders.

She stayed that way for a time impossible to gauge. It felt like forever, but that couldn't be the case because it was still night when the strange pose ended. Still the same horrible night after the same horrible day. Mercedes' arms stayed where they were, but her head lifted so her face could be seen again.

Sue felt her hand rise of its own accord. Felt it go over her mouth, stifling the scream and the gorge that both fought to escape.

Mercedes was dead.

The black threads had peeled themselves away from her eyes, but those eyes stared straight ahead, focusing on nothing, seeing nothing.

The woman's mouth was still cranked open. Still lined by darkness that pulsed as it pushed deeper into her.

Mercedes sighed. A last breath, the final exhalation as her body released its last stores of air from lungs that would do no more.

Then Sue saw something shift under Mercedes' shirt. It compressed. Released. Shifted again.

The dead woman's mouth opened wider, and she took a breath.

GLAD

~^~^~^~^~

Raven's hand shook. He tried to stop it, tried to keep it steady, and even as he did he realized what a foolish thing that was, how stupid it was to care about whether or not his hand was steady right now.

Mercedes was dead. Dead, but alive. Dead, but moving.

The woman opened her mouth. It gaped wide, wider, then so wide that her head tilted back like the top half was affixed to the bottom by way of a single hinge.

At the final moment, the instant it seemed that the top of her head must fall behind her, tumble to the hull of the boat and from there into the black water, at that instant it snapped back forward with an audible clap. Sprays of something flew out of her mouth and Raven realized it was her teeth, shattered by the impact.

Mercedes looked at each of them in turn. Only that wasn't exactly true. Her face turned toward them, but her eyes remained sightless. The eyes of someone long dead and happier for that fact.

The corners of her mouth curled up in a grin. Not a normal smile, with muscles doing the pulling to create a familiar, safe expression. This smile was caused by the snake-things at the corners of her mouth, drawing back, pulling in on themselves. A death-grimace created by things that Raven didn't understand, but that made him want to scream and run until he fell off the boat himself.

Only… only what was beyond the boat? What was down there?

He no longer cared for the idea of gold. No longer wanted treasure or riches or fame.

Just let me live, just a little longer.

That was what he wanted now. *All* that he wanted. To live. To breathe in every time he breathed out, just a few more decades, years – even *days* at this point.

He could hear the air wheezing in and out of Mercedes' body. But he got the impression that it wasn't real breathing – at least, not the kind of respiration he and Cal and Tim and Sue were engaged in. It was more a clever imitation. A pretense.

And what was behind the façade?

He didn't know. Was terrified that he might have to find out.

After looking from each of them to the next, her face tilted sightlessly them, Mercedes spoke. Her voice came in quick gasps, regularly spaced inhalations breaking the words at junctions where normal speech would not pause. The effect was mechanical, like she had been replaced by an audioanimatronic version of herself.

"You should… come in… and see… what's down… below."

Raven didn't know whether to scream or laugh at that. One might well lead to the other.

Does she expect us to just dive off? To just jump in and find whatever's down there? Whatever's doing this?

(*Why not? It's going to happen eventually. You know it is.*)

323

The small voice in the back of his mind terrified him. Not least because it was appealing. Something that beckoned him with the immediacy of an inevitable outcome.

(*Just go.*)

No. NO.

The thing that had been Mercedes took a step toward Sue. That was good. Maybe it wouldn't do anything to him. Maybe it –

Mercedes stopped. Her head tilted back as though she were smelling the sea air. Sniffing for prey.

Go. Just go. Take Sue if you want.

Take any *of them.*

The thing turned toward him. Took a step toward him.

He moved back. A step. Another. Another.

Mercedes followed. Kept perfect pace, maintaining distance between him and her –

(*it*)

– as he drew further away from her.

No one else moved. Everyone else stunned to silence and immobility by the impossibility of what was happening.

Raven stepped back again.

Mercedes' smile widened further. Pulled back by black strands until he thought he could hear the bones of her skull shifting and breaking. The mouth opened until the corners nearly touched her earlobes.

"Don't you... want to... see what's... down here? Don't you... want to... get the... treasure?"

And against his will, it came again. Just a fraction of an instant. A flash-image of gold, of treasure, of fame and women and the return to what he had once been and more. Greatness long-deserved and longer-denied.

He reached out. Barely a twitch in her direction. And at the same instant felt something burning his palm. He looked at it. A perfect circle of black shimmered there. Moving, writhing.

What's that what's THAT?

But at the same time his mind shrieked the question, it also – with a strange calm – voiced the answer.

Where you held the gold. Where you first had the thought.

Where you first wanted more.

The black disc on his hand erupted. A sticky, oozing strand shot across the gap separating him from the Mercedes-thing. It slammed into her mouth, which once again gaped in that horrible, too-wide grimace.

He heard a crunch. Saw something leap up. Her hair, a puff of red.

Realized that the thing that had come from his hand had just...

... just punched a hole in her head, oh dear God, please save me it punched a hole in her head and she's still standing how is she standing?

The grin on the face of the thing – not Mercedes, not at all anymore – just widened. Then a black strand seemed to flow around her neck, tightening like a noose, and

Raven realized it was the same one that went through her skull, the same one that led from his hand to her mouth and beyond.

He tried to pull away. Yanked back with his hand. It felt like he was putting a hot poker to raw nerve. He screamed.

The thing's smile widened for a second. Then her mouth closed around the strand. He saw it was pulsing, just like the things that led into her mouth. Throbbing, a grotesque umbilicus tethering him to the creature at the other end.

The mouth opened. Closed. Opened. Closed.

The thing was eating the strand. Eating its way toward *him*.

He thought of the scene from *Lady and the Tramp*. The two dogs, eating a spaghetti dinner, finding opposite ends of the same spaghetti strand and eating their way to a surprising kiss.

He didn't want to find out what kind of kiss this thing would offer him.

He pulled away. The pain came again. Worse this time, and when he looked down he saw that the disc had widened. His hand was now covered in black, with those same writhing flagella he had seen on Mercedes flickering back and forth under the skin of his wrist.

Then forearm.

Then biceps.

"Oh, oh, oh, oh," he said in a low voice, not knowing what it meant, helpless to stop. "Oh, oh, oh."

No one moved to help him. Not Cal, not Sue, not Tim. They remained motionless, either too terrified to move, or simply unwilling to put themselves on the line for him.

"Oh, oh, oh."

The thing was closer. Chewing the cord that separated them. Each up-and-down motion of its jaws pulled them a few inches closer.

"Oh, oh."

He started to cry. This wasn't how it was supposed to happen. Not fair, not fair at all. He was supposed to be rich, supposed to be famous, supposed to be everything good and not....

"Oh."

His hand jerked upward as the thing bit away at the last inches of cord.

Its mouth opened wide.

Raven shrieked. "*OH!*"

Then Sue was there. Slashing away at the strands with a knife. The steel parted the strands, and for a moment Raven hoped.

Tim joined her. He hoped still more.

Then he saw new fibers whip out of his skin. Dozens of them, and each one a spear-tip of agony as it pierced him. They flew out of his hand, his arm, his shoulder. Passing through the air and piercing the thing that had been Mercedes in its face and chest. Each a miniature version of the ropy growth that had come from his hand.

Tim and Sue started hacking at the new threads. A few parted. Then the Mercedes-thing shoved him away. What had once been a petite woman now was something not just different, but *more*. Because the shove sent them rocketing across the hull of the boat; almost sent them completely over the side and into the water.

The strings twined together. Shot back into Mercedes' mouth.

She kept eating.

She got to him.

He screamed.

UNKNOWN

~^~^~^~^~

Tim didn't know he had stepped away from –

(*no it can't happen can't be happening*)

– Raven until he felt his left foot plunge into water and realized he had backed so far that he had reached the edge of the hull. Had almost panicked his way into the water.

And what's down there? What's waiting for us?

Can it be worse than what's here?

Mercedes –

(*Not her. Not Mercedes. Not anymore.*)

– had… *chewed* was the only word he had for it… her way to Mr. Raven. To the older man's face. Then continued chewing. Mr. Raven's screams grew in volume, in pitch, in terror. Rising and rising into the starlit night and then being swallowed somewhere high above them.

And none of it helped.

A sucking sound came from the place where Mercedes' flesh joined to Mr. Raven's. From the seam where her mouth had split into a nearly perfect one-hundred-eighty-degree angle, so wide it engulfed the other person's head.

Mr. Raven's scream grew muffled. It quieted.

It was gone.

The sucking grew louder. Mixed with a noise that Tim could not define. It sounded almost like the noise a kid might make when getting to the bottom of a milkshake. But different. Heavier. *Meatier*.

Mr. Raven went limp. But he didn't fall. He hung from the junction where he joined Mercedes. Where his face disappeared into her.

Someone was screaming. Tim thought it was Mr. Raven for a moment, then realized it was Cal, screaming "No it can't no it can't no it can't!" over and over until his voice grew ragged and raw as that bloodless seam between two bodies that were becoming somehow one in the night.

Mercedes swung around, the body of Mr. Raven swinging with her like a grotesque phallus.

She ran to the edge of the hull.

Jumped off.

There was barely any splash. The water seemed simply to open around her, close soundlessly behind her.

Then there was only the slap of water on fiberglass, the sound of Cal's petering screams, the sound of his and Sue's jagged gasps.

Mr. Raven was gone.

The sea was deep.

The unknown had come to call, completely and openly.

ANCIENT

~^~^~^~^~

Sue felt empty.

She suspected they all did.

When the impossible becomes real, when something utterly upends your version and vision of reality, there is a moment when all must be questioned, when all is viewed with suspicion. When all knowledge leaves, and leaves behind only confusion, skepticism, fear.

She sat down. More fell. Her knees weakened and she let them, rolling to her side and barely managing to remain partially upright.

Tim came and joined her. He sat beside her.

Her father came a moment later. Sat on the other side.

Humans crave the comfort of company when in the darkness. Not darkness of vision, which they have trained themselves over long centuries and millennia to endure and overcome. But the darkness of soul. The darkness of spirit which cries out for help, for assurance that there is brightness in the dark, even if that brightness is only the spark of another human life.

For where there is life there is always a small measure of hope.

Still, in this place that hope was so dim, so hidden behind what had just happened, that Sue could barely feel it. Her dad put his arm around her, and she could barely feel that either. She shivered, and the shiver became a series of tremors that rocked her just as what she had seen had rocked her understanding of the world, the universe, *Creation*.

Tim leaned in. Shoulder to shoulder, hip to hip.

After a while – she didn't know how long – the shudders slowed and stopped. Not that she felt any better. Her body simply ran out of energy. The emptiness she felt in mind and spirit had reached black threads into her body, had emptied it as well.

Black threads....

Like what pulled Mr. Raven. Like what came out of Mercedes.

How long until something like that comes for us?

"What was that?" she said. And it turned out that she still had at least a small store of energy. Enough to tremble a bit. Enough for her voice to shake, to quiver, to become the sonic embodiment of her fear.

"I don't know," said her dad. His voice came out flat and used-up. Empty like her.

Tim spoke. His voice sounded only barely more lively. Perhaps because he only had to say a single word: "Stonefish."

"What?" said her dad.

"It's the most venomous fish in the world," said Tim.

Emotion crept into her dad's voice. Anger filling the empty vessel of his terror. "I know what it is. I meant what do you mean by saying it?"

"You know how it hunts?"

"It buries itself in the sand and waits for fish to pass by, then it sucks them into its mouth," said Sue. The words wearied her. All she could hear was the sound Mercedes had made when she... *joined* with Mr. Raven. All she could think of was him saying "no, no, no" over and over like the word might have some power to save him.

"Yeah. In the sand. And sucks them in. Some of them even secrete a substance that encourages plant growth on their backs," said Tim.

"So?" said Sue's dad. He sounded even more irritated. If unchecked, she thought he might turn to rage as a preferable substitute to his terror.

Finding ourselves alone in the dark, we often strike out against the night. And if we strike out also against another huddling soul, so be it.

"So he buries himself, and what you have is a lump, covered by sand. And a predator, waiting to suck in anything it can."

"I'm still not getting it." Irritation rising in her father's voice.

But Sue got it. Suddenly and completely. Wished she didn't. "You think there's something under the ground."

She felt Tim move. Felt the nod ripple through his shoulder, his trunk. "I think that's why the ocean floor rose up. I think there's something down there – something huge – and it's luring us in with things we want. Things we love."

"That's ridiculous," sputtered her father. "*Ridiculous*." The second word came out so hard and fast she knew it was his fear that Tim spoke true. "Something like that... we'd know about it."

"Why?" said Tim. He sounded calm.

No. Not calm. Resigned. Like he knows we're going to die.

"We know less about the ocean than we do about the moon. The deepest parts are all but completely uncharted. No satellite imagery can penetrate them, and there's no reason to even bother looking at most of it without some particular reason." He shrugged. Again she felt the movement, again she felt resignation in his whole being. "Ambush predators have lived in the ocean forever. Why not one more?"

"But this one... it knows what we're *thinking*," said her father. And now he sounded like he was nearly crying. "It knows what we want." The desperation in his voice was heartbreaking.

She knew what he meant, the reason for his despair. If the thing – whatever it was – knew them so completely, then how would they escape it?

Answer: we won't.

"What about the ships?" said Sue. "You said there are all those ships down there, pointed toward something at the center. And if that's true, then whatever it is has the power to drag things way bigger than us down there. And...." She pointed at the spot where Mr. Raven had been dragged under. "We just saw that it come for one of us, so it obviously doesn't need to wait for us to come to *it*."

"I don't know," said Tim. "Maybe there's some critical mass, some level of desire. Maybe part of what it eats is our thoughts themselves, and it needs to feel us *wanting* something, so bad it starts to consume us... and then it can feed. And once the ships are empty, it pulls them down. It hides again."

Sue felt something writhe inside her. A thing long-buried in her subconscious, a knowledge carried down through eons and epochs, from times before people walked on two legs, from times before we left the deep.

Times when we were hunted. By things spiny, things bony. Things toothed and tentacular.

And more. Something greater. Something at the forever-apex of a food chain of infinite variety.

"You're right," she whispered.

At the same time, her father said, "Ah, God," and it wasn't an oath, but a prayer. Another blind search for light in the dark.

"What do we do?" her dad said a moment later.

Tim didn't shrug when he spoke. Didn't shake his head, didn't nod. He remained motionless as prey caught in the power of the predator.

"We die."

CHILD

~^~^~^~^~

There are things people are not made to experience. Contrary to popular wisdom, our own death is not one of them. We are born to die, and on the day of our birth we begin the inexorable process of preparation that will end in the ground.

But we are not – cannot be – able to properly prepare for or face the death of our children. Though born to die, our deaths make sense only in the face of new life. And so when we see our children into the ground before us, it makes a mockery of the process, it cuts the circle off mid-arc.

Cal had not seen Debi die, but there was no doubt she had. He would not see Sue die, would not watch her pass away before him the way her mother and sister had done.

He was not made or destined to be the last branch of a horribly mutilated family tree.

He had already killed to avoid that fate.

He felt like giving up. But he knew in his bones that to give up would be worse than death. It would be damnation. It would be death with a side helping of insanity. An impossible destiny.

"We have to get off this boat," he said.

"No way to do that," said Tim. "Nothing to float on."

"Not here," said Cal. He didn't know where the words came from, didn't even really have a plan in mind when he said it. But *as* he said it, an idea began to form.

It was stupid.

It was insane.

It was the only possible thing to do. The only possible way to save Sue.

He had already killed a man to save her.

What was left but to die?

PLANNING

~^~^~^~^~

Sue shook her head the whole time her dad told them his plan. But shaking her head didn't change the fact that she knew what he wanted to do was the only way.

"So, we have Tim's three tanks," he said.

"Almost empty," she interrupted.

He shrugged. "So we drop like rocks. No slow descent. Just grab the anchor line and dirt-dart it." He looked at Tim. "You remember where the Nelson Chem boat is? Can you get back there?"

Tim nodded. "Yeah. I think.... Yeah."

"And that's another thing. We only have one go-home line," said Sue. "And just Tim's wetsuit."

"No, actually we have two lines, six tanks, and two wetsuits," he said with a snap of his fingers.

She didn't know what he was talking about. Tim did.

"Haeberle," he said.

338

HAEBERLE

~^~^~^~^~

Cal volunteered to get Haeberle's tanks and his go-home line. He was the logical choice: he knew where the man was.

Tim wanted to go, but Cal persisted.

He was the logical choice.

He was the right choice.

And Cal didn't want Tim looking closely at Haeberle; seeing the stab wound. Wondering if maybe he had been the first to act; if it hadn't been self-defense, but murder that happened down here.

So Cal went.

And Haeberle was gone.

But for some reason it wasn't a surprise. Not here, not now, not after all that had happened. It just seemed inevitable. One more impossibility that followed all the others in an inevitable chain of events leading to the deaths of all who still lived. So when he saw the empty area where he had left the other man's corpse, Cal didn't rant, he didn't complain. He just thought one thing:

Of course.

GAMBLES

~^~^~^~^~

Sue seemed livid when Cal got back, and Tim couldn't tell if she was mad at her father, or at the situation, or both. Probably both. The chances of whatever reconciliation they had been on the verge of enjoying was likely about to be cut short.

Cal separated Tim's tanks. One each. He attached the extra regulators Tim had brought back from his abortive dive earlier in the day. Gave one set to each of them.

They didn't test the tanks. They would either work or they wouldn't. They would either die or they wouldn't. Testing the tanks would use up precious air they couldn't spare.

Tim was the only one with a BC. He bled all the air from it. They had to drop as fast as possible or there was no way Cal's plan would work.

Step one: get to the bottom.

Step two: tie on.

Step three: get to the Nelson Chem boat.

Step four: Cal and Tim find a life raft while Sue finds scuba gear they hope to heaven is there.

Step five: they shift to the tanks, get back to the anchor line, tie the raft to the go-home line and inflate it.

Step six: they don't die on the way up, even though they're guessing at deco stops.

Step seven: they get to the top and hope the raft is there and hope the thing below leaves them alone and hope the Navy finds them.

Step seven, Tim knew, was the big one. The *impossible* one.

And it was all they had. Their only remaining hope.

They jumped off *The Celeste*. She had sunk so low that they were knee-deep in water before they jumped off. They wouldn't be returning to her, one way or another.

Back into the deep.

Tim took lead. He swam under the boat, then clipped onto the anchor line. He was aware that when *The Celeste* went under the anchor line would be useless.

Everything's a gamble. A bad one.

He felt himself falling as he swam. Heavy. Realized he hadn't drawn a single breath from his tank yet, either. Afraid. Of so much.

He inhaled. Air. But he had no idea how much.

He clipped onto the anchor line. Pointed down and swam.

Plummeted, the others trailing behind in a long caravan of ridiculous hope.

Typically, it wasn't a good idea to move *toward* the thing trying to kill you.

He tried not to think of it. Tried to think only of breathing in, breathing out.

The secret to immortality: breathing in every time you breathe out.

He had to try not to laugh around his regulator. Hysteria at one hundred feet wouldn't be a good idea.

He still had his dive computer, but it wasn't much use. They'd reach bottom when they reached bottom. They'd run out of air when they ran out of air.

He realized that they were alone. Unlike previous trips, there were none of the strange floods of sea life that had pummeled and pulled at him. He wondered what those had been. No doubt they were part of all this, creatures controlled by the thing at the center of the boats, just like Mercedes had been controlled.

That's what happened to the bodies. Taken out by Jimmy J… or just got up and left themselves.

But the fish?

No answer. Maybe they had been acting as sheepdogs to the sheep, trying to herd them closer to the center, trying to get the ultimate prey to enter of their own accord. Perhaps they had been driven mad by whatever power lay at the bottom of this trap.

Maybe it was something else. Something so alien as to be unknowable.

Maybe it didn't mean anything at all. That, for some reason, scared him the most. The things which we cannot define, which we cannot understand, are always the most frightening. It is not the dark that scares, it is the fact that *anything* could be in it… and that means we can never *understand* anything of what it hides.

They fell.

Touched down.

Tim clipped his go-home line to the anchor line. He felt hands pulling at his BC – Sue and Cal, holding tight to him so they wouldn't get swept away and lost in the nothing of the deep… or worse.

He felt a sudden urge to take them both in his arms. Especially Sue. He resisted only because there was no telling when one or all of them would run out of air.

Some regulators are designed to let the air out slower and slower as air runs out. Some simply cut out completely. Tim had no idea which kind he was currently breathing through. But his mind made it seem as though the air was getting thin, harder to pull out.

Was it? Was it imagination?

He pushed away from the anchor line, into empty water.

He didn't want to, but he bled some precious air into his BC. He had only found the *Evermore* – the Nelson Chem boat – before by floating well above the surface of the shipwreck to which *The Celeste* had anchored.

They floated up.

The current took them.

Please, please, please.

He didn't know if it was prayer or mantra or just empty words ringing through his mind, but the word repeated in time with his breaths. Please, please, please, in, out, in, out, the secret to immortality.

The wrecked destroyer passed beneath them. Quickly when worried about losing your way, but far too slow when sucking the last molecules of air from a dry tank.

Then it fell away.

Tim saw the *Evermore*.

And saw a problem.

ENOUGH

~ ^ ~ ^ ~ ^ ~ ^ ~

Oh, no.

Not enough.

Not enough to have a sunken ship.

Not enough to be out of air twenty-five fathoms down.

Not enough to have a monster *out to kill us.*

The current had them. And Sue saw now what Tim had described: the black light. The spinning globe of near-microscopic flotsam lit to a brightness that should have been white but somehow wasn't; somehow was a color neither white nor purple nor blue nor any other she had a word for. It invited the eye to slide off it, invited the eye to reject it.

It was right in front of them. They were traveling toward it.

And she didn't worry about barreling into it. Tim – or any of them – could stop their forward motion at any time.

But the *Evermore* was off to one side. To get to it they would have to reel out far enough that they would enter that whirling submarine storm. Would enter whatever lay at its center.

Nor did she think they could simply try and swim sideways. The current was too strong. Too fast. And she suspected that no matter where they went, it would pull toward the black blossom of light at the center of the ships that served as the only gravestones to uncounted sailors.

Something in there existed only to pull things to it. To suck in life, and spit out only bones, only death.

Tim stopped them. They jerked to a halt, and she saw that he was wondering the same thing she was: *What now? How do we get to the* Evermore?

UNDERSTANDING
~^~^~^~^~

Cal fumbled for Tim's arm. Shook it. Tim didn't react. Cal shook harder, wondering if the younger man had finally snapped. He couldn't blame him if he had.

He finally grabbed the back of Tim's mask and pulled on it.

That did it. He whipped around and looked at Cal.

Good. Cal needed Tim aware.

He turned to Sue. She was already looking at him. Wondering what was up.

Good girl.

He began motioning. There were some common hand signals in scuba diving: hold it, something is wrong, out of air.

But what he was trying to say… not so much. And this damned pounding in his head wasn't helping any. Not just the unrelenting fear that had taken up residence in his mind since the moment Mercedes became something else. It was narcosis, he knew. But knowing didn't make it easier to handle. Didn't make his thoughts less muddled.

What if this is a stupid idea? What if it won't work?

No one else has anything better.

What about just letting go? Would it be so bad?

He started. Jerked in place as the last thought found its way between the last cracked bits of his courage. Was it even his own thought? Or had the thing at the center of the strange light found some way to enter their minds – not just to read them, but to *influence* them?

If it had, they were all well and truly boned.

Just keep on. Keep trying. Save Debi.

No. Debi's dead. Gotta save Sue. Save Sue.

He kept motioning. Pointing to Tim. Pointing to the go-home line. Pointing to Sue, trying to make her understand.

Tim nodded. So did Sue, both of them motioning understanding almost at the same time.

But he didn't know if they did understand.

Didn't know if understanding was even possible in a place like this.

FLASH

~^~^~^~^~

Tim began pulling the go-home line. Yanking the three of them back toward the anchor, hand over hand, hand over hand. One foot at a time, wondering how far would be enough, how far they could go before running out of air.

Wondering if this could even work.

Normally he would reel in the line, use the spool clipped to his BC to keep the cord from getting tangled.

He couldn't do that this time. He just let it drag below them. Hoping it wouldn't snag on some outcropping of rock, some bit of wreckage, or even simply tangle on itself.

He kept pulling.

Something flared. A subtle change in the brightness around them. He had his flashlight, that pitiful yellowish globe that protected little and served at this point mostly to remind how much they were at the mercy of the elements and of whatever thing hunched at the center of the ships and below the sand at their feet.

But whatever happened behind him changed the quality of the light. Overpowered it completely, if only for a moment.

He did not look back.

He feared to know.

DEAD

~^~^~^~^~

As Tim pulled the three of them back, Sue joined her father in desperately swimming, pushing sideways, the opposite direction of the *Evermore*.

She felt sick inside. Not just from the horror of all that had happened; the decision she had made to follow her dad's newest plan caused her gorge to rise in her throat. Each second ticked away in time with the jungle beat of the narcosis raging through her veins.

There would be no way to reach the *Evermore*.

There would be no tanks there.

There would be no raft.

There would be no way to climb to the surface with proper deco times.

They would die.

She kept kicking. Finless feet so much less useful, but doing what she could.

A light flared. The direction of the strange thing in the center of the ships.

She looked.

The snow globe swirled harder than ever. Shaken by the hand of a malicious god, an evil child bent not on enjoying the beauty of the swirling motes, but rather on shattering the glass and allowing what was inside to spill out.

Something appeared at the bottom of the snow globe. Then something else. Many somethings.

They were small. Thin lines that went up from the sand like reeds on a riverbank.

But reeds did not move. Did not walk.

She saw arms. Legs. Hands. Feet.

Heads.

Bodies rotted by time, some so covered by slick black threads they were discernible as human only by their outlines; others barely touched by the obscene strands.

She saw Mercedes. Jimmy J. Haeberle.

No. Not them. Not them.

Because if I see them, what if I see her?

She kicked harder. Breath coming in quick gasps.

The dead seemed not affected by the current that flowed impossibly toward the bud of dark light. They walked upright toward the three people kicking away.

Cal touched Tim. Tim stopped pulling them up the line. Rapidly unreeled more cord from his spool.

The dead walked. Swayed in the current, but walked nonetheless.

Sue didn't look at them.

What if she's there?

Her dad wasn't looking, either.

He tapped Tim. Tapped her.

She and her dad stopped kicking as one.

Tim let go of his hold on the go-home line. The current took them, fully and completely.

They flew toward the waiting arms of the dead.

351

SWING

~^~^~^~^~

The current grabbed them, if that could be said of something that had never really let them go. Held them fast and threw them full-force toward the things –

(*Is that Jimmy J? Please don't let that be him, please no!*)

– that seemed to rush toward them impossibly fast. As though they were not constrained by the current or the laws of physics or reality itself. Propelled by hate and evil and a need to *feed*.

The go-home line reeled out between Tim's fingers. Fast. Faster. So fast it burned his palms, left thin slicks of blood that dissipated in red clouds behind them.

They were going too fast. Too far.

They were going to end up in the demons' arms. If not beyond. In the bulbous light that now seemed to pulse at the center of the still-whirling snowstorm of death.

Tim grabbed the go-home line. It burnt his hands, worse than before. Tore the flesh from his fingers. Wouldn't stop.

Then it did.

The sudden cessation of movement was so fast, so violent, it felt like it tore his shoulders from their sockets. But all the energy that had been mostly forward with a small bit of diagonal arc now transferred wholly to that arc.

They swung in the water. Swung just out of reach of the creatures' grasp. Swung past the center of the ships.

Swung to the *Evermore.*

LOOKING

~^~^~^~^~

Cal didn't wait. He pushed away from the Tim and the go-home line, then began swimming toward the deck of the *Evermore*.

He hoped Tim was coming, too. Looking for the life raft. And hoped that Tim wouldn't notice that Cal was going to veer off. Because Cal had no intention of following the younger man. No intention of searching for the life raft.

That was a dead end. For all of them.

And Cal had bigger fish to fry.

SEAT

~^~^~^~^~

Sue saw where the tanks were held almost immediately. Some boats kept dive gear in closed bins below seats, others kept them in open air slots. If the *Evermore* had the latter, there was no way they could have been brought down intact.

But she saw the seats ringing the outside of the aft deck. Saw no spaces below them, just solid wood. She made her way to the closest one and pulled on it.

Nothing. It didn't give.

So the dive gear must be kept somewhere else. Maybe at the forepart of the ship, maybe belowdecks. Either way, she could feel her air petering out. She wasn't going to have time to find it.

Think. Don't give up.

What if this one's just jammed?

She moved to the next seat.

Pulled.

PLEASE

~^~^~^~^~

Unlike *The Celeste*, Tim discovered that the *Evermore* actually carried a life raft where it would do some good: bound in a tight bundle, lashed to the point where the foredeck met the wall of the wheelhouse.

Please don't let it have any holes.

Please let Sue find some tanks.

Please let Cal —

Where the hell...?

Tim looked around.

Cal wasn't anywhere to be found.

PRESENT

~^~^~^~^~

The second seat pulled open. And it was full.

Tanks. BC. Fins. Regulator. All bundled together like the most glorious Christmas present ever provided.

Sue ditched her tank and regulator – which was so close to empty that the air was nearly impossible to draw anyway. She put the new regulator in her mouth. Made sure it was connected. Drew in a great gasp of air.

Good air.

Sweet air.

She got the tanks attached to the BC, then shrugged into the gear. Felt it all like a comforting embrace.

Now I just have to find tanks for Tim and Dad and wait for them to get back with the raft.

Please let there be a raft.

She didn't look toward the light that still pulsed around them. Because she knew what was there. What was coming toward them.

Hurry. Hurry.

Hurry.

TRY

~^~^~^~^~

Tim wrestled the life raft around the side of the wreck. Saw Sue.

Did not see Cal.

He pulled the bundle to Sue. She was waiting with tanks and regulators. Enough for him and Cal, enough for all of them to make it to the surface – assuming they were fully charged.

No way to check.

He ditched his tank. Shrugged into the waiting BC and tanks she had.

Trying not to look in her eyes.

Then he looked.

And saw beyond her.

The dead.

They were at the boat.

On the boat.

She didn't notice.

She pulled at him. Shrugged: *Where's my dad?*

He shook his head. Shrugged, too. *Don't know.*

But his movements were hurried. He pointed over her shoulder.

A burst of bubbles flew from her regulator. A scream that seemed to come from everywhere in the directionless sounding board of the water.

He saw that the first creature to board the ship wore a wetsuit. It had the Nelson Chemical logo on one arm.

It was a woman.

He knew who it was.

He grabbed Sue.

Turned.

Knew there was no way they could get away.

Had to try.

AGONY

~^~^~^~^~

Cal swam.

He swam, for the first time, wholly with the current. Not trying to escape, but swimming straight for the pulsing globe that seemed to be the genesis of the danger, the pain that had fallen over all of them.

He had worried at first that the creatures, the dead bodies spurred to an obscene semblance of life, would swallow him up. But they parted around him. He traveled through them as they ran their strange run past him.

Toward Sue. Toward Tim.

Not my daughter. Not –

He passed Debi. He knew it was her. She turned to look at him.

Her eyes were gone. Chewed out by fish, perhaps. Or perhaps something more primal, more ancient, more ugly and far worse. Small tentacles shot out of them as he watched. Black masses that pulsed toward him for an instant, extending about ten inches past her eye sockets before receding into her skull.

Then she turned back in the direction they were all going. Back toward the *Evermore*.

But in the final moment, the last instant of her turn, he thought he saw something. Perhaps it was only his imagination – it probably was – but he thought he saw her expression change. A flitting instant of pleading, a request to help. If not a plea to save her, then a prayer to stop her.

I'm coming, baby. Gonna do my best.

He had buried his wife in the ground, seen his dead daughter buried in the horrible embrace of the deep. He would not lose his last daughter.

He had killed for her. What remained but to die for her, as well?

The things parted around him, and none cared that he held something clutched tightly to him.

He knew the head of Nelson Chem – he'd represented Deanna Nelson and Nelson Chemical itself in dozens of litigations and administrative hearings with the EPA over the years. He knew all Nelson's dealings.

All their projects.

All their dirty laundry.

All their contracts, private and secret.

He held the culmination of their most secret, most private of contracts in his hand.

And swum for the globe at the center of the dead.

Hold out, baby. Just hold out.

Something reached for him. Pulled out of the center of the globe of light, out of the center of the storm.

Touched him.

He began to shriek. Because it hurt.

Agony took him.

EYES

~^~^~^~^~

Sue wanted to stay. Wanted to look for her father. But terror stole her will. She had no idea where he was. And the dead had surrounded the boat. Had swarmed the white sand around them and were now leaping upward, reaching for them.

Dad.

He was gone.

She did not know where he was.

Where he *could* be.

She turned to Tim. He was struggling to hold the life raft.

She didn't bother trying to help him. She knew the current would never let them get away. Knew they had no chance.

She pulled the cord on the side of the raft.

It began to inflate.

She grabbed the side.

It pulled them up.

She felt something hook her foot.

Looked down.

Debi looked up at her with eyes empty and black.

DOWN

~^~^~^~^~

Too many things. Too many things at once.

Too many things.

Flying upward, toward the surface and the bends and death.

The current dragging them away, to who-knew-where.

And something holding onto them. Dragging them down.

Tim could only do something about one of those things. He pulled Sue higher, dragging her with his one free hand, pulling her as fast as he could. The raft was inflating slowly, the gas canister struggling against the pressure of the deep.

It gave them time.

He reached for the thing holding to Sue.

Slashed at it with his knife. Slashed again and again and again.

It fell away.

Now to worry about –

Something wrapped around his leg.

Not one of the dead. Not this time. It was something long, something that trailed into the depths of the snow globe, the blue-purple-black light that existed impossibly where no light should be. The thing – something like a tentacle, a greater version of the black strands Tim had seen on the dead – pulsed with that same light.

It began to pull him – them – down.

He hacked at it with the knife.

The strands of the tentacle parted.

Swallowed his knife.

Pulled it away.

Pulled him down.

Pulled *them* down.

CLOUD

~^~^~^~^~

Cal screamed. The flesh flayed off his body in the depths of the brightness. Then peeled from his muscles in long strips below the brightness, in the dark below the light, the black beneath the risen sand where something ancient and fell and eldritch hid from prying eyes.

He screamed.

He was dying.

He still held the canister he had taken from the *Evermore*.

With a last gasp he twisted the top off.

A gray cloud escaped.

A final project Nelson Chemical had been testing for the government.

A final bit of dirty laundry Cal had helped cover up. Not meant to mine gold from the sea, but to *destroy* the enemy's seas, to cow them into submission by destroying their ecosystems and their economies.

He had seen so many die.

And now he died himself.

NOTHING

~^~^~^~^~

Sue felt something wrap around her legs.

Then, just as fast as it held her, it fell away.

The light around them pulsed brightly. Even brighter. So bright she shut her eyes.

Then, abruptly, it grew weak.

Died.

She felt something pulling at her.

Looked down and saw the sand below literally disappearing. At first she didn't understand what it was, thought narcosis must have caused a complete shutdown of her senses. Thought a nitrogen bubble must have caused a stroke that was making her brain misfire.

Then she realized: she wasn't seeing the sand disappear, she was seeing it *fall*. Seeing it recede to its previous levels.

The sea began to pull at her, to yank her down. She threaded her arm through one of the safety ropes on the side of the now-inflated raft. Saw Tim do the same. With the other hand she managed to hold up her dive computer. Saw they existed in a strange state of homeostasis, the raft pulling them up at roughly the same speed the water was pulling them down.

No, the raft was pulling them up ever-so slightly faster.

They held to it all the way to the surface. It took just over two hours. They let go about twenty feet below, Tim lashing his go-home line to the side, both of them waiting until their last tanks were almost dry, then surfacing.

They pulled themselves onto the life raft.

She wept.

Tim tried to tell her that maybe her father made it. But she knew it was a lie. Knew *he* knew it, too.

And for some reason it was all right. She was weeping a goodbye, but it was not an angry one.

She had seen Debi. Horribly, awfully. But she *knew*.

She also knew that her father had something to do with what happened at the end. He must. He wouldn't have just paddled off and left her.

The tears came, the tears went. She was dry, empty.

She turned to Tim.

"What are we going to tell the Navy?" she said.

He laughed. "First world problems, eh?" he said.

She laughed, too. It felt good.

The life raft had a canopy. They hid from the sun.

The only threat was sunburn. The only danger above.

There was nothing dangerous below.

FOREVER

~^~^~^~^~

The Navy ship was on the horizon.

Sue stood. Began to wave. Shouted until her voice cracked.

It turned.

Thank God. Thank you, God. Thank —

She froze.

"Tim."

He was waving, too. Shouting like her.

And like her, he froze when he saw it.

Something had popped to the surface.

A bit of green. A bill, so alien out here. A hundred dollars, just floating for the taking.

"Don't touch it," she said.

"I had no intention," said Tim.

They kept waving.

After a moment the money disappeared. Like the unwanted bait of a disappointed fisherman being reeled in after an unsuccessful day on the sea.

Or under it.

If you would like to be notified of new releases, sales, and other special deals on books by Michaelbrent Collings, please sign up for his mailing list at http://eepurl.com/VHuvX.

(ALSO, YOU CAN GET A FREE BOOK FOR SIGNING UP!)

And if you liked *this* book, **please leave a review on your favorite book review site**… and tell your friends!

ABOUT THE AUTHOR

Michaelbrent Collings is a full-time screenwriter and novelist. He has written numerous bestselling horror, thriller, sci-fi, and fantasy novels, including *The Colony Saga, Strangers, Darkbound, Apparition, The Haunted, Hooked: A True Faerie Tale,* and the bestselling YA series *The Billy Saga.*

Follow him through Twitter @mbcollings or on Facebook at facebook.com/MichaelbrentCollings.

NOVELS BY MICHAELBRENT COLLINGS

THE COLONY SAGA:
THE COLONY: GENESIS (THE COLONY, VOL. 1)
THE COLONY: RENEGADES (THE COLONY, VOL. 2)
THE COLONY: DESCENT (THE COLONY, VOL. 3)
THE COLONY: VELOCITY (THE COLONY, VOL. 4)
THE COLONY: SHIFT (THE COLONY, VOL. 5)
THE COLONY: BURIED (THE COLONY, VOL. 6)
THE COLONY OMNIBUS

TWISTED
THIS DARKNESS LIGHT
CRIME SEEN
STRANGERS
DARKBOUND
BLOOD RELATIONS:
A GOOD MORMON GIRL MYSTERY
THE HAUNTED
APPARITION
THE LOON
MR. GRAY (AKA THE MERIDIANS)
RUN
RISING FEARS

YOUNG ADULT AND MIDDLE GRADE FICTION:
THE BILLY SAGA:
BILLY: MESSENGER OF POWERS (BOOK 1)
BILLY: SEEKER OF POWERS (BOOK 2)
BILLY: DESTROYER OF POWERS (BOOK 3)
THE COMPLETE BILLY SAGA (BOOKS 1-3)

THE RIDEALONG
HOOKED: A TRUE FAERIE TALE
KILLING TIME

Made in the USA
Middletown, DE
28 April 2020

92292772R00231